A Dr. Eustis Mystery

Revolutionary
Murder

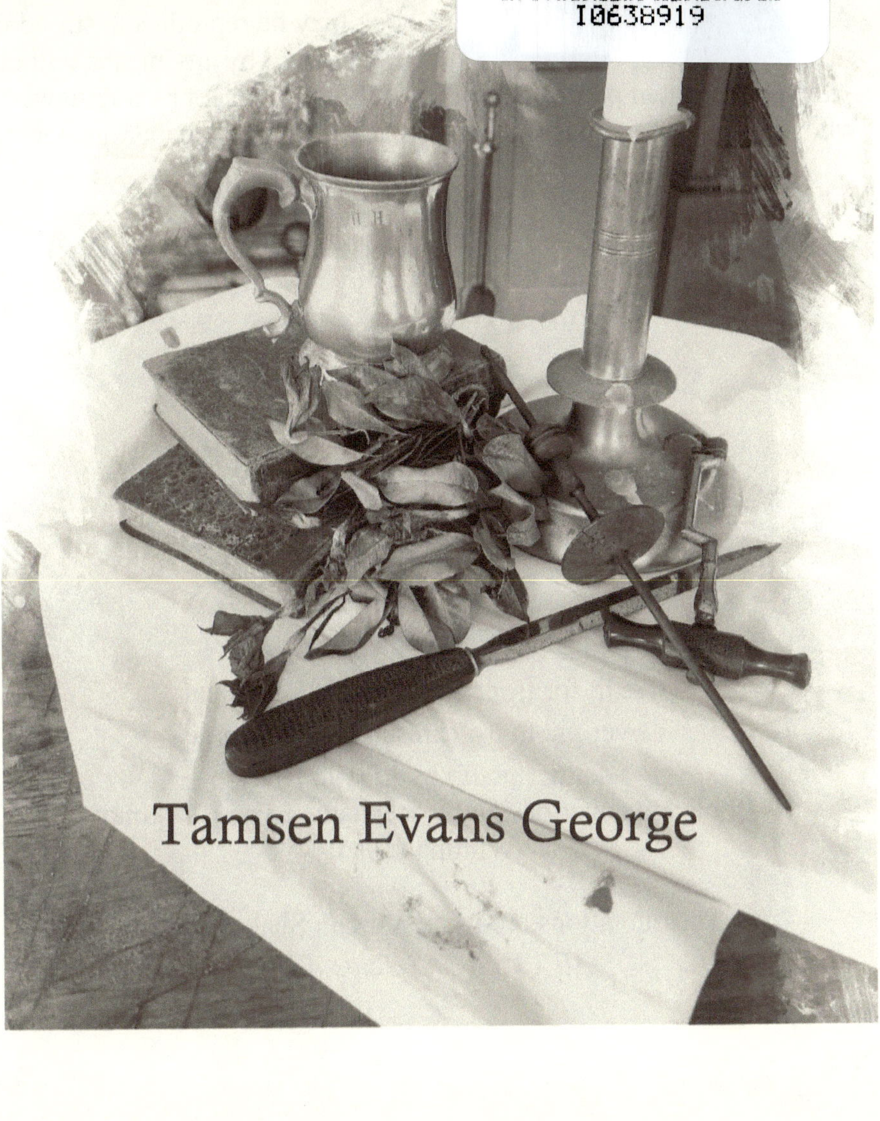

Tamsen Evans George

Revolutionary Murder: A Dr. Eustis Mystery is a work of historical fiction; all materials referenced may be found in the Bibliography and Notes sections at the end of this book.

Published in the United States by Riverhaven Books
www.RiverhavenBooks.com

ISBN: 978-1-951854-39-3

Printed in the United States of America

Credit for front cover: Brent Goodman
Cover photo by Tamsen Evans George
Author photo by Lisa Jo Rudy
Book and cover design by Stephanie Lynn Blackman
Whitman, MA

The quotations are from William Shakespeare's
All's Well That Ends Well.

Also by Tamsen Evans George

Allegiance
The Life and Times of William Eustis

For my father who encouraged my reading and brought me the stories of Nancy Drew.

Acknowledgements

The research that provided the background for this story is from my earlier non-fiction book, Allegiance: The Life and Times of William Eustis. Dr. Eustis's life seemed such a remarkable adventure that I wanted to make it into a fictional series using some of the highlights.

A great deal of appreciation goes to those initial readers who took a stab at understanding what I was trying to do – even before I had an ending worked out. I wish to thank Joan Canwell, Barbara Marcks, and Holly Hobart for being early readers. They were invaluable to me with their questions and suggestions. My grandson, Brent Goodman made a beginning observation that helped clarified the plot considerably. Lisa Jo Rudy and I had a long conversation that helped me see the cover possibilities. Friends like that are simply invaluable.

My gratitude also extends to the Falmouth Historical Society and its executive director, Rachel Lovett for letting me study and photograph certain of their artifacts.

And then there is my editor, Bob Haskell – the king of removing extra commas and putting them in the right places. Simply put, his hours of work made this into a much better book.

Thanks also to Virginia Young, whose final reading helped to polish out imperfections.

Many thanks to you all.

Characters in the Tale:

William Eustis – Surgeon stationed at Robinson House.

Noah (Diogenes) Royall – Assistant to Dr. Eustis, former slave.

James Mugford – Cooper (barrel maker), runs the forge at Fort Putnam.

Sandy Macdougal – Militia volunteer stationed at Fort Putnam.

Ezra Thorson – Lieutenant in a Pennsylvania Rifle Company.

Danny Grady – Apprentice to Mr. Mugford, cooper, at Fort Putnam.

Anna Grady – Danny's mother, a trader.

Nan Eldridge – Elijah's grandmother, a midwife.

Elijah Eldridge – Grandson of Nan, an herbalist at Robinson House.

Katy Bates – Woman at the settlement.

Norah Lindholm – Laundress at the settlement.

William Burnet – Physician from New Jersey stationed at Robinson House.

Sam Adams, Jr. – Physician stationed on the Northern line at Danbury, CT.

James Thacher –Surgeon with Sixteenth Massachusetts Regiment.

Mrs. Nardy – Hospital matron, supervisor of nursing staff.

Annabelle Tobey – Woman sutler or trader camped at Robinson House.

Jonathan Reed – A blond courier from Virginia Ninth Detachment at West Point.

Jonathan Reed – A dark-haired, bearded patient at Robinson House.

Colonel Amos Kendall – Manages General Arnold's business office.

Colonel Edward Aldrich – Relieves Colonel Kendall.

General Benedict Arnold – Commander at West Point.

Peggy Shippen Arnold – Wife of General Arnold.

Neddy Arnold – Six-month old child.

General Nathaneal Greene – Commander at West Point, succeeds Arnold.

Bridey McGuinness – Barmaid at Brouwer's Tavern.

General George Washington – Commander in Chief, Continental Army.

Colonel Henry Knox – Commander, Artillery division, Continental Army.

Marquis de Lafayette and Alexander Hamilton – Aides to George Washington.

Aaron Burr – Lawyer, former officer in Continental Army.

Colonel Richard Varick and Major David Franks – Aides to Benedict Arnold.

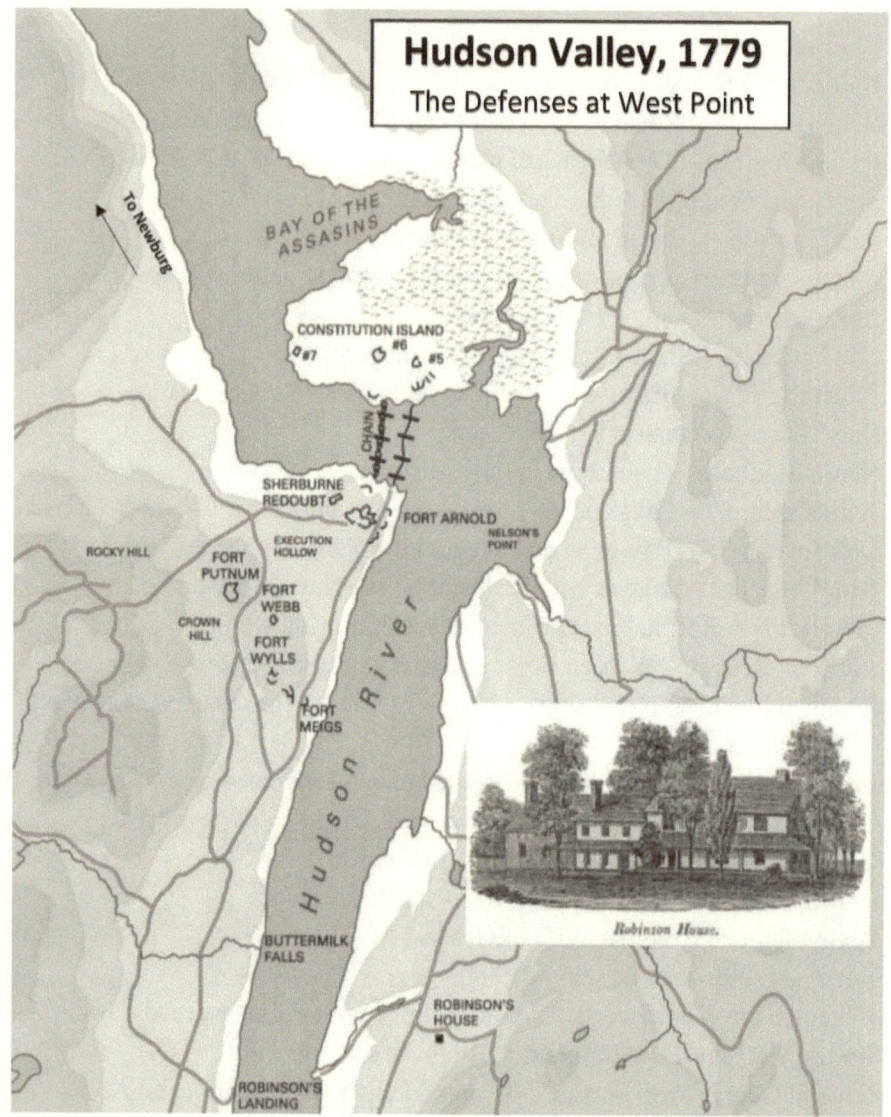

Hudson Valley, 1779
The Defenses at West Point

To Newburg

BAY OF THE ASSASINS

CONSTITUTION ISLAND
#7   #6   #5

CHAIN

SHERBURNE REDOUBT

FORT ARNOLD

NELSON'S POINT

ROCKY HILL

EXECUTION HOLLOW

FORT PUTNUM

FORT WEBB

CROWN HILL

FORT WYLLS

FORT MEIGS

Hudson River

BUTTERMILK FALLS

ROBINSON'S HOUSE

ROBINSON'S LANDING

Robinson House.

Year: 1780

Setting: West Point, the jewel of the Hudson Highlands, a steep and mountainous area, where the Hudson River cuts through a deep canyon. The broad, still tidal river turns and twists in tight curves before flowing south nearly sixty miles to the town of New York. Strategically located, with spectacular overlooks along the river, it features American redoubts armed with cannons to prevent passage of any British shipping.

Chapter 1

There was a heavy stillness in the early August heat. No breeze offered relief as clouds built up and the anticipation of a storm lurked on the horizon. At Robinson House, a young man in uniform strode eagerly into the surgical shed interrupting Dr. William Eustis during the tricky procedure of removing a bullet from a young man's chest. He held out a note. "Excuse me, doctor. I have this message."

"Move back, sir. Just wait. Can you not see? I am in the middle of this!" Eustis set aside his probe and reached for his long forceps. The patient was being held still by one of the doctor's surgical mates. It had taken two men when the procedure began, but after laudanum and whiskey, several gasps and then a gurgled scream, he had passed out.

"Ahhh. Ha," the doctor exclaimed as he located the round ball and accompanying small wad of cloth. Withdrawing both bits gently, he turned to his surgeon's mate, who had been lying across the patient's legs. "Pray, hand me the basin, then a needle and thread." Their patient moaned and rocked his head back and forth. "Aah! Bloody hell," he gasped.

"Hold still," Eustis tersely ordered.

Fortunately, the young soldier passed out again so they could finish efficiently, stitching the wound, packing it with lint, then applying a bandage. Eustis turned to look at the messenger who was peering over his shoulder – hovering, getting in the way. He wiped his hands on a rag handed to him by his aide Noah, grabbed his waistcoat and turned to leave the shed. Annoyed, he gestured to the messenger to follow as he went out the door.

"These interruptions are not acceptable, sir! And I still have two more patients in the barn." Reading the note, he realized that the message sent from across the river was asking, really ordering, him to come immediately to Fort Putnam at West Point. The note had not come from the fort's new commander, General Benedict Arnold, but from a Colonel Kendall whom Eustis did not know. He was directed to examine a corpse.

This did not seem like the outcome of the usual brawl in this area. It hardly seemed likely at West Point. The new and expanding fort complex lay across the mighty Hudson River from Robinson House, the hospital where William Eustis lived and worked. He would have to take the ferry from Garrison's Landing. God's teeth! Another major interruption and nuisance.

The doctor, a man of medium height, hazel eyes, and thick brown wavy hair pulled back with a length of twine, rolled down his sleeves and reluctantly put on his waistcoat, buttoning it almost to the top despite the heat of the day. His steady and reassuring look seemed to give patients the hope they would survive.

His sixteen-year-old aide and some-time servant, wiry Noah Royall, hustled off to get their clothing and mounts ready for possibly two days away. Whenever they crossed the river, they wanted to be prepared.

Eustis went to alert his fellow doctor and the hospital's physician, Dr. William Burnet, that he had been called away and that two patients still required attention. Eustis handled most of the cases calling for his surgical skills. Burnet was trained as a physician and worked more with illnesses.

Although using a crutch, Noah had an amazing ability to get onto his mule by gripping its mane, leaping up, and hooking his good leg over its back. He had lost his leg at the Battle of Bunker Hill and had taken care of their horses since coming to work with Eustis years ago. Back then, Noah's doctor boss had promised to get a wooden leg made for him as soon as he found someone who could do the job.

Entering the side shed where the horses were stabled, Noah tossed a saddle over the back of Eustis's bay horse, Hector. His own pride was a well-mannered gray mule called Sally. Both animals were in good physical shape thanks to the young man's persistent efforts to get them out to the pasture around the farm. It would be a different problem when winter arrived and forage was scarce.

Five years ago, General George Washington, appointed commander in chief by the Continental Congress, had arrived in Cambridge, Massachusetts to take command of the collection of local militias in July 1775. Under its new name, the Continental Army, and its new regulations, officers including doctors were allowed one servant to care for a horse and uniform, to get rations, and manage food allowances.

It had worked out that Noah, originally called Diogenes as a slave, more or less adopted Dr. Eustis. Having lost his mentor, Dr. Joseph Warren, killed during the June battle on Bunker Hill, Eustis appreciated the help and needed a companion of sorts. When Eustis signed on with Henry Knox's newly-formed artillery regiment as its surgeon, the boy had come along, and a carpenter attached to the company made a wooden peg leg for Diogenes who still resorted to his crutch when it was more convenient.

After about ten months, the British evacuated Boston, leaving on their ships for Nova Scotia, and the Continental Army marched south to New York. The doctor had acquired the mule for his aide by then, and as they rode through Connecticut with the rest of the army, Diogenes revealed his desire to have a new name to go with his new status as a free man. When the boy said he did not want a Roman or Greek name, Eustis suggested he think of Biblical ones.

He didn't know much about those Bible people, but the name he

3

chose would be all his own with no connection to his background as an enslaved person. Eustis suggested Daniel from the lions den story, or David for his bout with Goliath, and then suddenly thought of Noah, the man who saved animals by building an ark.

Diogenes certainly had the magic touch with Eustis's opinionated horse, Hector. Saving animals? It seemed perfect, and he took to it immediately. A second name? Did he need one of those as well? Usually for enslaved persons, it was the name of the owner, which would be Royall. He would have to think about that.

Four years later in 1780, Dr. William Eustis and his aide, now called Noah, were stationed at Robinson House beside the Hudson River in upper Manhattan, nearly directly across from West Point. The army had eagerly incorporated the deserted Loyalist property into a much-needed hospital. The self-supporting farmland with a house and two barns had soon become a busy place with comings and goings of wagons loaded with provisions as well as the injured and sick. Camped on its fields were various sutlers' wagons offering goods to purchase and several small military companies who needed their own areas. Some soldiers brought their wives who were not issued equal rations with their husbands so made a living by cooking, sewing or washing.

Dr. Eustis quickly briefed Dr. Burnet that he and Noah had to take time away and cross to West Point. Burnet was not pleased to be left as the only doctor, but he had to honor the orders coming from the fort. And he was not eager to go himself.

As soon as possible, Eustis on Hector and Noah on his mule Sally left for West Point. Approaching the ferry's wooden landing, Hector began to toss his head. He knew what was coming. Loading horse and mule provoked the usual disturbance from Hector who disliked this choice of conveyance. Once on the other side, the horse and mule, three sheep, and several caged brown chickens were unloaded. Some passengers headed south while Eustis and Noah rode north on the well-traveled, hard-packed dirt road toward the Continental Army's fortified complex.

Stone walls and tall grasses separated the road from farmers' fields and woods. The woods had been thinned out because the requirement for wood to supply the forts and families had increased. Local families usually owned woodlots to meet their needs for construction projects or cooking fires, but now a growing army encampment was depleting the area.

Eustis had not been out riding for anything close to pleasure in months. He took a deep breath. From a young age he had enjoyed horses but had not owned one until he was out of Harvard College. Now he just appreciated the fresh air and sense of freedom. Walking was fine, but it was not as good as riding.

The sun beat down. Soon Eustis, in his good black waistcoat, was sweating. The waning days of late summer brought mixed feelings about the cold weather to come, and he tried to enjoy the time despite the heat of the day.

Suddenly Hector stopped. He had heard something. He did not care for whatever it was, snorting in alarm and expressing it in sideways steps. Eustis dismounted to walk him along the scary stretch of road.

Then they heard the boys. One came toward them, skipping around the bend in the dirt road. He appeared to be about ten years old, a spotty boy with reddish brown hair. Barefoot. Skinny. His hand-me-down breeches were too large and secured by a belt likely made from a piece of harness. It looked like an old rein. "'Scuse me, sir. Please. Is this where they found the man?"

"I know nothing about any man. Was he lost? I'm Dr. Eustis, and this is my assistant, Noah Royall. We're on the way to the fort."

"A doctor? I'm Danny Grady. I know a lot of what is going on here 'bouts. A body was found alongside the road someplace here. I work as a 'prentice to Mr. Mugford, the cooper up at the fort. I can show you where to go. Follow me!"

Danny took the lead and Eustis followed along on Hector with Noah close behind. Thinking of what the boy had said, Noah, eyes wide and white in his dark face, nervously watched the sides of the road.

Surprises with dead bodies stirred up hidden and unsettling feelings.

There seemed to be few officers or soldiers in the vicinity of Fort Putnam. Several redoubts clustered near the central height of the fort helped make West Point into an imposing castle-like complex. Another bastion guarded the edge of the river and had been named after Benedict Arnold for his successful fighting style, particularly at Saratoga. Although recently built, the entire complex seemed oddly unfinished. But that explained why Washington had appointed Arnold commander, to take charge, make repairs, and finish building Putnam, the uppermost of the forts. Washington wanted it put into top fighting condition. As soon as Arnold had arrived the week before, he immediately began sending out units on tasks or expeditions.

Eustis thought fondly of the Putnam he knew, General Israel Putnam. He had fought in the French and Indian War with the famed Rogers' Rangers. Back in March 1774, when the British closed the port of Boston, the town was completely shut off. There was no transportation in or out. Other towns around Boston began to send supplies of fish, rice, and grain overland. The legendary Putnam defied the British by driving one hundred thirty sheep from Connecticut through the town's gates. That had been a sight to see!

Putnam was a Massachusetts native, a farmer, and an experienced fighter, known as "Old Put" by his men. White-haired with a hefty build at fifty-seven, he had eagerly risen to the occasion again. After escorting the sheep, he stayed overnight with Dr. Joseph Warren and his assistant, William Eustis, who remembered the old fellow as quite a raconteur with a story for any occasion.

The fort actually honored the name of his cousin, Rufus Putnam, designer of portable armament and defensive tactics that were first used at the Battle of Dorchester Heights.

Chapter 2

The trio entered the West Point complex and paraded uphill to the solid star-designed Fort Putnam. They came to a halt outside what appeared to be the gated main entrance in the outside wall and asked for Colonel Kendall, the author of Eustis's letter. Directed inside, they dismounted, and Noah held the horse and mule. Eustis was shown into Kendall's stifling hot office, where one small window looking onto the fort's interior parade area admitted light but no air. Immaculately dressed, a brusque officer with graying brown hair rose behind his desk.

After a rudimentary salute, Kendall curtly directed, "Explain yourself, sir."

"I am Dr. William Eustis from Robinson House. You asked for me to attend you, sir."

"Yes, I see. My other doctor has no time to deal with any unexplained death. He has enough to do combating the recent fever that has attacked many of the men. We have a detail that just takes care of getting our own dead into the ground. This unexplained body needs to be buried soon in this heat but there is an irritating annoyance holding us up. Have you any experience with anatomy?"

At Eustis's nod, Kendall continued. "If so, doctor, I want you to examine this body and give an opinion on how and why he died. There

7

was very little blood, and I have to say, it doesn't seem right to me. Are you able to look him over?"

"I have experience with autopsies, Colonel Kendall, and I am certainly able to examine him. Do you know who this person is, sir? Or where he is from? Who found him?"

"I do not know anything about him. And I am not interested in having any to-do over this. No complications. I don't know who brought him in. I just need that man identified and a cause of death for my report. Because of the dead man's shirt, my men say they know the regiment he is from, but they do not recognize him. You can look him over now."

Eustis considered, "You have no identification then? Perhaps he had only recently arrived at the fort and he may have come with his wife. It could be that he did not associate with others inside the fort. Did he live here? Or nearby?"

"Listen, doctor. My men said they did not know him, so he cannot be from here."

"Yes, sir, colonel. Has the body been searched for information? Maybe if I can determine how and when he died, we can settle these unanswered questions. With all due respect, I agree it is essential to do an examination and an autopsy."

Colonel Kendall seemed suddenly uneasy. "I am not sure General Arnold would agree to an autopsy. You must surely understand that it is against the church's teachings. We know that the Bible does not approve."

"If it is done with respect and good purpose, I do not see any reason not to conduct one. I studied with Dr. Joseph Warren, sir. You must know his reputation as one of Boston's best doctors and surgeons."

Kendall suddenly glanced around him, looking nervous. He felt out of his depth and unsure of the situation, wondering what to do. He had no instruction for this and did not want to call attention to himself, or the dead, in any way.

"Surely doctor, we know that wars get people killed, but also that God would not like having to reassemble bodies at the time of, you know – the rapture. Nowadays, with the war on, we simply bury bodies with respect and some ceremony and move on. We cannot afford to have the men lose confidence. They must not become too involved, too worried, so we don't talk about it."

Silent enim leges inter arma thought Eustis. "Amid the war, the law falls silent." He had run into this concern over autopsies in his conservative hometown of Boston.

"But the soldier's name is important to honor as well as determine the cause of death," Eustis countered. "Accurate identification might require an autopsy. Let me examine the body and then I can come discuss my findings with you. We can go on from there."

Colonel Kendall seemed to be wavering, backing away from his original idea, so Eustis pressed on. "May I at least have a full hour with the body before they remove it for burial? I can try to identify him." He paused, then added, "The man's commanding officer will also need to notify the family. Otherwise General Arnold will have to be called in."

At this point, sounds of a horse and then loud uneven footsteps were heard approaching. General Benedict Arnold arrived, limping as usual and out of breath. He slammed into the office, clearly not happy, loudly stating he was taking over from the inadequate fools he had to work with. Everyone in the room fell silent, exuding feelings of apprehension. Danny Grady backed into a corner.

"Good morning, sir," said Kendall, standing erect and saluting Arnold.

"What is going on, Kendall? And what are you doing here, Dr. Eustis? I thought you were over at Robinson House. You are not supposed to be visiting here!"

"I was called in to examine a body found down the road, sir."

Colonel Kendal looked worried. "I am sorry, General Arnold. I had not intended to disturb you, sir. I thought I would take care of it. But now it seems Dr. Eustis wants to examine the body more thoroughly than I had anticipated. I am not sure about that at all. But I would have given you a full report."

9

"I'll deal with you later, Kendall. First tell me about this man. How and where did he die? Was there some skirmish I have not been told about?"

Not sure if he should be relieved or not, Colonel Kendall explained that the body was found on the road to the fort by a man out riding that morning. It was just after dawn, maybe 5:00 a.m. The discoverer had hurried to the fort to report it to him as officer in charge, and Kendall had sent two men to check and immediately get back to him.

On their return, the two men reported they found the body of a man protruding into the edge of the roadway with his legs back along the verge. It seemed best to them to bring it to the fort, so they had slung the body over one of the horses and walked back.

"I looked it over when it arrived, sir, and it was not one of my men. We're not sure who it is," said Kendall.

Arnold looked exhausted and seemed to have many other things on his mind. Kendall was nearly wringing his hands. Eustis, stepping in, urged, "We need to identify the body to file a report."

"There is no need to alarm General Washington," Arnold said. "The man is dead, so there is little point to it. Probably rambunctious boys startled him into falling, and his horse ran away. Or he could have had a secret rendezvous with a woman, and her husband came along."

His initial angry snit over, Arnold sighed. "I will give you time with the body, Dr. Eustis. I agree that he should be identified, and we need to know how he was killed. I just do not want any attention drawn to the West Point area before we get it better fortified."

"I understand, sir."

"Maybe the whole episode was an accident," Arnold repeated. "As I said, perhaps it grew from an exchange for a woman's favors. But if so, where is the woman?"

Eustis could see that the general was beginning to realize the problem.

"Perhaps a woman was his killer. Or a lover? Many women live around these camps. I just don't want General Washington involved," Arnold said again.

10

With Arnold's permission, Eustis and Colonel Kendall left and walked along the inside wall to a shed used for building supplies. They told Noah and Danny to mind the horses. Entering the shed, Kendall grabbed a lantern and, using his flint, quickly got it lighted. He hung it from a hook in the ceiling beam, and left to stand outside the door.

And there it was on the left among the barrels and boards, a man's body laid out on two planks over sawhorses. It should have been covered. Flies were collecting for the feast. Luckily, there was not yet much of an odor.

Eustis removed his waistcoat and rolled up his shirtsleeves before moving closer, looking carefully at the body. Rigor mortis had set in. Death had occurred at least six to eight or more hours ago. It could have been very early that morning or last night.

The body's odor was more noticeable when he got closer. There were odd overtones. It seemed more like garlic than the usual decaying of flesh. Some herb? He knew he should know what it was and would have to come back to it.

The man's face and neck were a deep reddish purple, more so on his left side. He must have been lying on the ground for some time as the blood settled on a downward facing side. At first look, it was hard to tell what killed him, or at least it was not obvious. The purpling effectively disguised any bruising. There was a trail of dried blood around one ear and running down into and under the collar. Eustis pried open the mouth and was surprised to smell vomit and see some other material that seemed to be foaming saliva. Maybe he'd been sick, and they were dealing with some contagion?

The doctor quickly tried to ascertain what had happened. It was probably not a fight. The body had no obvious signs of directed violence – just minor bruising and scratches on the face and hands. In fact, it was startling. The man was clearly dead, but there was no major stab wound and not a lot of blood. If he'd been lying with his ear to the ground, more blood had likely seeped into the earth. Certainly he could not have died in his sleep as he was found on the side of the road.

He looked about Eustis's age – perhaps in his mid-twenties. He wore a fringed hunting shirt like the rifle companies did. He was not dressed as an officer and was wearing moccasins. His hat, black felt with the brim laced up on the right side, had been placed on top of a barrel with a belt and powder horn a few feet to the left. Possibly he was a sharpshooter, a rifleman. The powder horn was there. But no rifle. Where was his valuable weapon? Perhaps Kendall had confiscated it for another's use. Eustis would have to ask. Or it could have been stolen by the killer. Maybe theft of the weapon was the motive for this attack.

Eustis decided he needed to have the clothing removed, the body naked to complete his examination. Kendall remained outside, not wanting anything to do with this procedure. Eustis also did not want the boys involved, but his hour was running out. Eustis called to the colonel. Kendall stuck his head inside and then cooperated to the extent of calling for a militia volunteer.

While waiting for help to arrive, Eustis continued his exam. The end of the man's right index finger was missing and had been for some time. Under the dirt, his nails and hands appeared too good for a farmer. There were no signs of other obvious injuries. Bleeding seemed so minimal, he could have been killed elsewhere and the body moved to the road before he was moved to the shed here. Maybe he bled out on the ground or his heart stopped before he could be stabbed?

A big, red haired, heavily-freckled man, coatless, ambled in and introduced himself as Alexander MacDougal. "Eh, call me Sandy, sir. I've got family here 'bouts. If you need any more help just let me know."

With MacDougal's help, Eustis stripped the corpse, removing the fringed tow cloth hunting shirt, stockings, and brown woolen breeches. The shirt showed a small bloody patch on the left side shoulder where blood had seeped down and there was a definite small puncture wound in the man's left ear. Bits of grass and soil stuck to it. Dr. Warren had always admonished his students to not jump to conclusions and to look

12

for details before coming to any diagnosis. The slight odd smell was still puzzling.

They looked over the man's shirt and breeches. They were lived in but in better condition and cleaner than the usual well-worn, filthy Continental soldier's clothing. Those were generally homemade or issued many months before. The condition of MacDougal's clothes was typical for most soldiers. "If they'd a fit me, I'd be glad to have 'em, doc."

There were no patches, darns, or sewn up seams in his shirt or breeches. The stockings were remarkable for the lack of holes. His body looked in good shape with no ribs showing – not the half-starved appearance of most of the Continental soldiers. It all just did not fit. The man had to be a recent recruit. A strange thought intruded. What if the man was British out of New York but not a real Continental soldier? Then what was he doing here? Perhaps some assignment?

There was no end to the puzzling questions. Had someone used a thin-bladed knife? Who carries those? Anything requiring substantial strength might leave out a woman, he thought, until he realized there were plenty of women who could use one. Any of the women around the camp, in fact. This man might not have been killed right there on the wagon path. Where were locations around the fort for meetings? Redoubts?

It could even be a vast mistake, some mistaken identity. There were just too many answers needed. Arnold was breathing down his neck so they could bury the corpse, but Eustis wanted to consult with other people.

He covered the body with an old linen sheet sent over by Kendall and, grabbing his waistcoat, left the shed. The clean-smelling air outside was magnificent. Wiping his face with a handkerchief, he took a few deep breaths. Then it came to him. That was it! The dead man had probably been eating anise or garlic! That would account for the odor beyond that of the decaying body.

On a positive note, Eustis realized that once he had gotten into it, Kendall had become concerned with doing things the proper way, and he certainly wanted to do right by the fellow. Arnold had called for an informational meeting of officers before their early-afternoon dinner. As it was nearly that time, the doctor decided to get a mug of coffee and think about what he had seen so he could be more coherent.

He walked over to the officers' mess. While he was there, a man arrived looking for Dr. Eustis, introducing himself as Lieutenant Eric Thorson. He had served with the Pennsylvania rifle regiment and offered his help with identifying the dead man. Eustis took him back to look at the body, hoping to wrap everything up with a name. But the lieutenant did not recognize the dead man as being anyone registered with the companies he knew.

As they were walking back to attend Arnold's meeting, a rider arrived, leaping off his horse, shouting that he had a message for Dr. Eustis from Dr. Burnet. He must return to Robinson House as soon as possible! Dr. Burnet needed help immediately. It seemed that about twenty cases of the bloody flux had appeared among the soldiers around Robinson House that morning. Arnold's one-hundred-man personal escort was camped near the house, and they could all become sick. Something had to be done. Coming outside to meet Eustis, Arnold led him back inside and insisted he leave immediately.

The general paced back and forth behind his desk. "Dr. Eustis. I am very concerned. Mrs. Arnold and our son will be arriving soon. You must leave. Now!"

"I will be off as soon as I can, general. But we have to decide how to hold this unknown person's body for about two days. I could not complete my examination in the hour you allotted to me, and I would appreciate knowing what you have found so far."

The general sighed in exasperation. "Have you learned nothing, Dr. Eustis? Surely you must be aware of the temperature, and surely you have some vague experience with what happens with bodies. I cannot just save it in that shed for you even though you may wish to play with it further!"

Danny Grady knocked at the office door. He had heard the growing urgency in Arnold's voice. "Excuse me, sirs. Could I please say something?"

Arnold waved him away. Eustis, equally annoyed at the interruption, turned to continue his talk. The general was still urging him to wrap up the investigation. "This is no time to keep a body out of the ground! Think, doctor! There is no place they can put it! In a well? No! You will have to accept it in the end. Why not now? Just sign the paperwork, and we can get it handled."

Remembering how they dealt with some of these situations in Boston, Eustis wondered, "I have a possible solution, sir. Is there an icehouse nearby? Where it could be kept for a couple of days? That is all we need. An icehouse near or in the fort?"

"Doctor, you clearly do not seem to understand. I am tired of this stupid debate. You must have realized we cannot get ice easily from the river. It is tidal and rarely freezes here. Besides, we are in the middle of summer. Be realistic." He waved his hand. "Dismissed. Go."

Danny, still hovering in the office doorway and practically dancing in place, eagerly interrupted, incurring annoyed looks from both men. "I know about an icehouse! My master, the cooper, has sawdust and an icehouse. They get their ice from a pond every winter, and some is left."

Arnold, despite wanting Eustis across the river and back at the hospital immediately, reluctantly agreed. An aide was sent to clear the idea with the cooper and make the arrangements. They could use the wagon and place the body in the icehouse – but only temporarily. With summer temperatures, it was not going to be long-term storage by any means.

As he went toward the door, Eustis reminded the general that the body should be guarded and not become some object of scurrilous interest. It must not be disturbed. Reluctantly, hating to release any extra men but realizing the necessity, Arnold agreed and told Kendall to assign men to alternate as guards, but only for two days.

Eustis thanked Arnold, wished him good day, and left the office, pleased to find that Noah had already brought both of their mounts and gear to the door. He was talented at listening at a door and always made Eustis's life work smoothly. Rarely would anyone stand up to Arnold's arrogance and argue as Eustis had done, but thanks to their basic friendship and common accommodations in Robinson House, it was a risk that luckily had worked this time.

It would make his mind clearer and more settled, Eustis thought, if there was a time to discuss the situation and the vague possibilities of murder with Arnold. But the general clearly was not in the right mood and perhaps not the right person. He just seemed angry and distracted. It would require creative thinking and an exploratory mind. Riding out of the fort, he pondered. Who would be good? Who among his friends would be available? Eustis considered sending a message to James Thacher – his longtime associate and friend who was the surgeon with the Massachusetts Sixteenth Regiment.

But the regiment probably would not arrive to establish winter quarters for months. It could still be as far away as Pennsylvania, even Virginia. For the past two years, the Sixteenth had been quartered nearby for the winter and Eustis hoped that would continue. Thacher was a good friend and an excellent doctor. He had just the mind for solving these kinds of problems. He was the one who had treated Arnold's infected leg and managed to save it when others wanted to amputate. He also enjoyed a pint at the local tavern after payday, although their paydays came with less and less certainty.

Eustis thought of another lifelong friend, Dr. Sam Adams Jr. He had known Sam since they were little boys playing in the water at the edge of Boston Harbor and sledding down Beacon Hill. Sam was close to the West Point area and might be able to get a few day's leave to examine the body with him. He usually was located along the northern line that extended west from Danbury, Connecticut. General Washington had established it to prevent the British from reinvading New England by land. So now, Eustis had heard, the bloody British just went around by sea to raid seaport towns.

Eustis was worried, concerned to get back and see what had happened in the short time they had been away from Robinson House. Loading the mounts on the ferry involved the usual disagreement and dancing around. Hector apparently did not think he should have to endure this experience twice in the same day. Sally was patient with the kerfuffle. Always a sensible mule, she knew food awaited if she could get back to her home barn. And that reminded Eustis that they had no idea about the dead man's horse. Did he have one? If so, where was it?

When arrangements had been made to turn Colonel Robinson's estate into a hospital, a lean-to on the back of one barn had been assigned for officers' horses. Hay, a diminishing commodity, was stored in half of one barn's loft. Up to one hundred patients now slept on cots or on hay-stuffed mattresses in both barns. An outside shed was set aside for the surgery. Everything, all objects including farm equipment, had been cleared out and put in another shed elsewhere on the property. There was nothing anyone could do about the screams.

The much-admired Dr. Benjamin Rush considered barns the best hospitals because of their air flow. He perhaps forgot that northern winters made them very cold and that circulation was far from sufficient in the sweltering summer heat. The house itself, a two-story clapboard Georgian style with a side wing, had lots of rooms.

As Noah and the doctor rode into the yard, the smell of human waste overpowered everything else. Eustis could see small gatherings of sutlers and some members of Arnold's uniformed guard. They appeared to be talking with some sense of urgency, and when they saw Eustis approach, they started toward him. He turned Hector over to Noah who took both animals to the horse shed.

One of the beefier members of Arnold's guard approached. "'Scuse me, Dr. Eustis, sir. Dr. Burnet won't tell us nothin' 'bout what's goin' on. We've got some of our men really sick. And those traders ain't happy with us. They say we brought it to 'em. Can you tell 'em 'twas not us?"

"As you can see, I just got here from the Point," Eustis said. "I understand you are worried, but you cannot expect me to know anything yet. I need some time with Dr. Burnet, my good fellows. I will tell you what I know after I find out the situation."

The soldiers sick with the bloody flux, or dysentery, had been isolated in two bays in the barn farthest from the house. Eustis went in to confer with Burnet and the head matron, Mrs. Nardy. Burnet was from New Jersey, about five years older than Eustis with light brown hair, a cleft chin, and expressive dark eyebrows. He was trained more as a physician than a surgeon. Each man's experience and knowledge complemented the others.

The smell in the barn was more than the usual mix of hay, wood, and sick men. It now included odors of chamber pots and damp clothing and bedding. Eustis was reminded of wet dogs. Mrs. Nardy had done what she could, but it seemed to be a losing battle getting enough helpers to aid the acutely sick men. The situation was not good at all, and those who were very sick might well die. Could Noah help too?

The issues of cleanliness and diet needed to be addressed immediately. Most especially, more latrines had to be dug away from the sources of drinking water. Dysentery had not been a problem before Arnold's troop had moved in. Those men must have been unsupervised or not given proper instructions. Eustis was somehow surprised at that. The importance of a proper camp with latrines had been repeatedly stressed back in Cambridge per General Washington's orders.

Arnold returned that evening and conducted his own inspection, something he had neglected before. He issued orders that his men immediately construct and use the latrines. His men were not to just relieve themselves wherever they wanted. The river banks were not to be used. For drinking water, they must use the farm's well, not the river.

To Eustis's relief, Arnold was his usual charming self during their evening supper, a better one than their usual repast of bread and cheese. Noah and the other officers' servants ate at the large kitchen table before they served the officers in the dining room. Someone had had luck fishing, and the kitchen crew that day prepared a particularly savory fish stew. It was a welcome change.

Chapter 3

Arnold had been given time off to recover from the horrendous wounds he had sustained at the Battle of Bemis Heights during the second and victorious fight at Saratoga. He served during his convalescence as military governor of Philadelphia. Despite the scandals that revolved around Arnold during this time, General Washington believed he was a talented soldier. He valued Arnold's fighting experience as the most effective combat general in the young Continental Army. Earlier that June, because of his talents in the field, Washington had asked Arnold to assume the field command of a department in the army.

To Washington's astonishment, and disappointment, Arnold had declined, pleading that his still painfully injured and shortened leg made him incapable of vigorous active duty. He could not ride a horse easily, so he suggested instead that he command the garrison at West Point. After some thought, Washington granted the request. He had hoped that the arrival of the French would bring arms and ammunition to his army by July. That had fallen through and he realized it would be best to put what money and time the army had into strengthening the defenses – hence his concern about West Point. He really had wanted Arnold to be an active soldier, but nothing that year had gone the way he wanted.

Short and egocentric, Arnold had arrived with a grand flurry. It was another surprise that he had chosen not to live in the fortress that he commanded but across the river in Robinson House despite its being used as a hospital.

He explained that the rural surroundings better suited his family. The estate certainly suited his image. It was more gentlemanly, with an attractive country setting and a view of the river, and it would be much more comfortable. Ever cautious, Arnold had arranged for his hundred-man personal guard to camp in tents around the house. They were issued rations as was the household. He also arrived with an eight-oared, thirty-foot-long bateau, or longboat, to facilitate his travels on the river.

Remaining camped in the surrounding field were sutlers with their wagons. The sutlers' camp had nearly doubled in size, and the vendors moved their wagons closer to Robinson House, expecting to find more customers needing whatever they could sell – from leather to lace.

Hoping to remain in the house himself, Dr. Eustis welcomed West Point's new commander. He wished to avoid a repeat of that earlier winter when Major General William Heath had taken over the house and closed it to any medical use, thus evicting the doctors. This time the two resident doctors chose to share a bedroom rather than flip a Spanish dollar to see who would move to the attic or barns. The Arnolds would take two of the remaining rooms, still leaving several rooms and the attic.

Once General Arnold had moved in with his entourage, he and his aides and the doctors frequently dined together. Arnold had his own menu, budget and cook and sometimes the entire household benefitted. He and Eustis renewed their acquaintanceship from back during the siege of Boston. Arnold's wife, Peggy, a petite, blonde, nineteen-year-old socialite, would arrive weeks after her husband, in mid-September. As far as the doctors were concerned, despite all being more crowded, it was much better than the winter when General Heath lived there. And there was more staff in the kitchen.

Together the two doctors cared for the nearly one hundred patients, and Mrs. Nardy, as matron, supervised all nursing help provided by women living in the area. Dr. Burnet, trained as a physician, was assumed to be more experienced in diagnosis. Eustis did most of the surgery. General Washington had directly urged that every effort be made to avoid using men who could fight for nursing duty.

The sun rose early that August morning, the sky glowing pink, and the day warmed rapidly. It could be another unseasonably hot one, thought Eustis. An adequate breakfast of bread and coffee was set out for the officers and doctors in the dining room. As usual, both doctors made their early-morning rounds in the two barns to see how their patients had fared overnight. Later, after stepping outside, they made their plans for further necessary medical care or surgeries.

There was the usual stir around the property as the entire camp awoke. Cooking fires quickly created a smoky haze. The grounds as well as the nearest meadow were filled with tents, huts, sheep pens, and laundry lines. The farm's cows gazed at the horizon, ruminating over their breakfast in the farther meadow. Women with their skirts tucked up for safety had begun to chop kindling, haul water, build up fires, and set their large iron pots to boil in preparation for the day's laundry business. The smell of lye mingled with those of bacon and coffee throughout the sutlers' camp.

Mrs. Nardy met the doctors in the shade by the barn door. She had been head of the nursing staff for several years. A plump determined woman of middle age, with graying brown hair in her forties, she was invaluable to the operations at Robinson House. A born organizer, she knew exactly what had to be done to help their patients.

Right now, they needed to plan how, with limited surgeon's mates and nurses, to combat this outbreak of dysentery before it spread through the entire camp. As they talked, Eustis absently scratched at his waistline under his waistcoat, catching Mrs. Nardy's sharp eye. "And that reminds me, Dr. Eustis. We need to do something about our lice infestation. 'Tis increasing again. The men recently come in with General Arnold are askin' for lard to treat their clothes and are smokin' them over their campfires. They seem to have a variety of remedies, and I don't know which is best."

Eustis groaned. "Ahh, Mrs. Nardy. If it isn't one thing, it's another; lice, or those barn swallows. What can we do to discourage the birds in the barn from defecating? Some of the bedding is getting hit. And the lice can bring typhus. Do you remember what worked best the last time we fought lice? We can't make all the men go swimming and wash their clothes. Most would desert."

"Last time, we ended up turnin' out most of the mattress ticks and re-stuffin' them with fresh straw. Let me look into it," she said to his relief.

It was becoming a lovely summer morning and, with a cooling breeze, not as hot as yesterday. It was hard to believe a horrid disease called the bloody flux lurked around them. It brought fever, bloody diarrhea, and abdominal cramps. And Eustis knew it was particularly infectious, although no one seemed to know exactly how it was transmitted among people.

There were theories that the infection could be passed along by dirty hands, anything that might be contaminated with fecal matter, and even drinking water. Through their experience, the doctors knew that cleanliness seemed to help combat any disease, particularly the disposal of feces. Mrs. Nardy bustled about. She would see to it that the sick soldiers were given plenty of water and make sure they were kept as clean as possible.

The camp's residents, Arnold's guard, and anyone else living on the grounds were set to digging new latrines and directed to wash everything, including their clothes and themselves. There was a great deal of resistance among the men, and it took orders from General Arnold to at least begin cleaning the camp.

By the end of the day, new latrines had been set up, some surrounded by fences. General Arnold had issued orders for no defecation in the camp except in designated areas. Those sick with dysentery were isolated in two bays within the second barn. There seemed to be some sense of achievement, of fighting back against the disease, and everyone seemed pleased they were slowing its progress. They also understood that if not, they had Mrs. Nardy to face. She was fierce about doing things the correct way. And God bless her for that.

Eustis wanted to go back to West Point as soon as he could. He needed answers to a multitude of questions if he was to come up with any solution to the identity of the dead man and how he had died.

Oddly, it seemed like Arnold was distracted and just wanted the death and its accompanying questions swept under the rug. He had other matters to deal with, and it was clear that he did not want to disturb Washington. Among those tasks were preparations for the coming winter. His plans included sending a company from the fort to cut wood some distance away, and he was about to send another company over into northern Manhattan to patrol.

Eustis could not get his additional responsibility, this investigation, out of his mind. He hoped for good news and that one of the friends he had sent notes to would arrive or write that they might find time to come help him work out this puzzle. Sam Adams, as a fellow doctor, solved puzzles and medical problems all day every day and equally hated the unknown. He would be perfect.

William Burnet, his fellow doctor, offered sympathy. "I am certainly glad they chose you instead of me." He understood the turmoil Eustis was in and how much he wanted to figure out exactly what had happened at West Point. Luckily for him, autopsies were not part of Burnet's experience. Eustis was the one who had studied bodies with Dr. Warren and as a student at Harvard.

The following day at their midday dinner, Burnet generously reinforced the idea that Eustis go back across the river the next morning. Things seemed to have settled down, and their sickest soldiers were improving. He would manage with the help of their two surgeon's mates, their aides, and Mrs. Nardy.

Before Arnold retired that evening, he also encouraged Eustis to take a two-day leave to return to West Point. He showed no interest in solving the questions around the murder or discussing it, but he wanted the body out of the icehouse and buried. He also did not want Eustis to stray long from his medical duties. "I need you to be working to prevent the flux in my guard, Dr. Eustis, not just traipsing around, visiting in the countryside. I have other plans for those men."

Dawn came a little later the next morning as they crept toward the fall equinox. The doctors ambled out to the barn in the half-light to make their early rounds. Noah had the horse and mule saddled, ready to go, packed again with all their necessities. "Give me an hour, Noah. And get yourself something to eat."

Once Eustis reappeared at the door, they were off. Gathering the reins, Eustis mounted Hector, Noah leapt aboard Sally, and, waving good-bye, they started toward the ferry. As they rode from the barnyard, they could see sutlers' wagons filled with the end-of-summer harvest – corn, squashes, and pumpkins. Most families would be starting to preserve food for the winter.

Arriving at the sloping ferry ramp at Garrison's Landing, they faced yet again the chore of persuading Hector onto the ferry. Sally gazed placidly at the river as they crossed. Noah wondered if Sally was just older and more experienced. Why couldn't Hector be more like Sally?

Riding up the road to West Point, Noah trailed behind as he had been previously taught during his enslavement by the Royall family, feeling uncomfortably exposed by riding ahead. It seemed to Noah that some days were more hopeful than others. And he had Sally, an important part of his life. Maybe, when the war ended, he could get a proper document as a free man, go West, and Sally could carry him. He heard that free Black men were more accepted there and would be hired on at ranches or could make their own way as homesteaders. As an alternative, he could get to New Bedford in Massachusetts and sign on with a whaling ship. The great goal was to become his own man, and there were not many Black men around as examples. He had thought of trying to talk to Billy Lee, Washington's body servant and slave who went with the general everywhere. But Noah soon concluded that was a hopeless situation. For now, life was interesting, he had his place to sleep and food, and he was learning all sorts of things.

Noah believed his lucky star was shining when he came to work for the doctor. He had been working with Eustis in Massachusetts since the beginning of the rebellion. He met the doctor under the worst of circumstances in mid-June 1775 when he was brought in and laid out on a table in the Sun Tavern. His fellow fighters were brought down via barrows, stretchers, or friends' shoulders as the battle raged up on Mr. Bunker's hill to their east. It was the second failed British charge that got him, and he had been carried to the tavern. He remembered it as a very bad time with lots of pain.

About half of his left leg was missing from a cannon ball that had bounced into the redoubt where he was. He also had a sword slash across his left temple. Eustis did not hold out much hope for him but applied a tourniquet and went to work removing the damaged part of his leg as quickly as possible. Several aides helped the doctor and held him down until he passed out. Then they stitched and bandaged his head tightly. Enough pressure would control the bleeding there.

It took several hours for the young Black man named for a mythological Greek to regain his senses. Even then, he was not too sure about the reality of his painful injuries. Mayhap it was due to the trauma or the sword wound to his head. The doctor could not say.

At one point early in his recovery, Diogenes had told Dr. Eustis that he was not sure where he came from. He only knew that he had been bought in Barbados when he was maybe six or eight years old, and that a white man had taken him away to his plantation and named him Diogenes. This master, Isaac Royall, also had a big house in Medford, Massachusetts, but left to go into Boston in April 1775 when the rebellion began. With Boston suddenly under siege, Mr. Royall stayed safely behind the lines there. Diogenes, who had heard the speeches about freedom, maybe even for himself, ran away to join the local militia and could, at least, get food.

***

25

Anytime Eustis approached the West Point fortress, whether by boat or on horseback, he reveled in its collection of defenses and redoubts. They numbered about ten now and impressed him every time. The largest stronghold, Fort Putnam, squatted on a natural platform of rocks overlooking the sweeping bend of the river. Behind it, rocky ridges provided further natural defenses where more redoubts with cannon were being positioned. The entire complex, appearing as a strongly fortified medieval town or a large castle, overlooked the plain below where Fort Arnold sprawled near the edge of the river.

The West Point fortress was really the key to preventing the British forces from enacting their primary wartime strategy of controlling the Hudson River and isolating New England from the rest of the country. Although he had not seen it, Eustis had been told about a formidable barricading chain with huge iron links that had been strung across the river on floating logs. Batteries on both sides of the river guarded it, everything engineered to prevent British passage up the river. And General Arnold had the task of getting it properly fortified, armed, and manned in just a few months; fine tuning its ability to hold off an army of up to twenty thousand men.

Eustis, followed by Noah, cantered along the wagon road to Fort Putnam. From the cooper's workshop at the fort, Danny had been watching for the doctor's return, and as soon as they came through the gate, he ran toward them, calling. "Dr. Eustis! Dr. Eustis! I have something for you!"

"Greetings, Danny. And what have you got to tell me?"

"Doctor, sir. That dead man used to walk around here. I heard about him. He wanted to know things, like wagons 'n how to get to places. Said he was from a regiment."

But which one? Why transportation? Wagons? And what had been his name? No one had managed to get that information. Eustis thanked him and tried not to discourage the boy with these unanswered questions. What Danny did tell him set him to wondering what this man really had been doing.

Eustis intended to check in with Colonel Kendall but found General Arnold in the outer office with Kendall, assigning work parties to leave the fort for the next few weeks to gather wood for winter. They were not to remain near the fort or in any of the surrounding areas, but to go farther west in their scavenging.

As he entered, there was another officer sort of lounging in Arnold's own office. Eustis noticed his unusual, certainly different uniform. He had lots of very fine lace at his wrists and collar with a satin waistcoat and a jacket with wide lapels and tight breeches. He wore the usual sword and carried a small cane, or something like a swagger stick. In his white wig, carefully structured and coiffed, he certainly was not the usual Arnold type of associate, and Eustis inwardly classified him as an upper-class snob, probably a foreigner.

Arnold might have made this acquaintance during his stint as governor in Philadelphia, Eustis thought, but there did not seem to be a real explanation as to why this fancy gentleman was sitting in this West Point office. Most likely he was associated with the French. Maybe an officer? Perhaps he was headed to see the French in Newport or was going across the river to join the recently arrived French company in their new encampment. The women, children, and baggage accompanying the French had been sent across the river for safe housing at West Point where they now added confusion and annoyance to Arnold and took up precious campground space.

Before Arnold could reply to Eustis's question about gaining access to the body hopefully still awaiting his inspection in the icehouse, Arnold's guest interrupted their conversation. He had a long face affecting a constantly bored look, as was probably the latest fashion somewhere. "Zounds, my dear fellow, this is beneath us. I say, Arnold, you are the general, the authority, here. You should not have to deal with this, this nonsense about dead bodies."

Very strange around these parts to find a dolt with intellectual affectations, thought Eustis. And speaking like that to General Arnold! Maybe he was a leader in fashion somewhere. But here? Arnold turned back to Eustis, after frowning at the man, probably a Frenchman. He had laid his cane on Arnold's desk. It had a distractingly ornate handle of a vulture's head. Could this be the exaggerated fashion style called macaroni?

Looking somewhat embarrassed, Arnold spoke: "Good morning, Dr. Eustis. I will send for someone to guide you to the icehouse."

They were interrupted again by the guest calling through the doorway.

"Odd's fish, man! We have better things to do! I say my good fellow, Eustis, is it? Can you not take care of this? Move or bury the dead man? I detect a hint of aroma in the air." And he waved his lace handkerchief beneath his nose.

Arnold called for his aide, Richard Varick, who would take the doctor to the icehouse. Eustis knew Varick from their mutual residency in Robinson House. Noah and Danny Grady, affecting some kind of official capacity, followed along. Varick unlocked the door, and Eustis entered to look over the corpse again.

This man's death could not have been accidental. There had to be a reason, a motive. Someone had to gain by it. An identity was crucial. Then they could go on from there. The shed had a distinct odor that Eustis remembered from his days at Harvard as a member of the Spunkers Club, the secret group that learned about anatomy by performing autopsies on bodies stolen from the gallows on Boston Neck.

Varick left them there to figure it out, saying he would send over help to move the corpse. Noah and Danny helped Eustis assemble two sawhorses and planks outside the door as the icehouse itself was small with no room to move. It had only been meant to store blocks of ice buried in sawdust, not serve as a morgue. The boys stood back as a man they had never met arrived to help and, with the doctor, carefully carried the body outside, laid it on the planks, and unwrapped the linen, dusting off clinging sawdust. Although the air was better outdoors, it was obvious from its condition, appearance and odor that the corpse had to be buried very soon.

Eustis made some sketches, trying to note everything of importance or that he would need to remember. Doing so reminded him about getting an artist to draw the man's portrait for reference and identification. They could circulate it to the other companies to help find out who he was. His identity was a top priority.

He should take note of the teeth too. Teeth had been critical in identifying Dr. Warren's body when they finally recovered it after the battle on Bunker Hill. Paul Revere had made false teeth for Warren and recognized his own work.

Eustis looked the dead man over again. As noted, the end of this man's index finger was severed at the first joint. It was an old scar, perhaps from childhood. The man looked as if he might have been in a fist fight or a scuffle. Bruises on his face and one wrist. Eustis took special notice of the small wound in the left ear and the blood stain on the shirt. Measuring the incision, more of a puncture put it about a quarter inch across.

Then, with Noah backing farther away, Eustis took a steading breath and used his small scalpel to cut into the flesh, tracing the wound into the ear. It penetrated all the way to the brain. Usually stab wounds result in an exploding spurt of blood. But where was the evidence of that? There was not much on his shirt. Maybe it had gotten on the killer, but that seemed unlikely, or maybe his clothes had been changed. Pressure on the wound would not have stopped any bleeding. It made no sense. Maybe Eustis could find more information along the path or road where the body had been found, or find a blood stain where it had lain. But they would have to find the exact spot.

After moving the corpse, wrapped again in linen, back inside the icehouse and before leaving to look further at the area where it was found, Eustis went to the office to see Colonel Kendall.

"If you could answer a few more questions, sir, I can be out of here. For instance, does the army require an inquest? Do they consult a local sheriff? Was there some legal procedure to determine facts and cause of death?"

29

Kendall was only sure of procedures when a man died in the cause of duty or service, or was condemned. But they would certainly need some kind of paperwork. Eustis asked him to get an artist to draw the man and his teeth so they could circulate a portrait for identification.

Persisting in trying to get the job done the right way, Eustis asked to see General Arnold to request a certificate of death and to release the body for burial. After a few minutes of waiting, he was shown into the general's office and greeted with a brisk "Make it quick."

In times of war on what is contested territory, Arnold said, there is no rule for needing an inquest. There were no sheriffs that he knew of. It seemed since they were not yet an independent country, and had left English rule, there were no governmental protocols or legal procedures that he knew about for inquests on an incidental body, and he certainly was not going to send the question to the Continental Congress. The army itself, though, had proper procedures and accounts, and any death is recorded with its cause, just as was done for those who had died in Eustis's and Burnet's care. Eustis inwardly resented the implication and slur against their skills and efforts. Arnold rudely went on to say the doctor just needed to establish the cause of death as being a stabbing and put it in a report, then go back to Robinson House.

Eustis mulled over possibilities later as he ambled on Hector back along the wagon road, followed by Noah. Having gotten a description from Danny, who lived with his mother in a cabin nearby, he decided to take an hour or so to locate the area where the body had been found. It would be very helpful if he could interview the person who found it, but no one seemed to be forthcoming with that person's name. Perhaps they had not paid attention to it.

It was getting on toward afternoon, and Eustis needed to stay focused. He really should make a list and at least write down the situation as he knew it before he fell into his bunk in the officers quarters that evening.

Chapter 4

Heading south, they caught up with a young woman walking along the wagon road. Curling strands of russet with blonde streaks escaped her mob cap, and she carried a basket filled with what appeared to be dirty shirts. Eustis could see oily gray smudges around a collar as he came beside her. Tipping his hat, he wished her a good day as he rode past. She glanced up at him briefly, nodded, then appeared to look again.

"Excuse me, sir. Are you Dr. Eustis?" she called, darting forward. When Eustis said he was, she seemed to gather her nerve and told him she had been at the fort and heard about his attempt to solve the mystery of the man found dead along the road. Hoping for a little more information, Eustis dismounted so he did not loom over her. As a local, she might be a good source. Noah discreetly held back.

She seemed nervous, asking anxiously, "Please. Do you know who he is? They would not let me look at him. Why would they not let me see? My husband is with a Pennsylvania rifle company. I am just so worried. Can you tell me what he looked like? Please, sir? Is he dark or fair?"

"Tell me about your husband's regiment, mistress. Did you arrive recently?"

"Oh, no, sir," she said. "We have been here since early spring. We arrived back in April, and my husband went off with his regiment. I just wait."

"But how can you just stay here?"

She relaxed enough to explain. "My husband's posted to a new company with seven other riflemen. They added riflemen to their firepower before they went out on this year's campaign. But I don't know where they are now!"

"Is there anyone to look after you?" asked Eustis, thinking she might be in a difficult position without a husband. Women needed protectors. She was young and attractive, and he particularly noticed her breasts swelling to escape the confinement of her bodice. Her husband was a lucky man. A passing thought: With that bosom, is she pregnant? He studied her. Perhaps a belly beginning?

"Not to worry, sir. I stay with some other women. We have a strong camp where I'm with other wives. We make our money doing the officers' laundry or trading. We're hard-working women, sir."

Eustis nodded in understanding as she talked.

Clasping her hands. "Please, sir. Is he fair or dark? The man who died. I might be able to tell you who he was."

"Thank you for your concern, although no companies have returned that I have heard," Eustis said. "The dead man was young with hazel eyes and dark brown hair. But perhaps you can tell me. Were there any insignia on your husband's shirt? I am assuming he wore a hunting shirt? Is there any way to identify what company or regiment he was in? Or any other way to identify him?"

"Oh, sir." She sighed. "'Tis just that I am so worried about my Albert. He was very fair, like many of the men in our regiment. Our families were mostly from northern Germany. They had no fancy huntin' shirts. Just the regular tow cloth ones we made." She was obviously trying to stifle her fears. Maybe she was a newlywed to be so upset.

Eustis asked for her name and permission to find her if he needed more information or had anything else he could tell her. Maybe the man had been a friend of her husband. He would likely be back in the area he thought, and would see them again.

She answered with tears in her eyes. "I'm Norah Lindholm, sir. And thank you, sir. You don't know how much you have helped me. I've been so worried about when he might come back." She said she and the other women lived on a side path not far from where the body was found along the wagon road. She had thought her husband might have been coming home or his body had been brought in.

As he thought about the man, Eustis offered one more observation. "One other thing. Your husband is a rifleman in his company, am I correct? If so, then he could not be the body we found. That man had the right forefinger severed at his first joint. I doubt he could fire with the accuracy required."

The doctor then took his leave. Riding on down the road, he mused about there being a small settlement of some kind near where the body was found, where Danny's mother lived, and so it now seemed the gentle Norah. He hardly thought that the dead man could be from some regiment that Norah knew, but then, maybe he was. He should ask General Arnold for a list of his other regimental companies. And what was that other fancy fellow doing here? Oddly, the idea of a disguise floated into his mind. By God, he hoped a friend could get leave to come ponder all of this with him.

Noah pointed out a narrow wagon path to the right off the road. Leafy foliage of all kinds seemed to be edging onto the trail. Eustis turned into it, and Noah followed, Norah trailing far behind. "Do you suppose the body was here or back on the road?" Eustis wondered aloud. They dismounted and walked along single file leading the horse and mule, carefully looking on both sides. Noah seemed to know something about tracking, perhaps from his childhood.

Eustis wondered what Noah thought of this rebellion. What did slaves make of it? The Noahs of this world – those persons whom the law permitted to be bought and sold – hearing of the patriots' alarm, all that writing and talking about being made slaves to the British by paying taxes? There was no guarantee Noah would get his desire to go West as a free man. But indeed, as for that, there were no guarantees for any of them.

His mind came back to his surroundings. It appeared that due to time passing any indications of a body along the path they followed had disappeared, perhaps because of boys running or hoofprints. They saw no splash of blood on leaves or grass. The path appeared to be well-traveled, and there were some areas of grass that appeared to have been trod on around the entrance. He wondered why no one had found the body earlier when on the way to the fort instead of several hours later. Perhaps the man had been dumped after being killed someplace else. When they left they would look for other signs where the death might have occurred along the road.

Then he smelled it. A too familiar odor of vomit, well-known from his medical practice. Looking around, grass and weeds in the area seemed flattened, and he saw remnants of an odd spongy spray of yellowish material on the side of the path. It was totally dry but looked as if someone had been sick earlier that morning. Hector was not amused. Eustis was curious. Could the dead man have been on this path and gotten sick? And if Hector was disturbed, maybe the man's horse also got skittish, threw its rider and ran. Or maybe it was the dead man or maybe nothing at all. And could there be some nearby tavern he did not know about where the man had drunk too much?

They soon arrived in a small clearing with seven or eight cabins randomly arranged on its perimeter with several more along a path close by. A robust laundry operation was underway in the center. It reminded Eustis of the women's work at Robinson's House. Large iron pots hung over fires. Various lines were secured to trees, and white linen shirts and shifts were spread over the tops of bushes. A cluster of small children and dogs, clucking chickens and several pigs came over to inspect the visitors. Three of the women looked up. Two of the youngest ones stayed, watching at a distance, but one strode toward them. Not welcoming, she seemed cautious yet curious as she approached. Her sleeves were rolled up, a knife was in her leather belt, and she looked ready for anything. "Can I help you? Have you lost your way?"

Eustis dismounted and, leading Hector, slowly approached. He had the feeling that any abrupt move would put all the women on guard. There was vague uneasiness in the air. Something must have happened here.

He removed his tricorn. "Good day to you all. I am Dr. William Eustis, and this is my aide, Noah Royall. We are looking for answers and your help to identify the body that was found along the path into this settlement."

"Oh no!" the woman protested adamantly. "'Twas found out on the wagon road, not here in our settlement. Not here at all. No men are here." She seemed alarmed that someone might think they had a side business entertaining men, maybe for money. It was a possibility in women's villages such as theirs.

Eustis wanted to talk with Danny's mother. "Please, good wife, not to worry. We can go back to look along the road. But could you direct me to Mistress Grady? I understand from her son that she has a cabin here abouts."

"'Tis true, sir, she does," said the woman, directing them toward the cabins. "Emma Grady lives in one of the furthest along, down there."

After thanking the women, Eustis and Noah led the horse and mule toward the Grady cabin down the narrow path leading to the woods. From what they had heard, it seemed Mistress Grady was a trader, and likely a hard bargainer. She bought and sold useful items to make her living. Her substantial garden plot had just come into its harvest time and showed off carrots, squash, beans, and turnips. She was evidently known for her good vegetables and sundries. Perhaps she also traded in whiskey, known to be lucrative.

The log cabin they approached looked comfortable but limited in size and had one window cut in the front and one in the side that they could see as they approached. The openings were covered with thin oiled paper to let in light but keep out flies. Eustis guessed that due to its size, only Danny and his mother lived here.

On their approach Danny ran out to the garden area in front, excited that Dr. Eustis had come to his house. He exuded importance, more so than the two other children, likely his brother and sister who shyly poked their heads out the door.

A woman in her early-thirties, with tendrils of brown hair under her white cap and dressed in brown homespun, came out the door. "Good day, Dr. Eustis. Danny does not stop talking about you." Stepping back, Mrs. Grady welcomed them inside. She said her husband was a sergeant with one of the regiments, the Sixteenth Massachusetts, and when Eustis told her that he knew that regiment because his friend, Dr. James Thacher, was its physician, any concern she had disappeared.

Indicating the two other children behind her, Mrs. Grady said they were Rebecca and the youngest, Seth. She seemed eager to talk, perhaps to have visitors, and told them her story. She had moved to the West Point area from Barnstable, Massachusetts, following her husband, but decided she could do better for all of them if she settled here with their three children rather than following his company wherever it went. Her husband would join them every winter. He had built the cabin for them last winter so they could move out of the wagon in which she carried her wares. She still used the wagon for her sales expeditions into nearby villages and to the fortress. Her husband should be returning in another month or so; once it got cold, the season for campaigning was over, and the regiment returned to its winter quarters.

Eustis quickly deduced that gossip was another of Emma Grady's services. He wanted to ask her about the initial nervousness of the women who were doing laundry, but at that point he realized that an older woman with fluffy white dandelion hair barely contained under her cap was at the doorway. Emma Grady called her in.

"Dr. Eustis, may I present Nan Eldridge, our midwife," said Mrs. Grady.

When Eustis stepped forward to offer his greetings, Mistress Eldridge formally welcomed him to visit the women in the settlement and courteously assured him that it was unlikely they would have any need of his services. "I handle all the doctorin' needed in our settlement," she said firmly.

"I'm glad you are here to care for these women, Mistress Eldridge. But I came on a completely different mission. I'm hoping to find out more about the dead body found at the end of your path to the wagon road. We've been unable to identify him. I would greatly appreciate any information or help you could give me on that."

"I admit I am somewhat relieved, doctor. Men in the area keep tryin' to take control here, and we do not need or want that! We do just fine on our own, and do not care for any outside intrusions." Then as a woman who seized the moment whenever she could, she went on. "But I have an idea. If you could use another helper in your work, may I make the suggestion of my grandson, Elijah? He's seventeen, well-trained in herbs for medical purposes, and he's a very caring young man."

She went on to explain that Elijah's parents had been killed during an Indian raid in western Massachusetts some years ago, and he had been with her ever since. She thought he needed to be around men who had a healing purpose and not in the army. Elijah would benefit from a more worldly experience at Robinson House. Then the fluffy-headed older woman let out a shockingly piercing whistle to call her grandson over from their nearby cabin.

A tall, tanned, and well-muscled young man, in shirt and breeches with his dark brown hair tied back in a queue, came jogging to them carrying a pitchfork, calling "Here I am, Gran. Got your spindle fixed. Are you alright?"

Eustis made a quick assessment. His concern that he might have to escape from a sticky situation was quickly abated. He was particularly drawn to the young man, but not sure why, and thought perhaps it was intuition. This boy would take pressure off Noah and might be useful in their investigation as well as at Robinson's.

Mrs. Eldredge explained her idea to Elijah and spoke of his abilities, then turned to the doctor for his response. After further exploration of the opportunity, Eustis agreed to take Elijah with him based on his grandmother's approval. The best possibility would be that he became a surgeon's mate after training and further experience. His grandmother instantly agreed and left to pack his second shirt and stockings for his travels. When she returned with a small haversack, she squinted her blue eyes at Eli and sternly admonished him to always listen to Dr. Eustis.

As they prepared to leave, Eustis pondered how they would manage with only the two mounts. The boys would have to ride double. He wondered if Mistress Eldridge could spare one of her horses but realized they were needed for her wagon. Seeing the problem, however, and surprisingly eager to get Elijah on his way, she agreed to loan one horse for his immediate use. They would return it as soon as possible. Eustis was puzzled by the grandmother's enthusiasm and began to wonder what he had gotten into. Eli had not seemed quite as eager as she had been about the new arrangement. Had he misread the situation? Eustis explained that they would not leave for Robinson's until the next morning after spending a night at the fort.

As they were bringing out the other horse, a pleasant black cart horse, Mrs. Grady sidled up to Eustis, saying quietly for his ears only: "I just want to ask you, doctor, have you met Norah Lindholm? She is pregnant and should be due soon as her husband left more than six months ago. But she looks like she is barely a few months along. Could she be in trouble?"

Eustis nodded, wondering how much of a gossip this woman was. He had observed Mistress Lindholm's likely pregnancy reflected in her breasts and belly when he met her on the road.

"Indeed, I have seen Mistress Lindholm along the road. Surely Mistress Eldridge would be the one to talk to?"

"Norah is not telling people, and I was waiting for her to come to see me. I just hope there is nothing wrong."

"Mrs. Lindholm may have consulted with Mistress Eldridge, and it could be fine."

"But she has not. I asked her!"

"My advice is to give it a little more time," said Eustis, thinking it was none of Emma Grady's business.

Before they left, Eustis wanted to establish where the people he had met lived. Which cabin did Mistress Lindholm live in? Mistress Eldridge was hustling them toward the path leading out of the settlement when he managed to get an answer. Mrs. Grady pointed to a small cabin at the edge of the woods beside the central common area. It looked like one room with a loft above. "Mrs. Lindholm does what she can and has her garden over there. We all keep an eye on her."

Chapter 5

Once back at Fort Putnam, Noah showed Elijah where they would stable the horses and mule, after which they would check in with the sergeant in charge and find out where to sleep, then go to the mess hall for their midday dinner. Still wondering about the dead man's missing horse, Eustis could ask the stableman if any stray horse had been turned in.

Eustis went over to the officers dining hall. They were serving a meat stew, although he was not sure what kind of meat it was, likely squirrel or rabbit. He was reminded of the preparations for fall and winter that he should be considering. The farmers in the area had begun harvesting their crops, and the vegetables were plentiful. Turnips and parsnips now, potatoes to be dug up later. They would be bringing in corn now and getting it ground for meal or storing it for winter. Even the horses might be given oats when all the grains were in. The fall was the time for hard work; winter came soon enough, with its cold temperatures and eventual supply shortages. Eustis thought he had better try to get at least one new pair of knitted wool stockings. Drat! He should have checked to see if Mistress Grady had any.

His thoughts were interrupted by a man approaching.

"Excuse me, are you Doctor Eustis? And if so, could I talk to you after your dinner? It's somethin' private, sir."

Several of the men lined up in the mess hall after their meal for his medical attention. Most of the illnesses and complaints could be traced back to cases of syphilis. Eustis was prepared and could dole out the usual mercury pills. He cleaned out one man's infected cut, then added a stitch just to hold the edges together for a week, then looked at another man with a painful tooth abscess.

Even better, it being known that Dr. Eustis was staying overnight in the officer quarters, an orderly brought him his mail. It could have been delayed at the fort, later sent across to Robinson House, and he would not have gotten it for several more days at best. What a treasure trove! Eustis went out to find a private spot to sort through it and read alone. He found an archway that supported part of the fort ramparts and that had a bench and sat. There were four letters: from his father, his brother Jacob, his friend Dr. Sam, and an odd one with writing he did not recognize. He could feel his throat tighten. By God, he missed his family up there in Boston. And memories of his mother threatened to bring tears, the grief as close to the surface as when she died those several years ago. He had been away for so long, more than two years of not seeing them all.

First, he opened his father's letter written nearly two months ago, back in early summer. He wrote that he had decided to re-marry, and did Bill remember Elizabeth Lazenby, the widow who had lived near them in Boston's North End? He would move into her house, and he hoped Bill could come home to bring them joy. Jacob's letter offered a little more about their father's new venture, saying they were all happy for the old gentleman and his new wife, and that it left more room in the family home on good old Sudbury Street for Bill whenever he returned. With luck, that would be soon. The infernal war had to wrap up! Did Bill have any news on that? Jacob planned to rebuild part of their house, raising the roof on the back ell and adding a window to Bill's room so that he could see the harbor.

And then he held Sam's letter. Just breaking the wax seal and unfolding it brought memories of their time as boys sledding all the way down Beacon Hill to their school. They had hauled the sleds back to the top close to the base of the beacon tower so they could fly down again. Later his mother would help warm them up with hot cider in her aromatic kitchen in the North End. It always seemed to smell of baking bread and babies. After all, he had eight younger siblings.

A fast courier was heading in their direction, wrote Sam. He would take advantage of the opportunity and write quickly. The big news, he would come on a rescue mission – after all, what are friends for? And he would solve the mystery for Dr. Bill. It seems it was an opportune time and he had secured permission for a short leave. It might take him two or three days to ride there, but he could likely leave in a week. And should he find Dr. Bill at Robinson House? He was eager to see the place and would be willing to help with patients. Eustis immediately wrote out an answer so it could go back with the post the next morning. Come now! Come as soon as you can!

The mystery letter, when he unfolded it, was short and puzzling. The words, if that is what they were, made no sense. It seemed to be in code of some kind. Perhaps a message to someone? Maybe it was not meant for Eustis at all.

As he puzzled over the baffling piece of paper, he thought of Aaron Burr. His friend Burr! He regularly used code in his letters to friends because he was so suspicious, and rightly so, that anything could be made public. Burr was especially averse to his personal comments being exposed or misquoted. Perhaps that was what this writer was concerned about or intended. Burr had a certain point there, thought Eustis. Letters could be opened by anyone at any time. The mail was often left in taverns for others to pick up, and if the recipient could be identified, one might be opened for the edification of all who were there. Burr had mustered out of the army and gone to study the law down the river in Haverstraw, New York.

Maybe he could catch a boat up the river.

Eustis would get a note off to him the next morning, inviting him to come and to ask him for another key to the possible codes being used. The one that he and Burr habitually used did not fit with anything here. Probably people used different codes or changed them. Or did they expire in a certain time? Burr would know all about it.

Later that evening in a welcome gesture to Elijah, Noah and Eustis treated him to beer and cider at Peter Brouwer's nearby tavern along the road north of the fort. The tavern had a saltbox roofline with a side door toward the rear where customers were welcomed into a wide back room. It was a warm, snug place with low-ceilings and card games or earnest discussions going on at every table; all talking about the latest news, from General Gates's recent defeat at the battle in Camden, South Carolina, to the earlier arrival of the French in the Rhode Island colony. They were proud and grateful for General Lafayette's success in France because the colonies had desperately needed a loan or arms, preferably both.

When Lafayette had returned to France, his home country, a year ago, he had a mission to get King Louis XV to pay attention to the colonies. And if it was not Lafayette alone, perhaps it was the revered Doctor Franklin who helped persuade the French once the colonies had won that battle at Saratoga. If the French brought all the weapons and supplies the colonies needed, they could finish this campaign for freedom within months. It would be like a last-minute charge of the French cavalry galloping over the hill to save them. There were even rumors that the British had reevaluated their position in Newport, blown up their fortifications, and retreated to New York to regroup and build up defenses there. Things could hardly be better. The army was breathlessly waiting to hear about any supplies the French would bring, and some thought they would all move against the British in New York.

A burly man, red haired, came in, was handed his mug of beer at the bar, and wandered over to their table. He looked familiar to Eustis. What was his name? Seemingly irritated, the man pulled back the corner of a free bench and climbed in, eager to talk. "Sandy

MacDougal, Rhode Island militia at your service, doc. Met you before, over that dead body." His discouraging news interrupted all other talk.

"Well, gents, what do you think of the times now? I heard what you was talkin' about. It's not like that. The feckin' French did not bring us those supplies, arms, ammo, or anything else they promised. You're right that they did arrive with about six thousand troops, but most of them lily-livered frogs was sick from their time at sea. I mean, they could not even manage to get all their horses here alive. And what's worse, they eat snails! What can you expect? It ain't civilized! They were s'posed to come to us, not make a main base there in Newport. All along 'twas a pack of lies. We should'na ha' trusted a Frenchie. Just a bunch of cowards."

As the word went around, any excitement in the room was quickly overshadowed by a universal gloom. He's right, thought Eustis. Much as General Washington wants to attack New York and drive the British into the sea, we can't do anything without the French supplies. Congress has no money, and they keep printing more dollars that become increasingly worthless due to the circulation of counterfeit bills. Reluctantly, the general realized that the French may be allies, but they would do what they pleased. Strengthening his defenses would have to suffice. And that was what General Arnold is supposed to be doing – strengthening West Point.

A natural raconteur, MacDougal asked his rapt audience if they had heard about Claudius Smith, the leader of a band of Loyalists operating north of New York on Manhattan. "They're counterfeitin' money, makin' fake dollars, and cheatin' everyone. The bunch o' them keep movin' around so they're not caught yet." MacDougal allowed as how they should be taken to the nearest tree and strung up.

"'Tis that ill-begotten, limp-cocked Smith and his gang's work that makes our pay worthless. We got no meat, no money, no rum, and no contentment. Sorry, gents," he sighed. "My wee wife calls me a grumbletonian. Says I'm never happy with whatever situation I'm in. But look at it! Nothing is worth a damned Continental dollar anymore.

It's nae good. I just need to complain to somebody!"

A young woman working at the tavern, Bridey McGuinness, brought filled pewter tankards to their table. A saucy redhead, she flirted with the male customers. She wore an apron over her tightly-laced bodice and striped skirt. MacDougal obviously knew her. She cheerfully sat on his knee, an arm around his neck, and chatted, seemingly trying to obtain information as much as share any. Probably she had one or two customers on the line she could sell it to. Everyone enjoyed the way her cinched apron emphasized her ample bosom swelling over the top of her shift, her rounded bottom, and small waist.

The time skimmed by with the entertaining talk and charming young woman. The evening easily wore on longer than Eustis expected. He realized he had two younger men in his charge and that they all needed to be on their way across the river the next morning. It took some convincing, but he managed to get them back to the fort and their barracks beds.

Eustis had a growing anxiety and sense of urgency, a need to get back to Robinson's and his patients, even though he would like to have lingered to work on his problems at the fort, visiting the women's encampment one more time. There seemed to be a great deal he was missing in the turmoil here. But there was a light ahead. Sam would arrive at Robinson's in a week or so.

After a pot of steaming coffee and oat cakes had restored them the next morning, the three rode back to the ferry to cross the river. This time Hector seemed slightly calmer, reassured by Noah and with the additional company of Elijah's horse Belle, and they managed to load the horses and mule onto the barge without mishap.

The entire Robinson staff and household, surprised at the arrival of a new helper, welcomed Elijah, found a place for him to sleep and stow his gear. He would help in the barns under the supervision of Mrs. Nardy. She was delighted to have his strength to help move the seriously injured and unconscious. They soon found he worked out well in many ways – not the least of which was his knowledge of medicines and herbs – as well as keeping the injured men company and attending to their needs. He served meals and got water, happily talking to the patients. And they were more open with him than they were with officers or doctors – or Mrs. Nardy. They seemed to trust him immediately.

There was something about the two young men that balanced each other. Where Elijah was like a young puppy eager for any new idea or experience, Noah was watchful, more like a creature from the forest, maybe a deer.

***

The days crept along. They were coming into that restless time toward the end of one season and before the next could get established. The geese began flying in formation toward the south. Eustis was just coming out of the barn for a breath of fresh air when he heard a whooping yell as a horse cantered into the yard.

Sam had arrived! He swept off his hat and gave a low bow. "Happy to be at your service, sir," before rolling off his horse and grabbing Eustis in a bear hug. "Hey, Billy. I am so glad to see you!" They pulled apart and grabbed each other again, grinning, each pounding the other's back.

"Sammy, my boy! How are you and what news? Your hair has grown so much! How long has it been since I last saw you?" When there was a pause for breath, everyone including the gathering spectators got a chance to meet Sam Adams Jr., the son of Boston's famous rebel, Samuel Adams.

Sam said he had until mid-September, and that would be plenty of time, two weeks at least, to solve all of Eustis's problems. Sam did not have his father's high forehead, having retained his hair, but there were signs in his eager glances around and ever-present curiosity that he followed in his father's footsteps. It also made him an excellent doctor. He was fair, youthful, enthusiastic, and thinner than Eustis remembered. He fit right into the life of Robinson's.

On an overcast morning about two days later, slightly cooler than the week before, young Elijah Eldridge approached the doctors.

46

Adams, Eustis, and Burnet were sitting on a bench outside the barn door. The barn swallows were doing their usual swooping in and out of the wide-open entrance. The doctors were taking a break from administering smallpox vaccinations to a company of soldiers; harvesting some of the matter from pustules on an infected soldier's skin and, with a small scalpel incision, inserting it under the skin of their patients.

The rest of the waiting men were sprawled or sitting around on the nearby grass, taking the opportunity to relax. Most had their arms wrapped in linen bandages. They had all been quarantined for a week on a special milk-based diet and would be kept sequestered to see who contracted the disease, and then for another week or so until all signs of fever had left.

"Sorry to disturb you, doctors," said Elijah, "but I think you might be interested in what I have just heard."

"Happy to listen to you Eli, anytime. Come, sit down. Grab a stool." said Eustis.

"Well, you know how I appreciate you letting me be here, doctor. A few minutes ago, a patient was talking about meeting another traveler on the road north of Fort Putnam. Anyway, he said this traveler mentioned that he was working for the French, but he was very interested in where any regimental or company movements were planned, or if there was any news of what General Heath was doing."

"Well, that is interesting indeed, Eli. Anything else?"

"Absolutely," said Sam. "What did he look like?"

"That's the thing. He's inside now. He was wheeled in, brought in a wheelbarrow by one of the farmers who live nearby. Dr. Burnet put some stitches in his leg early this morning. But I wanted to tell you about it because I am not sure he wants questions. I doubt he's actually with a company. He wears a hunting shirt, but he did not seem to know much about any rifle companies. He stopped talking when I asked, but after I gave him some laudanum for his pain, he told me his name was Jonathan Reed."

47

"Good work, Eli," said Sam. "But what does he look like?"

"Well, why don't you just come and see? He did say he was looking for a man disguised as a Frenchman."

"Lead on, MacDuff," said Eustis with a sweeping gesture. Sam smiled and waved them on. Eli, after looking curiously at Eustis, led the way into the barn and up a steep narrow staircase in the back corner to the loft sleeping area. Hay had been packed into ticking mattresses, arranged in rows under the sloping beams of the roof. The center of the floor was open to below.

Eli indicated a man deeply asleep under a thin quilt. He was a tall man, taller than Eustis's five feet, eight inches, perhaps nearer to six feet. Heavy dark eyebrows and a beard emphasized his balding dark brown hair, sparsely tied back in a queue. His bandaged leg made a rigid outline under the cover.

Eustis made a mental note to ask Burnet more about the injury or wound he had stitched or if he had performed any other procedure on their patient. He decided to come back later when the man might have roused. Maybe the person this Jonathan Reed was looking for was the dead man they were trying to identify.

Later, when the three doctors made their evening rounds, Eustis and Adams climbed the ladder to check on Reed again. He seemed better, was conscious and propped on his jacket and several pillows. They introduced themselves and checked his bandage.

Reed told them he was looking for a man disguised as a Frenchman. Pierre de la Fontaine could be his name. He was not sure of the person's actual identity or nationality. He might even be British. "I do not know how I got into this," he sighed. "I was a shoemaker down in New York, fixin' British soldiers' boots, but then I decided to help the cause."

Eustis explained that he was trying to determine the identity of a man whose body was found on August eighth just south of Fort Putnam. He wondered if this Fontaine might be that dead man found by the road, when had Reed seen him last, and why did he decide he was French? Could he have been dressed as a fancy officer?

Jonathan Reed could not offer much in the way of a description or identification. He seemed inept, almost reluctant to be pinned down. "I may have lost the trail of this person, but I don't think he has been killed. I am sure I would have heard about it."

Eustis persisted. "Can you give us more of a description? Anything to help us determine that this man you were following is not the one we are trying to identify? How about hair color?"

"As far as I know his hair is black – but dye can cover many things," said Reed.

"Have you had any close encounters with him at all?" asked Sam.

"I am sorry, doctors, but I am just not sure enough to be able to help you much."

"How were you injured, Reed? Not in a fight, then?"

"No, I'm sorry I'm of so little help. I had an accident with my axe. I was setting up my camp, trying to cut some kindling from a log, you know, splitting the log, and got my leg instead. I have to say that I am much relieved I found that farmer, and that you all were here nearby. I am not sure I could have found a way to get across the river."

Sam and Eustis walked back to their quarters in Robinson House, trying to puzzle out if Reed had told them the truth. He had sounded genuine but was not much help. It would be more useful if they could get a better description. Sam thought that the Frenchman they sought, if it was de la Fontaine, could be the gentleman Eustis had seen in Arnold's office. But was he truly French? What if, indeed, they were the same person, thought Eustis, one man just playing a slightly different role? How do they find that out?

Perhaps others had run into this man on the road. Another trader or traveler? Two more wagons had recently arrived around Robinson House. The sutlers must have heard about Mrs. Arnold's expected arrival. Eustis decided he and Noah could talk with one of the new traders, and Sam could visit the other.

Chapter 6

Doggedly setting out to find answers, Eustis and Noah walked over to the sutlers' camp after making the early rounds the following morning. They passed assorted kegs, crocks of butter, and wheels of cheese packed in the wagons. The traders had been visiting the local farms, stocking up for more sales.

Approaching one of the recently-arrived wagons, the men found a tall, thin, middle-aged woman with an amazing nose that reminded Eustis of General Charles Lee, or maybe a flamingo. She was turning johnnycakes on a griddle hung over her fire as they approached and looked interested and slightly amused by almost everything around her. Her cap covered graying brown hair in a bun, and her apron needed washing. Clearly, she had been cooking since dawn. There was a lidded iron pot buried in coals beside her fire. Its enticing smell made the men's mouths water.

"Good morning, mistress. Let me introduce ourselves. I'm Dr. Eustis, and this is my assistant, Noah Royall." Her eyes twinkling, the woman introduced herself as Annabelle Tobey and offered mugs of coffee to both men.

"Yes, I know who you are, Dr. Eustis. In fact, I've heard about the two of you. Now, what can I do to help you, attractive fellows that you are? You look like you may have several young ladies to whom you pay attention. I've some lovely trinkets here. Perhaps I can show them to you?"

Eustis grinned at her. "You can really help me more with information, Mistress Tobey. Other than this marvelous coffee perhaps you could help us solve a few puzzles.

"I am sorry, doctor," she said. "I may see a great deal and all kinds of people in my travels but I doubt I can be of any help today. Still, you will not forget I have other sundries, and I will make you some good coffee, should you ever desire it."

Eustis persisted. "Have you met a Frenchman along the road? Or a man calling himself Jonathan Reed?"

"I'll think about it, Dr. Eustis, but at the moment I have no answers for you."

"Could you tell us where you have been traveling?" asked Eustis.

"It is not so much traveling and adventure as you might think, doctor, but more making a living out of the back of my wagon. When my husband died some years ago, although I was guaranteed my widow's third of his estate, it was my son-in-law who inherited through his wife and he is not, umm," she paused, "what you might call an easy person to get on with. I winter with my daughter and her family where I am given a garret bedroom and a place in the kitchen where I can help with the children. As I said, it's a living. But in my travels, I have enjoyed the people I have met and the good friends I have made."

"An interesting saga, Mistress Tobey," said Eustis. "And I am sure you have many stories to go with it."

"Ah, yes, that I do – perhaps when you return another time."

Eustis rose from the log he had been sitting on and handed her his empty mug, followed by Noah.

"Thank you, Mistress Tobey. Say you will consider my questions, and I will absolutely take advantage of that offer of coffee. I'll certainly be back, and soon." smiled Eustis.

Walking back to the barns, he asked Noah what his impression was. Noah said he had liked her but he thought there was a lot that she did not tell. Eustis agreed. Fully aware of what was going on around here, she was being wisely cautious. It would probably take him several visits to gain her confidence, but she made delicious coffee.

Their day began. Sam helped process the sick and wounded who had just come in, so there was not the usual backup of men waiting to be seen as often happened when additional accidents or fights occurred. A skirmish with several British regulars to their east had sent a wagon loaded with five men, all requiring the surgeon. Sam proved to be so helpful that both Burnet and Eustis wanted to keep him there permanently; and he had charmed Mrs. Nardy, not an easy thing to do.

Just thinking about him had Mrs. Nardy making plans to improve efficiency at her hospital. Three doctors! I wonder if we can reorganize the process of admittance, she mused, "Such a shame how long some of these poor boys must wait before we can tuck them into a bed."

After midday dinner and late rounds, Sam and Eustis sat out on the steps of the side porch of the house. The late August evening was mild with the hint of fall's cool weather just around the corner. The seasons were changing, but it would take a frost, probably in mid-October, for the trees to magically change their colors practically overnight. But they had been so busy that Sam had used up several days. And he was supposed to be helping to solve the murder, if that is what it was.

Eustis kept thinking of ways to keep him. It would be wonderful if he could have Sam around all the time. "Is there any way you could just stay on?"

"I do wish it, but I made a promise to General Heath that I would only take a limited leave and be back by September tenth. I would like to stay here with you too. Not just for you alone, my friend, but your location is so appealing with the fields and gardens and view out over the river. I admire how you and Dr. Burnet are running this place. I would love to be part of it, but . . . I cannot, and we still have a murder to solve."

"I thought you were going to do it!"

"Ah, Billy boy, can we just make a plan? Let's see where we are now."

Eustis's mental list had grown longer each day. He took a sheet of paper from his pocket, and read aloud from it. "Things we need to look into:

"*Imprimis*, oh, forget the Latin, I'll say first. Who was at the fort on August the eighth, the day of the murder? Has anyone in the area heard or seen anything?

"Second, what was the identity of the dead man? And what was the weapon used?

"Then, where did the coded note come from, what does it say, and to whom was it intended?"

"And, also," he added, "what about the fancy officer seen in Arnold's office? Is he in on it? Was he wearing a sword?"

There was something just at the edge of his memory. Eustis did not remember any introduction to him, and Arnold had not spoken of him.

"Indeed," said Sam. "It seems critical to me that we do more interviews with area folk across the river. I would also like to see that barmaid you told me about." Sam raised his eyebrows at him. "Noah will remember her name. I'll bet that she might know who the posh gent in Arnold's office was."

Eustis pounded his fist softly on the decking. "There is just so much we do not know." It seemed they kept getting bogged down with patients and in thinking or talking about what they should do rather than actually doing it.

"And by the way, thanks for your notes on the dead man's wound. The murder weapon might be a fancy officer's weapon. It seems even smaller than that but not a needle. Maybe something slightly larger, and longer. Perhaps an officer's poniard or a French epee? Those do have very thin blades, but they are only worn for dress. Makes me wonder too about what that French officer was wearing. Huh. Could a blade cause a puncture?"

53

"Hmmm. Sam, I was wondering also what weapon might a woman carry? Maybe the dead man was an officer who came after a young woman, and she defended herself? Maybe it was an assignation gone wrong and they were caught?"

"But then, if he was an officer," said Sam, "someone would have to have changed the man's clothes and put him in the hunting shirt. I don't want to just sit around and speculate. You know we can go on and on, and there are too many possibilities. We must narrow it down."

"And I also want to go find that girl Norah Lindholm so you can meet her, Sam. And we should talk to more of the women there in the encampment. I am still not sure why they seemed so alarmed at my appearance. I think something happened there."

"Well," said Sam laughing, "Did I never tell you how women fear you?"

An owl hooted and swooped overhead. They could hear footsteps through the grass and glanced quickly at each other. Who?

Noah came around the corner. He brought the day's late mail including a letter for Eustis from Aaron Burr. "Thanks, Noah. Stay and sit a bit. Maybe you've heard something too." Eustis then eagerly broke the letter's seal, unfolded it, and read the main points to Sam and Noah. "Burr says send him a copy of the coded note and he would work on it. He might get up the river next week and has a few ideas to pursue. He wants to visit us at Robinson's."

Not surprisingly, Burr also wrote of his new love, Theodosia Prevost, saying he would be stopping by Robinson House on his way to see her in Sharon, Connecticut, describing his courtship adventures. Eustis was amused by Burr. He always was seeking the favors of someone and knew where all the ladies available for visiting or courting were located. Usually though, they were not married as this one was.

Noah seemed uneasy; unable to settle on the porch with the doctors. He had sat out with them numerous other times but he appeared nervous, and his eyes were in constant movement. It occurred to Eustis that Noah wanted to talk to him but was unsure how to begin. The doctor asked him what his news was. After wringing his hands and standing up, then sitting down, Noah blurted out that as he had worked for Eustis for nearly five years now, he wondered how much longer he would be with him, and then what? He explained that he had begun to worry about what might happen next. He had met another Negro who worked for an officer over in West Point who had told him that they would be sold back into slavery once the war was over.

"Doctor, I been so worried. Canna sleep." Noah bit his lip. "I'm hopin' you can help me. You know I want to go West and be my own boss."

"Ah, Noah, I am glad you came to me. I do hope this war will not last much longer also, but I'll do everything I can to make sure you can get on with your life. I can't guarantee anything about gaining your freedom here yet, but I know the colony of Massachusetts leans in that direction. I can keep listening for news, and if we must I'll say I own you and I can get you out of here in time to get over the mountains. But I don't think it will come to that."

"Thank you, doctor." Noah grasped his hand. "I knew you'd tell me. I just didna think it'd be as bad as that man said."

Sam spoke up. "Count on me as well. Count on us both."

The three decided to call it a night and rose together to walk back around the house. Eustis and Sam decided their greatest immediate priority was to get across the river and spend several days poking around the fort and the women's settlement. It would have been so much easier if they were stationed there. The problem was getting time away from Robinson House without leaving Dr. Burnet in the lurch. The doctor knew Eustis had these orders, and they needed to talk with him about what could be managed.

Eustis reassuringly patted Noah on his shoulder, and Noah headed up to his attic room. Before retiring for the night, the two doctors intercepted William Burnet just coming in from his final rounds at the barns and suggested meeting around the dining table. Arnold was in his office. Eustis was still baffled that the general had not seemed concerned about solving any questions surrounding the dead man or about him completing the assignment.

"I can see the two of you are anxious about something," Burnet said, bringing a mug of beer in from the kitchen and opening the discussion.

"You are absolutely right," said Eustis. "It's about investigating that wretched murder along the wagon road across the river by Fort Putnam. I have no solutions, but I have a few ideas. There is much more I should be doing. As you know, I have recruited Sam to help me, but we are running out of time."

"If I can be of help, I am happy to do it," said Burnet, "but you know yourself, we cannot be understaffed here for long. I am not expected to be responsible for this whole hospital and you're really supposed to handle the surgical patients."

"I agree. But I have to get back for at least another two or three days, doctor. Later I would welcome your comments on what I uncover. I do realize that I can't be gone from here for longer than that at any one time."

"Hmmm. You want to go again? I have to say it doesn't seem right to me."

Interrupting, Sam said that he would be leaving soon, and right now he and Eustis needed to get across the river.

"What is your best suggestion for how we can do that?" he asked.

Burnet did not look happy or cooperative. "I don't like being left behind while you go off on this jaunt."

"But I have orders, doctor," Eustis reminded his colleague. "General Arnold told me to do this. But perhaps I can do something for you. What could we exchange for the time?" asked Eustis.

Burnet paused and shrugged, finally giving up. "I'll not fight you. I know they're your orders, but I will ask you to support me when I apply for a leave this winter to go visit my family. You will guarantee to do that?"

"Absolutely," said Eustis. "We can draw up a schedule with you, and we'll promise to be back within three days. Noah and Elijah will stay here while Sam comes with me."

"Well then, I'll not interfere. I suspected you two would need more time anyway, but I'm worried about those new cases of malaria and diphtheria arriving here. And did you see the young man with those symptoms of smallpox who came in late this afternoon? We'll need to start another vaccination program. I'll teach Elijah to administer it. He already handles bloodletting well. And we'll need to find where to obtain that new cowpox serum. There is just too much to do. And," he added grimly, "no pay."

Promising to be totally committed to the hospital once they solved the mystery of the corpse, Eustis and Sam decided to leave the next morning. Returning across the river would also enable Eustis to return Mrs. Grady's horse at the women's encampment. The next morning before leaving they would inform Noah and Elijah of their responsibilities to keep everything running smoothly for Mrs. Nardy, Dr. Burnet, and the two surgeon's mates.

Finding Elijah in the shed hanging some different looking plants from the rafters to dry, Eustis noticed some with particularly attractive, trumpet-like flowers. He reached to touch them and was startled by Elijah's shout, "No! Don't touch those flowers!" As he pulled back his hand, Eli explained that the plant was poisonous and called devil's trumpets. It had several other names, sometimes called jimson weed or devil's snare. He found them nearby, he explained. A tiny bit of the flowers or leaves brewed in tea was useful in easing pain. Eustis left pleased, reassured that Elijah was mastering the apothecary trade.

Chapter 7

The day dawned overcast, windy, and chilly. Looming gray clouds threatened rain. Not the best conditions for crossing wide waterways.

Eustis and Sam rode down to the ferry, leading Belle and taking in the early shades of autumn yellow in the swamp maple trees, always the first to turn. Virginia creeper edging into its brilliant red coloring crowded the edges of the wooden planked ramp of the landing. A red-winged blackbird watched from atop a tall, scruffy pine rooted at the edge of the brackish water.

The river itself was moving swiftly and, again, Hector refused to approach. They needed Noah. He had the touch to reassure any upset creature. Even with Sam's horse and Belle leading the way, it took an extra fifteen minutes to get him up the ramp and on the barge, pushed by Sam, Eustis, and one of the barge's oarsmen. Although he'd been across many times, Hector behaved as if this was his first. And the ferryman was angry. "Oy, you two. I dinna care if you're in the army, I have to keep to my schedule. Get your horse in control!"

Impatient passengers laden with baskets of goods glared at the cause of their delay. "Eh, jus' shoot 'im," muttered one of them, and Sam was getting close to agreeing with him.

In contrast, all three horses unloaded faster than expected upon reaching the other side. Hector bolted down the ramp and up the slope to the road. Once everything settled down, and Sam stopped laughing, they mounted and rode to the fort. Insects buzzed in the surrounding fields where the corn and grains had been cut. Crows gathered, alert for any advantage.

Eustis pointed out the place along the road where the body had presumably been found. Any traces other than some slightly trampled grass had disappeared long ago. Taking the left turn and leading Belle, they headed for the women's encampment down the narrow pathway.

About a half mile farther along, they detected the smell of smoke and cooking and the murmur of human voices. Both men were hungry and inwardly hoped to be offered something to eat. As they came to the clearing, they were greeted by the familiar swarm of children, barking dogs, scratching chickens, and nosy pigs that Eustis had encountered before. Mrs. Grady and several other women were tending fires. Some were heating large tubs of water with a bucket of lye nearby to add for the laundry. There seemed to be more business, more activity than when Eustis had visited before. Drying lines were strung between trees. Sticks were balanced across the backs of pairs of chairs with twine or yarn hanging from them. Buckets of what looked like fat or lard were by one of the fires.

Several women cautiously withdrew back toward the cabins as the two men approached. They dismounted, tied their horses to a post, then walked over to greet Mrs. Grady. Her black horse, Belle, stepping lively trotted to the back shed on her own, seemingly happy to be home.

"Greetings of the morning, Mistress Grady," said Eustis, removing his hat.

"Well met, Dr. Eustis," exclaimed Mrs. Grady, chuckling. "Tell me the news of Elijah. How is he adjustin', and is he behavin' himself? Our whole settlement is interested."

"We can report that Elijah is more than doing well. He is a tremendous help to us. And may I introduce my associate, Dr. Samuel Adams?"

Mrs. Grady immediately looked in awe at Sam.

"Is he? Oh, my heavenly days! Are you related to himself? I almost don't dare to ask."

"Indeed, Mistress Grady, he is my honored father," said Sam, bowing as he swept his hat off his head.

Mrs. Grady was charmed. "What can I ever do for you?"

"Dr. Eustis and myself are as usual confused and puzzled, Mistress Grady, and need your help with some answers," said Sam. "Then we'll go on to the fort. Perhaps the charming Mistress Lindholm is around as well? And Mrs. Eldridge? I have heard about her from my colleague."

"Oh my, yes. She's here. We're beginnin' our busy time, preparin' for the long winter to come. Today the chores are both candles and soap as well as the usual laundry. Luckily some of our boys found a bee tree this summer and have kept an eye on it ever since. They didna want anyone else to claim it!"

Melting the beeswax and making tallow soap could not offset the unpleasant smells of lye and lard coming from a bubbling large pot being stirred by a girl of about twelve. "Later we will be into preservin' the harvest and then dryin' and saltin'. And then there is always gettin' more wood cut."

"Ah, yes," said Eustis. "I remember it from my parents' yard in Boston. Our fall preparations were somewhat different, but we certainly stocked up on wood, and my mother made soap and candles."

Norah Lindholm appeared from behind a cabin, cheerfully carrying a basket-like chicken coop. She put it on the ground near one of the tables, removed one of the chickens, and held it quietly in her arms. She nodded in greeting, smiling at both men, then explained, "They're biddies, gettin' too old to be layin'." Eustis was startled when, grasping her chicken around the neck, and with a quick abrupt downward twisting move, Norah efficiently broke its neck and tossed it beside two other dead, though still twitching, chickens on the ground behind the table. She smiled happily at them again, and reached in the coop for the last chicken.

"She's not disturbed by killin' the animals, so we give her all those jobs," Mrs. Grady quietly told Eustis. "It's amazin' how quick she can dispatch a pig. And she'll be gettin' to those soon. And we'll get to makin' sausages, and smokin' the pork, hangin' it high in our chimneys."

It was evident to Eustis that Norah, with her rounded belly, was at least six months into her pregnancy. The doctor would like to get a moment to talk privately to her, but in polite society that did not seem likely unless she asked to talk with him. As the local midwife, Mrs. Eldridge, Elijah's grandmother, would certainly be in charge.

Mrs. Grady invited them to her cabin for refreshment. The two men followed her along the path. "What news from you, Mrs. Grady? Is Danny still at the cooper's shop?"

"Dear me, yes, doctor. It is workin' out so well. And you have seen Mistress Lindholm."

"I'm glad to hear of Danny. And Mistress Lindholm seemed to be dispatching chickens very efficiently. I expect you will be eating well. But I have other questions for you. Have you seen a Frenchman or a man named Jonathan Reed?"

"Goodness, Dr. Eustis. I don't know about any Frenchman, but I know Mr. Reed! He is completely charmin' and has been bringin' us the mail that's come to the fort. Such a help to me. I do not have to walk that far to get it, and Danny, as you know, is all over the place."

"Where is Mr. Reed from?" asked Eustis. "Can you tell us what he looked like when he came to see you?"

"I thought you knew him. He is tall, has light hair, brown eyes and a scar on his chin. With the Ninth Detachment from Virginia, he said."

Eustis was startled. This did not sound like their patient Jonathan Reed. Surely there could not be two of them. He glanced at Sam.

"Ah, yes," said Sam quickly. "My old friend. Did he say where he was heading? I would enjoy seeing him again."

"Well, I seem to remember that he said somethin' about being a courier and having one more day at the fort. Then it was back off south again. Perhaps you will catch him, if you hurry."

"We would certainly like to catch him," said Eustis, suddenly realizing that this Reed might know something about their murderer. If they could find him, it might answer a great many of their questions. He suggested they get on to the fort soon and leave further visitation in the settlement for later.

The two left the cabin after profusely thanking Mrs. Grady for her cake and the most interesting tea she had served them.

Riding out of the encampment, they passed through the settlement clearing where three aproned women repeatedly dipped yarn strings in large iron pots filled with a redolent combination of melted candle stubs, lard, and beeswax. The young girl was still stirring her soap and had set up a table covered with blocky wooden forms. It smelled as if she may have added some herbs, perhaps rosemary, to one of the two developing pots of soap. They could see Norah approaching a pig with a rope, and the duo began a ballet of sorts, the pig moving opposite from Norah and dodging back when she followed.

Sam still wanted more of an introduction, and they interrupted her pig-catching effort.

Eustis called to her. "Good day, Mistress Lindholm! You looked busy earlier."

"And a good morning to you, Dr. Eustis. What can I do for you?"

"I would like to introduce my friend, Dr. Sam Adams. And I have a question."

Norah gave up stalking the pig and cheerfully came over to them.

"I will help if I can, and I am glad to meet Dr. Adams. I also hope you will soon have more information for me on the arrival of my Albert."

"A pleasure to meet you, Mistress Lindholm," said Sam. "Can you remember back to the day in August, the eighth it was, that the body of the man was found on the road? Where were you that morning? Were you here earlier? My associate, Dr. Eustis, said he met you on the road later that day."

"Oh my. I must have been comin' back from collecting laundry at the fort."

"Who did you see there? Was there anything unusual?" asked Sam.

"Let me try to remember. 'Twas some weeks ago. I usually sit outside the main office, and the men bring me their shirts throughout the mornin'. There was that odd Frenchman and the man who brings our mail called Jonathan Reed waitin' around too. Both wanted to get in to see General Arnold. Is this the kind of thing you mean?"

"Exactly. I am interested that those two were there. I can locate them in time that way. I apologize for not being more specific, but I am not even sure what I need to know. We still have not been able to identify that dead man."

"I wish I could help you more." Norah turned aside, looking around for the pig she was stalking.

Sam turned on his charm. "I hope we may return to ask you a few more questions. Would that be permissible?"

Norah was focused on the pig. "Certainly, Dr. Adams, I ain't goin' to be anywhere else. We've so much to do right now."

The men were aware that the young women working around the fires were keeping an eye on them. Despite Norah's friendly attitude, the others did not greet the men but watched surreptitiously instead. As they'd approached, one woman had moved back toward the nearest cabin.

When they were out of earshot of the encampment, Sam turned to Bill. "Would you believe it about Reed? There must be two of them! And whatever was that liquid she called tea? And what was going on with the women?

"Something made with mint and herbs, maybe sassafras, I suppose, Sam. They're trying hard, you know. And without that herbal tea, I would never have developed such a fondness for good coffee. But the women? And Reed? What can we do with that?"

They talked as they rode on to the gate at the fort and, once recognized and admitted, went directly to Colonel Amos Kendall's office. His aide let them in after they waited for a few minutes outside on a bench by the door.

Kendall stiffly welcomed them, clearly finding them a nuisance, and seemed particularly concerned they might be adding problems to his day. Eustis guessed that perhaps General Arnold had been pressuring him to get more work done, but they had not seen any evidence of construction or improvements to the fort that they had expected would be underway. Or maybe it was some other problem. Supplies?

Eustis explained that they had crossed the river to try to get more answers about who might have killed the unknown man. They also hoped to see Danny Grady again but thought they should check in with Kendall first to see if he had any further news for them.

He introduced Dr. Sam Adams, and he was amused that Sam did seem to open doors. Kendall told them he had no comments or news for them. He seemed to choose blissful ignorance and tending his official duties over anything else. They were heading back to their horses to look for Danny when they heard the boy's excited shout. "Dr. Eustis!"

I don't know how he does it, thought Eustis, as the boy ran up to them.

"Good morning, my good man. Are you ready to help with our investigations?"

Danny grinned proudly. "Oh, yes, sir, Dr. Eustis."

Eustis introduced Sam Adams, and the boy's eyes brightened even more. "Is he?" The doctor explained that Dr. Adams was another investigator called in to help solve the mystery of the dead man.

"But I know. I know who he is!" said Danny eagerly. Both Eustis and Adams were dumbfounded. If the boy knew the identity, why had Kendall not been told? Or if he knew, why had he not told them?

"Who was he?" asked Sam.

"He was a spy," said Danny. "I know because he liked to ask questions around here."

"You talked to him?"

"No, sir. But I listen to everyone. They said so. And I think so too."

"Who were they, these people who said so?" interrupted Sam.

The boy explained that whenever men from the fort or neighborhood came into the cooper's shop, they gossiped about the day's news. It was their opinion that anyone found wandering around as that man had been was obviously a spy. Otherwise, they would have heard who he was by now.

"The boy's got a point," said Sam. "But is that reason to kill him? Had he discovered something that others wanted kept secret? Huh! Let's keep that in mind."

Eustis asked Danny to be on guard for the rest of the day, and they would be back to talk with him later.

"It's important, Danny. Listen around you. You be the spy this time. Maybe you will overhear something else of interest to us. Take notice if anyone is trying to talk secretly with anyone else. One other thing. Find out whether anyone knows if the murdered man visited the women's settlement where your mother lives."

Danny skipped away at the sound of the cooper's voice calling for him.

It was Sam's turn. "Good question about the man's destination. You are right. We do not know which way he was going or if he was even interested in the settlement. He could have been going along the road to the fort. But you might be careful with that boy. You don't want to put him in any danger."

"Oh, I doubt anyone will even think of him. He's just a youngster. But there are a few more things that I just thought of, possibly recent developments. Let's go back inside, see if Colonel Kendall has more time."

Although he did not seem at all interested in spending more time with them, Kendall knew that they were on Arnold's business, and he could not refuse.

"I just have a few more questions, sir," said Eustis. "The women in their settlement mentioned Jonathan Reed bringing them mail from here. I wondered if you ever sent him into the women's settlement and how he knew it was there? Also, has he left here?"

"I had very little contact with Reed. He seemed to want to make sure General Arnold knew he was here, that's all. May have carried messages for him. Oh, and I found a note for you. I meant to give it to you. It's here somewhere." He pawed through the various piles of notes, letters, and reports on his desk.

"Here it is. Been here a few days."

"Thank you, sir," said Eustis. He glanced at the note and saw that it came from the Massachusetts Sixteenth Regiment in which his friend Dr. Thacher was serving as its surgeon. Possibly from him? It would have to wait until he got outside. He knew if he left now, he might not get another chance with Kendall.

"One or two other questions, colonel, then we will be out of your way. What can you tell me about the officer who appeared to be French, who was visiting here? I saw him meeting with General Arnold."

"That would be the representative of Admiral Rochambeau," said Kendall. "He was here just for a few days to coordinate maneuvers with General Arnold. Name is Comte Pierre de la Fontaine. But I cannot tell you more than that. He's a count or something."

"I am assuming you have circulated the drawing of our victim, but I am also wondering about any lists of missing persons you might receive. Is there anything that comes in from the different regiments listing personnel? Also, has there been any news about a missing horse?"

Kendall looked at them as if they were not making sense, and drew for more papers from a pile. "Doctor, I have other matters to deal with at the moment. If anything comes in for you, I will hold it."

I am sure you will, thought Eustis, and keep holding it for weeks if it is inconvenient to have it delivered.

"One other thing, colonel," said Sam. "Could you tell me if Reed was blond or dark?"

"As I said, I do have other responsibilities, doctor," said Kendall as he rose from his chair. He seemed to be annoyed rather than helpful. "I do have my own duties and have had no special orders from General Arnold. These interruptions are becoming irritating to the smooth operation of Fort Putnam. As for Reed, I thought you said you knew him. He's tall, has a beard, and dark hair." Clearly, he wanted them gone.

"I understand, colonel. But I assure you we do have the responsibility for solving this puzzle, and we hope you will continue to be of assistance." Eustis thanked the colonel to ensure they could return, and the two left.

Outside, as they were untying their horses, Sam said, "There is surely something about this that makes him uncomfortable. How can there be two Reeds? One on our side of the river and one here who visited the settlement? Same name. And he seemed to think Reed was dark and bearded like the one who was our patient. We need to find a better spot to talk. Good point to ask about the horse. But he didn't answer that."

Chapter 8

Leading the horses, they moved toward the nearly empty mess hall where they might get coffee and look over the letter. Inside with steaming mugs in hand, Sam indicated a nearby table. "What's the news from the Massachusetts Sixteenth?"

Eustis broke the seal and opened the letter. He read quickly, then gave it to Sam, watching him carefully as he read. The note was indeed from their friend, Dr. James Thacher, who wrote that his regiment would be arriving sooner than expected, probably in late September. Rumors about various correspondence and recent orders led him to believe the regiment would be needed in the north as soon as it could get there. It seemed, Thacher wrote, that security had grown lax and there was talk of some British effort to capture West Point.

"Deo volente." Everyone should be more alert.

***

Late that day at Fort Putnam, Danny noticed two men as they entered the cooper's shop; one short with an odd-looking bushy beard, the other taller, dark hair, pale as if he had never been in the sun. Everything about him was thin including his blotchy beard and hair. He seemed to have just grown too tall for it all. The men had appeared

68

before, customers of his boss, James Mugford.

Danny edged his way around the men. They were looking carefully at a small wooden barrel that Mugford had made as a sample, trying different ways to install and remove the top.

"How easy and quick can this be done without leaving any damage or any sign it has been opened?" one asked. "Does it need some kind of handle? And how long would it take to make a score of 'em?"

Danny leaned in, and one of the men, annoyed, glowered at him. "Eh, don't mind the boy," said Mugford. "He's my 'prentice, Danny Grady. He should learn this too."

"I don't care for it, Mugford. Don't need any snooping boys around. Get 'im out of here." Danny wanted to hear more, but his master told him to go outside and said to stack up the barrel staves he had been making. Discouraged, but knowing he had to obey, he moved out into the yard to collect the staves lying in a pile of sawdust.

When the men left the shop, the one who had frowned at Danny called to him.

"Hey, boy. I've seen you before. Where do you live? Here?"

"Yes, sir. Except when I go see my mother. She's down the lane."

"And where would that lane be, boy?"

"Out of the fort and down the road there," he pointed.

"Hah, where the women live." said the man, exchanging glances with the other one. "Do you ever take outside jobs, boy?"

"Sometimes, sir." Danny was feeling uncomfortable. He edged toward the shop door.

"You stay here and mind your business, boy. Meanwhile, remember I've got my eye on you."

Danny went into the shop full of questions, but was silenced by Mugford, who told him not to interfere in any customer's business. And that it would be better not to talk to or about those men in particular. "I'm warnin' you. Stay away from 'em, Danny. They're not good sorts."

Outside the cooper's shop, the two men conferred. Had the boy recognized them from some earlier encounter? That might make a mess of their plans. But how could they find out what he might know without giving it away. They untied their horses and rode off, talking. Danny watched them from the shop window. He could not quite hear what they were saying.

***

After stabling their horses, Eustis and Sam had gone to find dinner in the mess hall. Only a few men seemed to be there, and the doctors hoped for a quiet hour. But some of the diners were eager to talk to them about medical problems. After eating, they set up shop. Sam hauled in his kit of medicines with which he always traveled, and after Eustis talked with each one who had concerns, Sam dosed the ones sent to him. One major complaint about a toothache required more care than laudanum. They would have to remove the tooth, a back molar of substantial size.

"Let us tackle it early tomorrow morning," said Eustis, glad that he had brought several tooth extractors in his kit and that Sam was there to help hold the man down. "Meanwhile, take this until then, and you better talk with your corporal," he instructed. He handed over a tiny bottle of laudanum.

The doctors treated all the men in line, stitched and bound up a wagoner's crushed foot, and arranged for a convenient time to deal with the toothache. They then walked back to the stables, got the horses, and rode out of the fort and down to Brouwer's tavern, the one that Eustis had visited before.

"That was a good session," Eustis said. "I actually feel we helped those men back there. I get to feeling low more often now. Many of the men who are brought to us are so injured or sick, they are beyond my feeble help. This business of not being able to do anything for many of our patients eats at me, Sam. It's very discouraging. I just wish I knew more. You know what I mean?"

"I do know, my friend. It is a problem for all of us in medicine," acknowledged Sam. "And I'm sure the regimental surgeons wish they

70

could do more for their people too, but they are moving constantly."

"Remember back when we learned about the smallpox vaccine? I thought that was the beginning of many great discoveries. Vaccines for lots of things. Perhaps one for pneumonia or consumption or typhus. But nothing more has developed!"

"I know, I know." Sam grimaced and sighed. "I have to stifle all emotions and become very centered to care for the ones that are dying when I can do nothing for them except hold their hand. And I know that's not enough! Sometimes it's hard to come back from that removed state to being human again. Remember, no soldier thinks of their own death when they enlist. It may be good that they don't know how easily it can happen. I know it is not my fault. 'Tis just the way things are in this world."

"I'm so glad you came. At least I can talk to you. I don't know how long I can go on in this." Eustis shook his head.

"A day at a time, Billy boy, a day at a time."

It was early when they arrived and before going in, Eustis prompted Sam to chat with Bridey McGuinness. She might know more now, he thought. It would be good if they could talk to her outside or someplace without a bunch of men hanging around. She was like a man trap, or what was that type of metal that pulled other pieces to it? A magnet.

"You can charm her, Sam. I have not the slightest idea how to proceed."

After tying the horses to a ring on a post, both men ducked automatically when they entered the tavern, Eustis putting his hand up to the door's lintel. Sam chose a table on the side. It was a warm, comfortable place, the coals from a fire glowing in the large hearth centered on the wall. The room was not yet full or hazy with smoke, and most tables were still clean. Their business might be falling off with fewer men at the fort, mused Eustis, but there must be many travelers who stop here, even if just for food and a bed for the night.

He waved to the bartender, and soon Bridey came over after delivering an order at a table nearby. She looked as alluring as she had

71

the last time that Eustis saw her. She remembered him from that earlier visit and was interested to meet Sam Adams, saying she would be right back with their ale.

"Hoo, boy," whispered Sam. "You were right about her. I'm happy to do the talking." He hitched forward on the bench and, on her return, eagerly took the pewter tankard she offered.

"Any chance you can sit with us for a minute, my girl?'

"Well, ye see, sor, I'll have to see that ever'one is settled first. Then I might be gettin' back." This last was said with a promising twinkle and smile.

"I may stay here awhile, Bill," said Sam. "My wallet has a case of consumption, but I can make the sacrifice."

Eustis grinned at him. "Just so we find out something of what she knows, my friend."

A while later, Bridey came back to their table to ask if they wanted another round and then sat close to Sam on the bench. She gazed at him with fascination, and he was enchanted. Eustis waited for him to get to the questions, finally gave up, and began asking them himself.

"What's the talk? Have you heard anything new since last time, Bridey?'

"The most interestin' news is that General Washington is travelin' to Hartford up in Connecticut to meet with the French admiral. I surely would love to meet them. And if the French come here, I might learn to say French names right, do ye see? I might get one of 'em to teach me."

"I thought there was a Frenchman stopping by to see General Arnold at Fort Putnam. Perhaps you could ask him. What was his name now?" asked Eustis.

"I'll be sayin' this. I think 'e's nae but a fake frog. He was so fancy that I don't see how 'e could lead a regiment 'tall! But 'e did come here two, three times to talk to some men. They seemed to know 'im. Said Fontaine was 'is name. But 'e's gone now."

"Who were they? Are they here now?" Sam had recovered his wits.

"Ah no, sir, Dr. Adams. Not since a week now. They've not been back after the Frenchman left, or at least, 'e's not been coming in any more. That boy, Danny, up at the cooper's says 'e heard they were spies."

"Anyone that seems out of place is thought to be a spy. But the spies are cleverer than that. What do you think, Bridey?"

She seemed to pause to consider, and Eustis wondered if she was waiting for some kind of compensation. The barkeep signaled, and she abruptly left with a smile to get back to her job.

"Arrgh," muttered Sam.

"*Dum spiro, spero*. While I breathe, I hope." said Eustis. "We are not done yet. She'll be back." That said, he looked up later to see Bridey cheerfully coming toward them with a full pitcher to top off their tankards.

"I can tell ye about two of the men that the Frenchman met if that'll help. One of 'em had the most amazin' beard. Full and bushy. Ye practically could na' see 'im behind it. The other one was skinny thin. They were odd ducks, those two and the fancy Frenchie, but they knew each other. They didna speak French though. Spoke American, like we do."

"Have you seen anyone named Jonathan Reed? He came into our surgery across the river several days ago," asked Sam.

"Jonathan Reed – real pretty with fair hair but a scar on his chin. 'E should be off back south to 'is company by now. Nice man though. I liked 'im."

Sam looked at Eustis. It seemed this was the same man mentioned in the women's encampment – but not the one they met at Robinson's. And he was secretly glad Reed had left. She said she liked him!

Eustis wondered who else this other light-haired and beardless Jonathan Reed had been talking with when visiting the tavern, and asked Bridey.

"'E talked with everyone," she said. "Even spent time with that Frenchie Fontaine, if 'twas his name. I think the Frenchie used this place as a gen'l meetin' area, but Reed, 'e carried messages and said 'e was soon goin' back to Gen'l Washington. 'E seemed real friendly and nice."

When they left the tavern, Sam was singing. His father enjoyed the neighborhood taverns in Boston, especially the Green Dragon, and his son did the same. Eustis was sure that if they had stayed another hour, Sam would have been considering a marriage proposal. The niggling feeling that he was missing something continued. He hoped it would come back to him.

"I'm worried about you, Sam. What have you been doing in your slow time up there on the northern line? I'll have to ask Burr where the ladies are for you to pay court."

"Not to worry. Back there, we have no slow time. You know what it's like. We've talked about it. But did you see how she liked me?"

Eustis did not have to ask who.

They returned to the fort to claim two bunks in the officers' quarters. Rising early the next morning, they went in search of coffee and, hopefully, corncakes. The day began with light rain, looking unfriendly to travelers intending to cross any rivers. They needed to deal with the toothache, get that molar pulled. Both hoped it would not be a tough extraction.

A chair and small table commandeered, they set up a makeshift surgery in a corner of the mess hall. The man, private Henry Durgan, came in holding his jaw with one hand, helped by a friend. They got him seated and gave him some laudanum and a glass of rum to ease his pain and nerves. Eustis had laid out his extractors and scalpels on the table and covered them with a scrap of cloth. He found it was better for the patient not to see the instruments. He had lost a man out the door that way.

Sam positioned himself behind one shoulder, and Durgan's friend took the other side. A few other men gathered around to watch. Eustis said "Open wide," and probed around inside. The gum around the molar was as swollen as before and he felt sympathy for the patient but quickly got down to business. Hoping it was infected enough to come out easily, he clamped his best extractor onto the tooth and, leaning over, putting his knee against the patient's leg, began to twist and pull.

Tears rolling down his cheeks, Durgan howled and bucked. Eustis indicated he would pause to reposition the extractor, and Sam gave the man more laudanum. Then, after cutting an opening in the gum with his scalpel, Eustis reinserted the hook of the extractor, twisted it and, using his leverage, managed to withdraw the tooth in a bloody finale. They had a bucket of water for cleaning up. Rum for the patient, and wiping away more blood with a rag, wrapped up the surgery.

His patient panted with relief, and after about ten minutes, with the help of his friend, shakily got to his feet. "When you get to your tent or quarters, rinse your mouth with a little more rum, and do that again every time it gets too bloody until it seals over," Eustis instructed. "You'll be fine in a day or so. But don't eat anything rough. Keep to liquids, milk is good, and soft food."

Later, the two doctors walked over to check in with Danny at the cooperage and found him by a huge wooden box raised on legs over a small fire and a large iron pot of boiling water. A makeshift tube from a lid covering the top spouted steam into the box which hissed at its seams. Danny was preparing the barrel staves to put a curve into them. Earlier in the summer, it would be an impossibly hot job. Looking at Danny, they could see it was not pleasant even now.

Red-faced and sweating, Danny eagerly told of his day. Eustis was pleased to see that he also kept working, his eye on the steaming box so that staves came out of the box and could be braced and curved at the right time. He told them about the two men who came to look at the small barrels. Mugford came to the back of the shop just then to check on the boy, reminding him to pay attention to the steaming.

He then turned to Eustis. "I don't want you distractin' this boy, Dr. Eustis. You know I do jobs on the side, and I was just makin' some small barrels. It's a private job. I make extra money doin' work for customers other than the army, and these two will pay. And you know we all need money these days. The value of the Continental is about zero. 'Sides, I have to feed Danny, and he's a growin' boy."

"I understand, Mr. Mugford," said Eustis, smiling. "We don't want to interfere at all. We just came by to check in with one of our favorite friends. These are difficult times, so please keep an eye on him for us."

Mugford nodded and told Danny that he had five minutes and should then get back to work. Meanwhile, he went back to his own work, picking up his mallet and hammering an iron hoop around a large barrel.

"What is news in your world? Discovered anything, Danny?"

"I ain't heard nothin,' Dr. Eustis."

"We were just down the road at the women's settlement and checked on your mother. I wondered if those women or your mother had a bad time there sometime?"

Danny looked down at his feet and then peeked back up at the doctors. "My mum said not to talk 'bout it."

"Well, if you want to talk it over with anyone, Dr. Sam and I are available. You know we're on your side, Danny, and if you didn't want us to, we would not tell anyone."

Danny looked back at his feet. "I dunno. It makes me worried. Some men are just bad and mean."

"What I said stands, Danny."

His face screwed up in puzzlement. "Why did those men here not like me, Dr. Eustis? I just watched 'em. I did 'em no wrong. No pranks, nothin' like that."

"You are right. That is curious, Danny," said Sam. "I wonder too. But you best stay away from them if they come around again. Keep your distance, boy. And no more spying on them. They probably are just traders or carters."

"Where do you sleep?" asked Eustis, now concerned for his safety and closely watching the boy.

"I got a nice spot in the attic, Dr. Eustis. My mattress and my best stuff's there, just up that ladder."

The men walked to the door of the shop. "Well, you stay alert, my boy," said Sam.

Eustis added, "We're serious about that, Danny. And if you decide to talk with us more, just send over a message. Meanwhile, no larking about. We'll be off now, but we'll be back soon."

Eustis and Sam eased their way out of the shop and back to their horses, intending to ride down the road to the women's settlement. The clouds had cleared away. Each man was deep in thought as they wound their way down the lane through the late summer day. Butterflies were visiting the milkweed along the side of the road, and some of the wild flowers were turning to seed. Sam realized with some regret that he would have to get back to Danbury and his hospital duties in another week.

"May the devil take it, Bill. I am going to hate leaving you to work this out. We are running out of time, and we don't know enough yet."

They decided to discuss their situation with Dr. Burnet as soon as they got back. Perhaps they could make arrangements to cross the river every other day. Or stay longer. The increasing awkwardness of trying to find a solution when the information they needed was on the opposite side of a vast river began to seem insurmountable – perhaps just what Arnold intended. It seemed the answers they needed were to be found with the people around the fort. Both men wanted to find out more about the Reed on this side of the river. What about Colonel Kendall? They wondered if those two had ever been seen together. And the very odd Frenchman? He had to be in disguise.

Riding down the road, they decided they would have to pass up another settlement visit to get back to Robinson's when they had promised. Instead, the plan would be to discuss their problems with Dr. Burnet and see about finding more than two days away at a time. One half a day, an overnight, and another half day was not enough time, particularly when medical obligations and treatments intervened. And what had happened to the physician at the fort?

Chapter 9

The next day, late in the afternoon, there were hoofbeats and a flurry of activity in the Robinson House barnyard. A gentleman approached on an elegant horse. Aaron Burr had arrived! He would overlap with Sam for a day or two.

Burr was a small, neat, dark-haired young man of twenty-four with intense eyes. As Burr approached, one of the surgeon's mates ran to the surgical shed to alert Eustis, who had just finished stitching a cut on a man's forehead. It could be left to Elijah and Mrs. Nardy to bandage. Eustis wiped his hands on the nearby rag, grabbed up his waistcoat, and went out. Burr was just as Eustis remembered from their days back in Cambridge, stylishly dressed and smooth in social settings, even while riding into the barnyard.

Burr cordially greeted Eustis with a clap on the back and shook hands with Sam who, hearing the news, had followed Eustis out of the barn. Burr said he could stay only two days because the beautiful Theodosia was calling to him. She awaited him, and he was the moth to her flame. Her soldier husband was somewhere in the South, and despite her having five children, she and Burr had conducted a secret romance for months. What could Eustis do but be amused by Burr's audacity and flattered that he would even come to see them. That seemed to be his usual reaction to Burr, and he fell into the spell again.

Burr was offered a sleeping space in the house, sharing a room with Sam next door to Burnet and Eustis. To quell their concern, Burr told about his experiences as an experienced camper, hunter, and western explorer. He was not discouraged by any sleeping arrangement, he said, although he preferred being under a roof, reminding them that he had been on that failed expedition with General Arnold to capture Quebec. It had snowed and they were all starving. Had Eustis heard the story of eating Henry Knox's dog? And he could assure them that a leaky canoe is not the worst place he had laid his head.

After getting his gear upstairs, they cheerfully dragged him to their favorite nearby public house, the Queen's Head in the village around the ferry landing. The pub was on the first floor of a large square hip-roofed building set back from the road. The proprietor, his wife, and several children lived on the second floor. The battered sign over the door displayed a woman in a crown and a few scars from what looked suspiciously like bullet holes. Eustis wondered if the shooters thought they were commenting on Queen Charlotte to spite King George.

The beamed-ceiling taproom welcomed them with a dim haze from pipe tobacco, the smoke circling into halos around the candles. Squinting to adjust after the bright daylight, the men headed toward the assorted tables with candles and chairs. A tidy bar occupied the corner. This opportunity to go over their thoughts with Burr seemed perfect. Sam claimed a table and they reviewed for Burr what was known about the man's death. They still had no definite answers, no resolution, just questions.

Eustis was not sure how it would all end or if it ever would and regretted his enforced involvement. At this time, he could see no way out. He knew he would fret if Arnold swept it under a rug, as was likely in time, and he worried that he could not come up with answers. He had enough to do with tending to his patients without this other perturbing responsibility nagging him, and he wanted to get it wrapped up.

Burr, playing his lawyerly role, said, "Let's see where we are." The three developed a list of things they should do and other people they still needed to visit. Burr corrected their method of inquiry. It seemed they were not asking the right questions. Instead of a pleasant, getting-acquainted conversation, and instead of just visiting, they had to be more specific, more focused. Find out where all these people were on the night of the murder. How exactly had the murdered man reached that point on the road? Had he been in the women's village at all?

They were working on the assumption that the murderer was a man – not a woman, right? And why is that? Answers would narrow down this vast field of suspects from anyone and everyone who was in the neighborhood. Burr assured them that they should not be afraid or concerned about insulting people in the cause of finding a murderer. "Be rude if you must."

Burr wished he had been there to get a look at the Frenchman in Arnold's office at the fort. Eustis told amusing tales about him as they relaxed over their cider and ale, relating how this officer, if he was one, swished his lace handkerchief around. And it seemed he kept a distance from others too. But they were not sure that the Frenchman, if he was one and not someone playing the role, was still around; he might have disappeared by now. Colonel Kendall might know. And Eustis remembered that was exactly the question he should have asked. As always, they needed to be across the river but had to find time to be at the fort when they would be free.

As they sat around their table, Eustis brought from his pocket and carefully unwrapped the coded letter. He regretted that he had not managed to send a copy to Burr earlier. After looking it over, Burr thought it was a simple substitution code and that it would become clear once he found that key. He asked how long Eustis had had it and said they should be prepared for old news since so much time had gone by. He hoped it had not been an urgent affair.

Eustis spread out the piece of paper on the table top, careful not to get it on any wet circles left by the tankards. Elbows on table, the three leaned in to look at it. There were shapes, numbers, as well as letters printed in three lines on the small page.

T3OKFKDΔ

3 QO3M 2BFKD OBQ CLO

ΔDT LK OL3A QLΔKPCG

Burr went over to the publican for a quill and paper and, sitting down again, got to work. "Usually, as I said, it is a matter of substitution. The simplest is to use a number one for an A, but that does not seem to track. Let me just play with this a little."

"Bloody-backed thieving dogs." Sam and Eustis listened with some amusement to two farmers engaged in a heated discussion at the next table. One was expounding on the sense of entitlement shown by a British officer. His farm had been subjected to a British raid recently, and he was still furious. "Damned rascally scoundrel bog rats! Seemed to think they owned this country and me too!" he sputtered. "No offer to pay, just took what they wanted. You'd think we were their serfs or slaves. Well, not me, boy-o, not me!"

Burr was still occupied about a half hour later while the others discussed the latest news of the French in Newport and sipped their cider. Then he suddenly exclaimed: "I have it!"

This caused the two nearby farmers to look over and wonder if they should come to see what he had, but Eustis gestured to calm everyone down. He did not want the message to become public. Sam immediately realized the situation and made a joke, laughing to cover the disruption. "So, my friend Burr, read it to us. You got it to rhyme, eh?"

Burr folded the paper and the note and put it carefully in his pocket. He spoke to them quietly. "Not here. I would rather head back to Robinson's, Sam. It is getting late, and we all will have an early morning." He rose from the table and led the way to the bar. They paid their tab, left the writing materials, and, waving thanks to the publican, made their way out, the two doctors hoping Burr would explain.

Burr stopped a short distance from the public house and said, "This is a dangerous note, my friends. I do not want it known before we can consider what to do. As soon as we get a light, I'll show you both."

Back at Robinson House, they entered the empty, tidy kitchen where that day's cooks had cleaned all the dishes, put food away, and set out preparations for the next morning's breakfast. A large scrubbed table occupied the center of the room. The three moved to sit on two benches near the banked fire, its embers still glowing. Eustis took a twist of paper from the supply on the mantel, lit it in the hearth then put flame to two candles. Burr passed around the note and Eustis and Sam sat in stunned silence.

Warning

A trap is being set for

GW on the road to Htfd

Is GW who they think it is? They didn't know the time frame. Wasn't General Washington already on his way to meet with the French in Hartford?

Sam turned to Eustis. "Good God, what can we do now?" Burr was to leave the next day, and they knew the message must get immediate action.

"Bill," said Sam. "You must alert General Arnold to warn General Washington." Burr, his legal mind at work, was not sure that was a good idea, troubled that Eustis would be asked how he got the information. Eustis knew Arnold was a suspicious man and seemed especially worried about conspiracies. His personal guard soldiers were always snooping around, and Eustis could become a suspect of some kind, might even be accused of being a spy himself. What then?

They worked out a plan. Despite their concerns, Sam and Eustis would have to inform Arnold at breakfast before Burr left.

The day began sun-less, overcast and threatening. The aroma of freshly baked bread drew them to the dining room. Coffee, and fresh bread with gravy, better than the military's corn cakes, eased them into the day. Arnold, however, was not at the table. It seemed he had stayed at West Point late into the night and had arrived only a few hours before.

Noah led Burr's horse into the barnyard, with his gear tied to the back of the saddle. Burr looked intently at Eustis, and wished them all well. Determined to get to his lady love by evening, he could not stay and must head out.

"Thanks, Noah, for all you are doing to keep my friend here functioning." He clapped Eustis on the shoulder. "And Eustis, if I hear anything further, I will get back to you. Please find the general as soon as you can. You'll have to."

After calling out "safe journey" to Burr, Eustis went back into the house, hoping to catch Arnold before he left or got involved in his work. He knocked on the door of the general's ground-floor office. Hearing "Enter," he stepped in and stood before the general's desk. Arnold continued reading the dispatch in front of him then looked up. "What is it, Dr. Eustis?"

"Excuse me, sir. I received information that General Washington will come into some trouble while riding up to Hartford. It seems there will be an attempt on his life."

"What?" Frowning, Arnold stood abruptly, shoving his chair back. He glared at Eustis. "What? That is absurd! Where did you hear this ugly rumor? Was it some patient of yours? What can they possibly know?"

He took an angry step to the side and then back. He looked like he wanted to hit the desk or at least start pacing but apparently felt both actions would be beneath his dignity. He seemed anxious, agitated like a trapped wild animal.

"Look, doctor, I cannot have these rumors spreading around. It is just not acceptable. You will have to stop it right now. Just stop them!"

"But, sir, I thought you needed to know and that you would want to deal with this. Please, sir, perhaps you can look into it, get further details? What would you have us do to help?"

"Hmmm." Arnold calmed down, and Eustis could almost see his brain working on the situation. "You do nothing, doctor. I will handle this. And I will need to get on it right now." Then gesturing with his hand, "Dismissed." Arnold followed him to the door muttering, "You would think I have enough to do." As Eustis went out, he yelled, "Colonel Varick!" bringing his aide running.

The sky glowered, dark clouds billowed overhead, and Eustis jogged toward the barn. The worsening weather seemed to reflect Arnold's temperament. Rumbles echoed around the river cliffs and ruffled the water. It looked like the entire Hudson Highlands was in for a storm. Burr would have a nasty, wet ride.

Eustis hurried into the barn. Relieved that he had spoken to the general, the doctor now had to shift his attention to a patient with constant pain in his lower right stomach area. Neither he nor Sam was sure what caused it. Elijah sat holding the patient's hand, hoping he could sleep. It was most likely not operable. Any surgery in the main trunk of the body was hugely dangerous, almost guaranteeing death. Eustis planned to ask Dr. Burnet for his opinion. Perhaps he had run into this during his years of practice in New Jersey. As it was, only laudanum had helped with the man's pain overnight.

Eustis passed on to Sam that he had told Arnold what was in the coded note, reporting that Arnold called his aide and said he would take action.

"He seemed shocked? Do you know what he will do?" asked Sam.

"Absolutely no idea."

"I've been thinking about how it just hands the entire war, our cause, our revolution, to the British if they take New England and our inspiration is gone. Without Washington and the Continental Army, we are surely lost."

"'Tis not a done deed yet, my friend, not hopeless until we know it is, and meanwhile, we go on," Eustis countered.

Another new patient required their attention. Under their care for two days now, he had been shot and had damage to his lungs causing a significant lung collapse. They had already revived him once. Eustis wanted to bleed him again, but he and Sam differed. Eustis followed the teaching of Dr. Benjamin Rush who always advocated bleeding, and he was the most respected physician they knew. After all, he had signed the Declaration of Independence. That was enough for Eustis. Sam wanted to hold off and had taken the early morning watch. The two of them and Elijah had taken turns through the night watching over the man. They wanted to ask Burnet if he had looked the patient over and what he thought.

The skies opened in a downpour. Watching from the doorway of the barn as sheets, rods of rain drilled into growing puddles and rivulets running down the drive, Sam and Eustis talked over what they knew.

Stretching his arms overhead, arching his back, Sam commented: "I wish there was a way to identify who people are. In our part of Boston, the North End, everyone knows nearly everyone else. If I don't happen to know a person, there are dozens in the town who do. But here, with people coming in from everywhere, even from as far away as Virginia, we can't know who they really are. They can say anything, give any name, and you would not know if it was true. It makes me very uneasy, as if our security is gone."

"I know what you mean," said Eustis standing at the door. "I reckon that in this new republic we are trying to create, there will be a great deal of change and invention. Here, right now, we are between two countries, as it were, with no rules but those of the army. Maybe there will be some kind of registry invented. What do you think? I can go to the Maine territory and no one will know who I am at all. Just whatever I tell them. So how can we know the truth or identify this dead man?"

Lightning and the crash of thunder rumbled overhead. Mrs. Nardy pulled the barn door shut and lit several lanterns. Noah came in carrying buckets for leaks. Sam might be due to leave soon, but they still had much to work out.

"Where are we, Bill?

"In a barn, you lame brain!"

"No, c'mon, you know what I mean."

"I do indeed. And one thing that bothers me is Danny's situation. I had not realized the kinds of characters who come into the cooperage. Do you think Mugford is trustworthy? I realize it is an ideal place to pass information around. Even Danny says they are all talking about the war. You could cover up anything and pass information to anyone you wished there."

"'Tis true. I thought the same thing. I'm glad you cautioned him, but what boy is going to remember that for long? You and I never worried. Remember how we just knew we were invincible? But I keep thinking of the women's settlement. Something is going on there too. We or you have got to spend more time there and talking to Danny. Something happened to put them all on guard."

"Agreed. But I'm committed here. I think more and more that Arnold knew that when he gave me this assignment. He must have realized how difficult it would be to conduct any investigation across the river with the number of patients we have here. He's no fool. I wonder if possibly he does not want me to figure it out. Maybe he knows something that could be relevant."

"Whoa! You are on dangerous ground there! But I know what you mean. *'The web of our life is of a mingled yarn, good and ill together.'*"

"I could answer that with all's well that ends well or something else Shakespearian, but let's not get started on this. We could spend hours and it would be a duel of quotations. Fun, but . . ." he chuckled.

***

Early in the day after the deluge, the two doctors strolled over to see how Mrs. Tobey and her coffee had come through the storm. The flattened grass was soaking wet and the trees still dripped. Puddles pocketed the barnyard. Eustis and Sam had spent most of the evening talking, sitting by the barn door, all the while keeping their ears open for any disturbance from their patients. Their soldier with the problem lung had come through the night without further bleeding, and they at least had some hope of his recovery. The one with the severe stomach pain to Eli's dismay had quietly died.

They found Mrs. Tobey sorting her cargo in the wagon, making room and organizing her wares. Drying the material that had gotten damp.

"Dr. Eustis," said Mrs. Tobey while pouring him coffee, "you might want to check into the rumors flying around the women's settlement. When I was by there just a few days ago, several were talking about their suspicions of Elijah having violated Norah Lindholm and that her expected baby was not her husband's. I know his grandmother is worried about something."

God rot it, thought Eustis. The quidnuncs were at it. He sighed. "Can we be saved from gossip? I'll talk with Elijah."

Mrs. Tobey tutted and said, "Oftentimes we find there is some truth in all rumors, doctor."

As a result of their discussion the night before, Eustis had new ideas and had developed various theories about how the murder of the man across the river had been committed and who might be on their list of suspects. It was all because Sam had asked: "What if?"

The two men had become speculative, and Sam had suggested they explore various scenarios.

"What if we are on the wrong track altogether?" he began. "What if these other things are all distractions, and the counterfeiters or smugglers do not come into this at all. Indeed, they are working for the enemy, but perhaps the real motive for the murder is something deeply personal, some question of financial gain or advantage such as a lust for power or envy? It could be several months or years in the murdered man's past with someone else."

"But Sam, without an identification, how do we find that out?"

They had to try to make a deal with Burnet for at least alternate days away from Robinson's. Sam had very few days left. When they had gone in for their midday dinner, Eustis realized the importance of getting across the river, and soon. Too many questions without answers were piling up in his mind. He needed to talk with Dr. Burnet later that evening, undistracted by the food and people around their dinner table.

The kitchen women had outdone themselves: wonderful fresh fish from the river, and several other dishes including one of stewed apples as well as leafy green salad and bread fresh from the oven. Eustis remembered how dreadfully lean it was last winter, their worst year ever. It might get as bad again this winter. Last year when there was deep snow, they even ran out of the basics like flour for bread, and hay for the horses and cows. Although grateful for the ample meals of the present, he felt apprehensive.

By the end of the day, as expected, his request for more time away irritated Dr. Burnet, but when reminded again that it was an assignment from General Arnold, there was nothing that could be said to object. If Eustis could put more time into it, everything might be resolved sooner. It was agreed. Eustis would leave with Sam the next day.

Elijah, adept now at maintaining their stores of herbs and medicines, would remain behind as their developing apothecary and deal out medicines as needed. Eli had spent time since his arrival getting to know the surrounding woods and fields and seemed to always return with more supplies or simples than he had the day before. He was particularly interested in finding ways to alleviate their patients' pain. He had gained much folk wisdom about the plants' curative powers and dangers from his grandmother.

Later, as they retired to their rooms, Eustis commented that they had to discover what had happened at the women's settlement. After all, the dead man had been found very near there, and it might be related.

***

Early the next morning, Eustis and Sam were rushing to wrap up several tasks before crossing the river. They were striving to get to a late morning ferry when Eustis was interrupted by a military aide who hurried to his operating shed to report that a man's body had been found not far from them along the road to Garrison's Landing, near the Queen's Head. Eustis quickly sent a message to Sam, finished wiping his instruments, and called for Noah to bring Hector to him. The doctor made haste toward the ferry landing, less than two miles away. He hoped this unexpected turn of events would not interfere with their planned return to West Point.

88

Further adding to that week's commotion around Robinson House had been the appearance of Peggy Arnold, driven into the barnyard in her carriage with Alpha, her slave, Edna, the nursemaid, and her baby son, Neddy. She moved into the two second-floor rooms, arranging them to suit herself and son. Her servants went into the attic.

The dining routine was adjusted to the Arnolds' schedule. Although rarely there for the midday dinner, in the evenings the general was always eagerly welcomed by Peggy at the door. Edna brought the baby in a lacy cap and gown to briefly see his father after he had settled in the parlor. When there were no outside guests, Peggy often planned a private light supper in their rooms while the rest of the staff and officers supped on the first floor. Alpha would bring their meal upstairs from the kitchen. When the general and Mrs. Arnold had guests for a proper dinner, the doctors might or might not be invited to join them.

Chapter 10

Elijah fretted over the edge on the blade of his knife. He gave it a few more swipes on the whetting stone, wanting it as sharp as possible to easily shave bark from willow twigs. Then again, too sharp and he was in danger of removing part of a finger. Not a good thing, he mused, as he picked up a small branch to test it. He had gathered plants in the woods and fields around Robinson House earlier and was preparing his medical supplies.

Eli was maturing into his self-assigned job of creating the best possible source of medicines for the hospital. He knew they were dangerously short of some of the imported medicines like Peruvian bark that used to be among their staples. He sought local alternatives for easing pain.

An infusion of willow bark tea was the best they could do to relieve a mild headache. They had to use laudanum if pain was more severe. And laudanum meant extracting the opiate from the poppy plant, its strength in the infusion depending on the amount of opium in the alcohol mixture. Sometimes codeine or morphine could be mixed in as well, all part of a new science of alleviating pain in patients. Eli believed the world was just getting started with these possibilities, and he hoped to experiment with hallucinogens as well.

Noah called to him as he approached the shed, his arms full of plants. "Eli, come quick. The doctor needs us! There is another dead person, and we gotta move him back here."

"Oh, may the devil take it!" said Eli. "I have to set this up here first. Can you hitch up the wagon? I'll be with you, soon as I can."

***

Eustis, riding Hector, appreciated his minutes of calm before he had to get busy again. Then about a mile and a half down the road, he saw them. A number of people stood in a cluster looking at something in the middle of the road. Drawing closer, Eustis could see a man's body. Crushed grass and brush made a trail down the bank to the edge of the river. Probably drowned and been pulled out of the water, he surmised.

Noah, on Sally arrived to find the doctor crouching over the soaking-wet body of a fair-haired man dressed in a shirt, brown breeches, stockings, and shoes. He looked to be about twenty-five.

Sam rode up just as Eustis was beginning to establish facts, asking the men standing there if they knew who had found the body and where exactly it was found. They shuffled their feet, looked at each other, and seemed not sure of who should speak. After a pause, a stout bearded fellow in dirty breeches, filthy stockings, and jacket said he found it. Said his name was Anderson and that he had a farm just over the hill. He had been walking toward the public house.

"I'm headed to my just reward for gettin' my mornin' plowin' done, plantin' winter rye, ye see, and there was this man – just lyin' in water down at the edge of the river. Hauled 'im up to the edge of the road, ye see, and then I hollered for help. Dunno who 'tis."

There were no wounds on the body other than several bruises, although it almost looked like purple fingerprints in one place on his neck. The blue tone of the lips and slightly gray skin left no question that he was dead. Probably a drowning accident. More men walked over to stand around the body, attracted to the novelty of the doctor examining it. They were interrupted by a horse-drawn buggy coming

91

down the road. Two of the men quickly slid the body out of the way to the roadside, watching the buggy as it passed, its occupants staring back at them.

Eustis intended to check the deceased over carefully back in his surgery at Robinson's. He asked for help and gently rolled the man over onto his back, then ran his hands over the head and down to the shoulders. He suddenly realized that it could not be just a drowning accident. This man had been strangled. The hyoid bone in the neck on the left side, the U-shape bone at the base of the tongue, was broken. Eustis would have to check the dead man's lungs to see if he went into the water before or after the injury to his neck.

As Eustis turned the body back over, intending to examine the underside again, something bright caught his eye near the grass where the body had been dragged up onto the road. "What's this?" he wondered, stepping over and peering around, seeing nothing at first. Then there it was. A long slender cane with an ornate handle. It did not seem to suit the dead man. Of course, maybe he was not the owner and had nothing to do with it. Anderson said he had hauled the dead man up from the river bank.

Perhaps this was not the only corpse and there was another in the river. It seemed like a recurring nightmare. Sam carefully worked his way down to check along the river bank, climbed back, and shook his head. Nothing.

Eustis sighed, vaguely recalling a cane like that from some other time. But where was that? Probably back in Boston. He wondered if the cane had been with the dead man at all. Or if it had somehow fallen from a passing coach or wagon. He looked around. Where was Elijah to help? He should have arrived by now.

But then he saw a small cloud of dust up the road, and Elijah soon approached in the wagon, coming to gather the body and take it back to Robinson House. Noah and Sam helped Eli lift the dead man into the back. Eustis planned to examine the corpse carefully, probably do another autopsy before burial.

There seemed to be the usual confusion over the victim's identity. Eustis checked the victim's pockets, finding nothing to help. No one standing around knew who he was, so probably he was not local. Surely someone had seen something? Eustis sighed again. This would call for another autopsy. And someone would have to make sketches to circulate in the area and perhaps throughout the army. He might have been a traveling trader from another village, and if so no one would recognize him at all.

Sam asked the bystanders about traffic along the road as they all stepped aside so another wagon could pass. It seemed to be busy whenever he or Eustis were there. Someone may have seen something and then gone on to the village. They would have to check at the Queen's Head.

Back at Robinson's, Elijah and Sam laid the corpse on the table in the surgical shed. Dr. Burnet joined the two other doctors. After a cursory glance, Burnet easily turned the problem over to Eustis, saying he was the one experienced in all of this and that he should continue being the chief investigator of unexplained deaths.

"Lucky me," groaned Eustis. His day's plans were quickly slipping away.

Several things had to be done immediately. First, they must notify General Arnold about the second dead man. Eustis asked Burnet to do that, and Burnet left to comply without enthusiasm. He dreaded the general's annoyance with him for delivering the news.

Then they had to find Jonathan Reed.

Noah reminded Eustis that he'd last seen Reed in the barn organizing his gear and preparing to move on. Eustis quickly sent him with a message asking Reed to come and look at the new corpse. Reed complied immediately. Handing his horse over to Noah, he walked hurriedly into the shed. He stood for several minutes looking silently at the body laid out on the planks. Eustis and Sam stood nearby, waiting. Then Sam said helpfully, "He fits the description of another Jonathan Reed who operated across the river. Fair and the right age.

Reed replied: "Can we speak privately? Perhaps take a walk?"

"Certainly," said Eustis. The two men walked across the nearest pasture, watched by several curious cows, and stopped by a gnarled apple tree filled with nearly-ripe red fruit.

Eustis frowned and began. "I apologize for not knowing your official title, if you have one, and I suspect you are not just a wanderer or dealer in trade goods. I have to say I am prodigiously concerned by hearing of another Jonathan Reed across the river who cannot be you. Or are you someone else altogether?"

"I understand," said the tall, dark-haired man who called himself Reed. He leaned with his hand on the tree. "And I do have a purpose being here as you have surmised." He paused before continuing. "I know you will keep this in confidence, doctor. I am a colonel in the Continental Army but am working without any identification, trying to uncover who is circulating counterfeit Continental dollars. It is a particular wish of General Washington that we stop this, and he has given me free range. I too am concerned with this other Reed."

"Thank you for telling me, colonel. If there is any help you can give me on our dead man, I will be forever in your debt."

Reed frowned. "Hmm, there are a few things, Dr. Eustis. This man may have been involved with some shady business, possibly smuggling. I don't want to encourage you too much, but I believe I have seen him several times. His name at that time was Peter de Vos, Dutch for the Fox. He seems to use disguises frequently. You may be on the edge of something major here."

Eustis felt a rush of excitement. Progress! After their past difficulties, this seemed too easy. But then Reed went on.

"I'll need a day or so to double check with my superiors, doctor, and get back to you. Can you do a decent identification and make some good sketches? I realize he needs burial soon. But I must make sure. Perhaps I can find an identifying description as well. If this is that other Reed, as I said, he used disguises a great deal."

If they were this close, and answers were forthcoming, Eustis felt he could wait, but it would not be easy. He hated feeling helpless, and he still had questions. He offered his hand. "I can do that, colonel. But hurry back. We need answers. Solutions."

The men returned to the barn, Reed mounted his horse and, gathering the reins, called a farewell to both doctors. Eustis wished him Godspeed and good luck on his early return.

Turning back, he sent Noah to relay Reed's request for a good artist to the surrounding camps. He knew there was no scar on the chin of this new corpse that would match the description of the blond Reed, so this dead man was probably not him. After giving Sam an update, Eustis began his own sketches and notes, his own medical record. As it happened, Sam and Eustis missed crossing the river on the noon ferry, not realizing that when they decided to do an autopsy, it would not be a day but an entire week before they could get back across the river to West Point.

***

Having lit several lanterns in the surgical shed and leaving the door open for light, Eustis began laying out his instruments for the autopsy. Sam assisted, looking carefully for anything Eustis might have missed. They needed to check the man's lungs for water. Was the man dead before he went into the river or had he fallen and drowned?

Hours later, two discouraged men went in for their evening supper. Sam had helped the surgical work move more efficiently as he held retractors, made suggestions and comments during each step, and took notes. They found nothing to indicate that a weapon had been used. Except now they knew that he had died before he went into the water. Probably a physical fight had resulted in this man's death. They still did not know who he was.

That evening, as they glumly sat around, a courier brought a message for Sam. He had to leave, called back to his hospital post on the northern line. "God's teeth!"

Could the day have gotten any worse? He would have to leave in the morning and not have the days they had planned. What wretched

95

timing! And the constant interruptions! Sam had said he wanted to help with the puzzle of the dead man, but he knew it was self-indulgent to stay longer when Danbury said they needed him back. There had been a serious skirmish resulting in many wounded men, and neither doctor knew how much longer it would take to find any solutions at Robinson House. Sam's responsibilities loomed, and he would not neglect his own hospital's patients.

"I wish I could stay, but I just can't do it, Bill." He sighed. "And here you are with two dead men, one on this side of the river and one on the other, with very little evidence of how they died and no way to discover their names unless someone shows up who can identify each of them. Each killed differently in up-close ways, but no obvious connection between them. If they are in an organization, there seems to be no sign of it. I think your best bet is to try making the rounds of the fort and women's settlement again. Maybe someone will remember something." Knowing he had an early morning and a long ride ahead, Sam headed for his bed.

After dawn's early surgical rounds in the barn, Doctors Adams, Eustis, and Burnet met briefly as usual with Mrs. Nardy outside the barn door. Burnet then headed for the house to get some coffee. Elijah helped several ambulatory patients move slowly out to the yard and onto benches in the sun along the southeast barn wall. The outside sun and air seemed to have a very favorable impact and was a major step forward in regaining the men's health. They could talk together about going home, their friends in regiments, or watch barnyard activity.

Noah brought Sam's horse carrying his traveling pack, as the two doctors waited in the barnyard. They would all miss Sam. In that short time, he had become an important member of the Robinson House family. Sam turned to Noah, offered his hand, told him how much he appreciated his help, and that he should take care of Dr. Bill.

"Same to you, Eli," he said, patting Elijah on the shoulder. "And teach Noah to write." Then he turned to his longtime friend.

Eustis took Sam's hand and, overcome by his distress at the

separation, reached out to hug him. "You have been a great help to me, Sam. I wish you could stay. You know that. But you have advanced our investigations, as it were. Pathetic to call them such. It seems we are no nearer to solving the puzzles, but for all we know some of it may become clear, and we will find the solutions soon. At least it has been of incalculable value to talk everything over with you. Travel carefully, my friend. *Manere incolumem esse felicem*. Stay safe and happy."

"I will, and you take care of yourself too. Until we meet again, and I hope we can make it soon."

Swinging aboard his horse, Sam gave a cheerful wave and rode out of the yard. Eustis wanted to yell: "Stop! You are leaving me alone with this murder mess." But he held back and gloomily returned to the barn to begin checking on his patients. Both Noah and Elijah felt his despair and hung around, willing to help him as much as they could.

Several hours later, feeling the need for some different conversation and after seeing his most recent mystery body wrapped for burial as an unknown, Eustis strolled over to see the affable Mistress Tobey. He perched on the log she had positioned by her fire, pleased as always to accept a mug of her notable coffee.

"I can see that you are not at your most cheerful," she observed as she also sat down smoothing her apron over her lap.

"No," he sighed, "I'm sorry to say, Mistress Tobey. Another dead man was found on the road, as you have probably heard. Another problem of identification, and I am quite sure this one could have been murdered as well. I have to wait another day to go across the river to see if they know anything. I wish I could just talk directly to them."

Mrs. Tobey murmured her understanding and Eustis unburdened himself, did not hold back his frustration.

"And my good friend Sam Adams just left to return to his hospital along the northern line. He came down for a short visit to help me solve the question of who murdered that man on the road over near Fort Putnam. Sadly, for both of us, Sam got a note requiring him to return sooner than expected. I guess fighting is renewing up there along the coast. For all his time here, we have not gotten very far. I realize we deal with the dying all the time, but a person deliberately killed! 'Tis sorely discouraging."

She was sympathetic. "I can see that, doctor. Plans oft times go awry. I was told about the additional corpse. I wanted to pass on to you what gossip was afoot as I made my usual circuit of places this week across the river. I know that interests you.

"First, I have to say, I'm surprised by how little is happening at West Point. I thought they were supposed to be improving and finishing the defenses. Seems to be an air of uncertainty all around, even in my business. It could be that people are not interested in buying because everything is costing so much more now. Our money is worth less by the week, and I do not understand how some folk can even afford basic supplies."

Several men in Arnold's personal guard came riding by, staring hard at Eustis and Mistress Tobey. Heading out on some secretive mission, Eustis supposed. But they gave him a very unsettling feeling. Made him begin to wonder if some self-identified patriots perhaps were not all on the same side, not necessarily allies. He sipped his coffee. "Suspicious bunch. And here we are going into autumn. What will you do this year when it gets cold?" He hesitated to ask anything more personal.

"I usually start ambling toward the southwest 'bout now, heading for my son-in-law's house. As I told you, my daughter inherited the farm, so her husband owns it now, and tolerates me living there over the winter. I'll be leaving soon unless I hear of a safe spot at West Point where I can stay for the next five months. But back to what we were saying. Have you learned about how those wicked men are making and spreading counterfeit Continental dollars?"

Eustis frowned. "I thought the money was being printed and spread from somewhere southeast of us down on Manhattan Island. There are rough groups of men roaming around that middle ground between the lines there. I don't know much about how such dollars can be printed or moved, but they must have some portable system. Do you suppose they have a press they can move around?"

"Well, Dr. Eustis, you might want to talk to the cooper at the fort. Goes by the name of Mugford. He was telling me about two men who came in to get specially made small barrels. And it seems to me that generally we want large barrels to get more of our produce or products to their buyers. Nail barrels are much bigger than those they were interested in. Even regular rum kegs are bigger. Those were like canteens, but I don't think they intended to use them for water or beer or even whiskey. And they wanted them to open and close easily too."

"Interesting, Mistress Tobey. What would anyone use a barrel that size for?"

"Really, doctor! Think about it. Probably not sheets of paper. Too big. But already printed bills? Or smuggled rum? No one would suspect them. It is just a curious thing. Go see for yourself."

Eustis added that to his growing mental list of things to look into as he walked back to the barn and remembered the pointed questions Burr had suggested. He had to be more specific with his questions. Well, he was learning how to conduct an investigation while on the job. It was like going into a different sort of country, and you had to learn all the new rules.

Chapter 11

Meanwhile, in a public house in the Hudson Highlands, two grimy men, one tall, bearded, with dark balding hair and the other shorter and fair-haired, both about twenty-five, arrived separately, quietly easing into a back room at midday when customers were few. They looked like day laborers or nearby farm hands. A third man with brown hair and a bushy beard, dressed in an old sweat-stained shirt and dirty breeches, also slipped into the room. The first two grunted greetings, and the three remained standing, apparently waiting. About ten minutes later, an almost hidden back door creaked open, admitting a uniformed general immaculately dressed with his aide close behind. The waiting men instantly stood straighter. This was their new commander.

After pulling a stool out and back from the table, the general sat and motioned the others to sit also. His aide, upon receiving a signal from the ranking officer, went to the inner door into the tavern, spoke to someone inside, and soon received four tankards of ale. After carefully setting the tankards on the table, the aide backed up to stand silently against the wall.

The general glared, took a long drink, then said, "Alright, tell me what you know."

The men looked at each other, wondering who should start. "You, Bowen." said the general, pointing at the last arrival with the full beard.

"I looked around that women's settlement as you asked, sir. Seems they do not know anything useful. 'Twas a very comely young woman living there though, too good to be the wife of a rebel, an' she caught my attention. She's a pretty piece of work, but resisted most everythin' I tried to get information. I was hopin' for mebbe a quick tumble but she gave me trouble on that. I like the feisty ones. Might make one more visit in a bit to see if they know anything about Gordie. Why he's missin', all that. She didn't know when their men would be returnin'. I was real friendly, an' told her my name was Reed. Confuse 'em." He grinned at Reed who did not appear to be happy.

"Hmmm," the general pursed his lips. "Keep checking on them. And you, Reed. What have you got for me? Any luck over in Manhattan?"

"Yes, sir." The dark-haired tall man answered, "The Westchester militia are out and around. Seemed disorganized, but spread out enough to be a nuisance. I ran into some difficulty, injured myself and went to that hospital at Robinson House to get my leg checked. They seem focused on their doctoring there, and that Dr. Burnet stitched me up good. The one named Eustis checked it later. He got ahold of me a day or so after that, just as I was leaving. He seemed to think I might know something, or at least he was snooping around. Asked if I knew something about a murder across the river. He pokes into things, but 'tis keeping him distracted enough not to look closely at us.

"And I don't appreciate someone else using my name," he looked pointedly at Bowen.

The man they called Bowen spoke up. "That doctor's been over at the women's settlement more than once. I'll bet he has an eye for the young woman there too. She's like bait for bears."

The general looked at them, chewed on his lip a moment, then asked, "Any sighting of action down along the river? All quiet? Williams?"

The last of the men answered. "Nothin' happenin', general. I been waitin' for the Vulture to show, but she's not there yet. You got problems, we can take care of 'em."

"That will be all then, Williams, I'll get back to you in about a week. Keep up your good work."

With that he rose and moved to the rear door. The aide opened it, looked out, then said, "All clear, general," and they left. There was a faint sound of hoofbeats, the men then finished their ale, and departed, one at a time, through the tavern.

***

Unknown to anyone at Robinson House, the British sloop Vulture, usually lurking farther south, silently crept up river flying a flag of truce during the night. The Vulture's launch docked at Robinson's early in the morning to deliver a note for the general as he was breakfasting with the officers and doctors. When his missive was delivered, Arnold thanked the messenger and sent him to the kitchen for his own bread and coffee. The letter bore the signature of Loyalist Colonel Beverly Robinson, the man whose vacated house they now occupied as a hospital.

Reading his letter, Arnold first looked concerned, then he informed those at the table that Colonel Robinson requested a meeting with him. It was a conundrum. Maybe Robinson wanted to ask about the condition of his property. There could be no obvious explanation. Arnold asked what his aides thought about making contact. Colonel Varick asked: "Aren't you scheduled to meet General Washington in Peekskill? I thought he was stopping there on his way north."

"Yes, he is," said Arnold. "He's off to consult with the French admiral, Comte de Rochambeau. I just wondered what you thought of meeting with Robinson." He eyed the men around the table from under heavy eyelids. Eustis wondered if he was serious or if he just wanted to check on his officers' loyalty. Something seemed off. They, in turn, continued to suggest that he should not decide without discussing it with Washington.

Eustis decided not to mention the strange coded note he had received with the information that he'd passed on to Arnold. He had no assurance that any warnings had gone out, but he had to assume that Arnold, or Varick with Arnold's information, would manage to prevent any ambush. Perhaps they would discuss it at their meeting, although it was not his place to ask. After all, it was supposed to be secret, and there seemed to be a great deal going around that was not general knowledge.

***

A day later, Arnold headed back to West Point after meeting with Washington. Riding along, he told his two aides that based on Washington's advice, he had declined the invitation to meet with Colonel Robinson. He had not told Washington or any of his officers that he'd secretly included a private note for British Major John André, head of the British spy organization and Arnold's particular contact. He had immediately recognized that André was the actual author of the secret letter purporting to be from Robinson, but he had no intention of revealing that.

***

At Robinson House, a burial detail dug another grave among the many that were marked with simple wooden posts in a sloping pasture overlooking the river, and Eustis puzzled over his autopsy results. Identification awaited the return of Jonathan Reed, gone for two days now, and Eustis had no idea when he would return. He did know that the dead man had died before entering the water. He had not drowned. Curiously, there were no marks on his body other than bruises, making it less likely he had fought back but instead had been ambushed, betrayed by a confidant and taken totally by surprise.

The barnyard roosters welcomed the sun's appearance in a striped pink and pale-yellow sky, on the following late-September day. General Arnold, with events crowding his mind, rose early and was busy in his office at Robinson's before the sun fully crested the horizon. He joined his officers in the dining room, and his orderly poured his mug of coffee as he sat down.

Looking sternly at his officers, he announced, "I will be taking this day and possibly the next off to inspect some fortifications and redoubts a little farther down river. I expect you to carry on as usual – and make sure this house remains a safe site for my wife. Should anything seem strange, get her to safety, but do not cross the river to West Point. That could be too dangerous for her and my son."

"Rest assured, sir," said Colonel Varick. "All will be well." The others nodded and echoed assurances. "We'll watch out for her." "There will be no problems, sir."

An orderly had Arnold's horse saddled and ready. There was a mounting block in front of the house to help people gracefully board a carriage or mount a horse. The general made use of it, easing the stress on his perpetually painful shortened leg.

A crew of eight men waited in his longboat, tied up at the stubby wooden pier. On Arnold's arrival, they snapped to attention, and after he'd climbed aboard, at a word from their captain, the men lowered their oars, and the launch pulled away, heading down river. The orderly brought Arnold's horse back to the largest shed.

Meanwhile, the doctors and Mrs. Nardy gathered outside the main barn door to discuss their plans for the day. They looked up when the honking of geese flying south brought the changing seasons to mind. This time it was Burnet who scratched at his right side. Eustis reminded them of the issue of lice and fleas. Lice meant the possibility of typhus. They seemed to arrive together. Did Burnet know if maybe one brought the other? That was more in his realm of knowledge.

A memory flitted through Eustis's head. Washing everything is probably the best solution. He remembered his mother bringing out the large tin tub and placing it before the fire, filling it with well water and adding boiling water from over the fire. His father usually got the first chance at the hot water. Then he and his skinny little brothers were scrubbed and dunked. The water was replenished before the younger girls got in. He never knew when his mother got her turn. Maybe after they all went to bed.

"Dr. Eustis, have you decided?" The question invaded his reverie, and he scrambled to remember Mrs. Nardy's suggestions. There seemed no possible way to clean all the men or to get them to bathe in the river, particularly in the fall. Most stayed away from water and did not swim.

Recovering quickly, he said, "Cleaning seems to be the proven answer. Surprisingly, Doctor Franklin advocates removing all the clothes and actually immersing the body in water and swimming, but it is unlikely we can enforce anything like that. Let's get fresh straw or hay, change the bedding, and then sprinkle salt as we did last year. I have also heard that rinsing with turpentine is good for head lice."

"Very well, I agree," said Dr. Burnet, nodding. "We'll try to enforce cleanliness whenever we can and wash clothes. We can make sure they are using only clear well water."

Eustis concurred, and everyone went off to their respective chores, Eustis and Burnet going back into the barn to check several patients. They seemed to be in a lull. The near plague of the bloody flux or dysentery was clearing up, and they had time to breathe. Elijah followed along.

***

His gran is certainly right, thought Elijah. Life here at Robinson House is so much better than over in the women's settlement. Here he is fighting for the cause and doing serious things with other men, something he'd missed without knowing it. Just to feel useful was not enough because he had been useful before. But here! He helped the wounded and contributed his knowledge of herbs and simples that he had learned over the years.

His plan for today included searching for leeches to add to their supply. Dr. Eustis had pointed out to him the reduced number of the slimy black bloodsuckers in their jars. Maybe Noah would be able to come along. He might have a good idea about where to look. A spring and small brook flowed on the far side of the largest pasture where Eli had found many medicinal plants during his previous gathering expeditions.

That evening, having slipped up the river again as soon as it grew dark, the British ship Vulture hovered off Haverstraw Bay, carrying the impeccably dressed British Major John André.

The ship's crew rowed the cloak-wrapped André ashore, depositing him on a designated beach near the home of Colonel Joshua Smith. Colonel Smith was retired, likely a one-time Loyalist who opted to change sides so he could stay at his estate, keeping it safe. He had been at Robinson House as a dinner guest of the Arnolds just a few days earlier and happily offered the use of his home as a favor for the general.

In the darkness, a brisk, autumnal wind whipped the branches of the trees and made eerie shapes, sounds, and shadows. Several bats looped and soared overhead looking for interesting prey in the beach area. Arnold's launch had earlier brought him to the shore where he and André planned to meet. Sitting beside a fire hidden by trees and wrapped in their cloaks, the two fine-tuned a plan to surrender West Point to the British Army.

Discussions of money and enticing military advancement intrigued Arnold, a shiny promise dangled alluringly before his eyes. His thoughts about the unfair and insulting way he had been treated by Congress stoked his barely-contained temper. Those inept villains! They had never repaid him the money he had loaned to the army. Worse, they had advanced men for far less valorous deeds than his. And they called themselves a Congress, yet had ignored him, and he had been seriously wounded! Congress believed it was "fair" for all the states to have the same number of senior officers, but he had taken control and turned the tide for the Americans at Saratoga. Without him they would not have gained the help of France. And now he had to wear a built-up heel in his boot because his injured leg had healed two inches shorter.

He calmed himself and smiled inwardly, thinking of his beautiful but expensive young wife. He believed he could finally get the recognition he deserved if he served the British. And, after all, he was merely reverting to his original loyalties. It was hardly treason, although those numbskull, truly treasonous colonials might say it was.

Somehow the conversation, the planning and details took longer than the men expected. Daylight approached, and the eastern horizon lightened from gray to pale yellow. André would be exposed getting back to the Vulture unless they came up with a better plan. Arnold helpfully escorted the worried officer to Smith's nearby home where they woke the retired colonel. Arnold told him that André was an American undercover agent, and Smith helpfully offered the British officer one of his guest bedrooms.

For his part, Arnold sent a message back to his wife and aides at Robinson House indicating he would not return until the following day. He took another room to catch up on his sleep. A message arrived in the early afternoon informing André and the Smith household that the Vulture had been damaged by American cannon fire the day before and had retreated farther down the river to seek repairs. It would be the following morning before the ship could return. André had planned to get back to the Vulture that evening, but he now was stranded ashore at Smith's house.

They had to do something. It was getting too risky. Arnold was anxious to get back to West Point knowing that General Washington planned to come into the area on his return from meeting with the French in Hartford. There could be unpleasant repercussions and difficult questions if he was not there to greet the general.

As it happened, Washington and his entourage, their meetings with the French over, were at that moment on their way back, stopping at Isaac Keeler's tavern in Ridgebury, Connecticut, for some rest and food. At best, Arnold probably had two days before Washington's arrival.

Arnold consulted with Colonel Smith who, thrilled by the drama and secretiveness of it all, offered to loan André a horse and said he would be honored to escort him across the river to Manhattan and south to the edge of the British lines. That way Arnold could head back upriver to greet Washington.

It became clear that André's elegantly tailored British uniform would not do. He could not expect to safely travel across rebel-held territory wearing that red coat. He needed to be in some disguise. Smith offered his guest a change of clothes, and André shifted from his uniform to Smith's choice but kept his boots. He had put the accounts of troop strength and plans of West Point given him by Arnold in his stockings. Once all seemed ready, André and Smith set out, leaving a relieved Arnold free to return from his inspection tour. Much to Mrs. Arnold's delight, after arriving just the week before, she and her husband were able to sup together privately that Sunday evening. It was their last quiet time together.

Chapter 12

Henry Knox, traveling as part of the escort for General Washington, had an idea. His entire focus in the Continental Army had been the development of its artillery forces grounded in information he had gotten from the books he sold in his Boston shop. With his brother, he had hauled fifty-four cannons overland from Fort Ticonderoga in northern New York to Boston and formed an artillery company in those early-rebellion days.

He yearned to review West Point's defenses, currently being completed and strengthened by General Arnold. He secretly thought he probably could do a better job of it. Urging his horse closer to the general, he suggested adding a visit to West Point during their stop at Robinson House. Washington agreed. He too, wanted to look over the anticipated improvements at the fortress.

The general sent a message ahead to alert Arnold and the staff that he hoped to breakfast with him and would stay overnight at Robinson House. He had used the house the year before to meet with Benjamin Tallmadge about the spy group referred to as the Culper Ring. Washington and Tallmadge had worked out the responsibilities of the group, including how it could get information obtained in New York across Long Island Sound and back to Washington at West Point. Their plan had been successful so far, with the use of invisible ink and codes they had devised. Would that all plans turned out as well.

At Robinson House, Washington's forty-man escorting guard would camp out in the fields, and his officers could stay in whatever space was available in the house. Armed with the knowledge that the commander in chief was about to arrive, Peggy Arnold, in a swirl of activity, planned a breakfast reception for the commander in chief. Eustis, meanwhile, resolved to speak to Arnold and Burnet again about his murder investigation and the need to cross the river as soon as Washington's visit ended.

The Robinson House staff turned out before dawn that September day to attend to last-minute preparations. The chief cook and his assistants checked the ham warming in the Dutch oven and stirred a large pot of oatmeal. Earlier, a fire had heated the bake oven for several hours. When it was at the right temperature, pies as well as risen bread dough were placed in the oven's center. Eggs, still vaguely warm from the chickens, waited in a large bowl. The table was set, all would be ready soon, and only their guests were needed.

After a restless night, his mind refusing to quit reviewing his problems, Eustis rolled out of his creaking bed, yawned, and stumbled downstairs behind Dr. Burnet. He found that two of Washington's aides, Samuel Shaw and James McHenry, had arrived at Robinson's earlier and were already seated at the table.

They brought the message that the larger party would arrive later, not for the early breakfast as previously planned. Just as well thought Eustis after joining them. He needed coffee and then some time to organize himself and his surgical shed. Mrs. Arnold returned upstairs to her bedroom saying she would join them when Washington arrived. They were directed to let her know when he was approaching.

General Arnold sat down for breakfast with the other officers. The room was redolent with the smells of coffee, ham, sausage, and freshly baking bread wafting in from the kitchen. The general's orderlies had just served coffee to the doctors, visitors Shaw and McHenry, and Arnold's aide David Franks, when an express rider arrived with a dispatch and a letter for the general.

Arnold immediately excused himself to examine his messages privately. Opening the letter, he was stunned to read that John Anderson had been captured by Westchester militiamen and that an assortment of papers found on his person had been sent on to Washington . . . including a letter of safe passage from General Benedict Arnold.

The color drained from his face, and he could not breathe for a moment, staggering as he put one hand against the wall. His plans! Realizing that the commander in chief was due to arrive momentarily and what it might mean if Washington had already received this information, he knew he had to get away! He abruptly called for his horse to be made ready then hurried to talk with Peggy.

Within minutes, Arnold's aide, Major David Franks, went upstairs to knock on the Arnolds' bedroom door, informing him that they had received word of Washington's approach. Was Arnold coming down to welcome them? On that news, Arnold brushed past Franks and hastened down the stairs saying he was off to West Point. He hurried out of the house, mounted his horse, and cantered to the boat landing where, jumping aboard his longboat, he ordered his crew to take him immediately down the river.

The Vulture had returned to her position about twelve miles to the south. Arnold's launch reached it within a few hours, but despite the general's urging, his crew refused to go onboard. They might transport him there, but they would not board an enemy ship.

Arnold climbed up the landing steps on the side and had a quick conference with the captain. Immediately, the bosun's whistle sounded and the ship's crew surged into action. Orders were barked, sails unfurled, and the anchor raised as the British ship sailed for New York, leaving the launch behind with a worried, confused crew to row the miles back up river where they might possibly get some answers or an explanation about this unexpected turn of events.

General Washington, with his personal flag, blue with thirteen stars, leading the way, and Henry Knox, the Marquis de Lafayette, Alexander Hamilton, and his usual escort arrived in front of Robinson House about a half hour after Arnold left. They expected him to come out to greet them, but it was an apologetic Major Franks who told them that Arnold had gone to West Point. Issuing his orders, Washington decided to grab a quick breakfast then follow Arnold across the river to inspect the fort, taking Knox and Lafayette with him. Hamilton would remain behind to tend to Washington's correspondence.

Eustis arrived at the house from the surgical shed, looking forward to the welcoming breakfast, only to hear that Washington, after a brief respite, had already left aboard a hastily-rigged, awning-shaded barge for the crossing to West Point. At least Eustis got to greet his friend, Alexander Hamilton.

Washington and his two companions anticipated finding Arnold prepared with a noisy welcome, perhaps a cannon salute, accompanied by flag raising at the fort. But, at West Point, they were puzzled. There was no greeting. The officers found a deplorably maintained complex with Fort Putnam not nearly as finished as they had been led to believe. They wandered around and found no signs of Arnold anywhere. No one seemed to know anything about his whereabouts or any planned construction. Something was clearly wrong or information had been mishandled.

Washington was more than irritated. "What the devil is going on here?" And where was his host, the person supposedly in charge, General Benedict Arnold?

Chapter 13

Back across the river by noon, the confused officers gathered in the dining room at Robinson House. Washington directed Hamilton to find Arnold immediately, then he decided he should speak with the absent general's wife.

"Would you be so good as to inform Mrs. Arnold that I am here?"

The message was sent, but there was no response. Peggy remained upstairs in seclusion, suddenly unable to greet the commander in chief. Confusion reigned throughout the house. Washington, impatiently craving a moment of peace, decided to retire to his room.

Just as Hamilton was about to mount his horse, intending to look for Arnold, a courier arrived with a packet of letters from Colonel Jameson of the Westchester militia. To his horror, when Hamilton looked through the packet's contents, he saw copies of his own letters that had been sent to Arnold with confidential information about Fortress West Point. A note in the packet stated the documents were found on a man who called himself "John Anderson" who had been captured just before entering New York.

Hamilton quickly took the letters to Washington in his room. Washington became alarmed as he read through them. What was this?

Plans to West Point? He immediately saw that the fort guarding the river was in imminent danger. Unbelievable! It could not be possible! He had suspected nothing and trusted Arnold fully. Everything seemed to be falling apart. What was happening? "Lafayette! Knox! I need you right now! Come quickly!"

When they saw the messages, both young men were equally horrified. Not Benedict Arnold! They could not understand what was happening. He was one of their own – a military hero. Yet it appeared that he had sold West Point and three thousand American lives to the British. "*Mon Dieu!*" "God rot the bastard! How could he?" If West Point was lost, the entire American cause would be in jeopardy, and the British plan to isolate New England could very well succeed.

Fearing that a British attack could come at any moment, and needing to act quickly to secure the fort, Washington sent out desperate messages by courier including an order for General Nathaniel Greene to come north immediately. Then he left to shut himself in his room to vent his fury. His inarticulate expressions fueled his officers' concerns.

Knox worried about how far the plot had gone. Turning to Lafayette, he said, "We need to secure everything and make sure of those companies stationed across the river. For all we know, they may have turned their coats as well. We'll have to quickly change all those officers, and perhaps shift the companies, or bring others in. As it is, the manpower over there looks to be way below what it should be. General Arnold may have sent men away."

Lafayette nodded and looked toward Washington's door. They hated the idea of disturbing him, knowing he needed privacy to control his temper, to steady himself.

While Washington's entourage was returning from West Point, Dr. Eustis went over to Robinson House to deliver some medicine to one of Arnold's aides, Colonel Richard Varick resting in Arnold's ground-floor office. Varick had been a victim of the same contagious dysentery traveling through the camp over the last few weeks, and the doctor had a new concoction for him to try to settle his digestive system.

At that moment, when they were talking in the office, the men heard Mrs. Arnold shrieking upstairs. "Help! Help! They are putting hot irons on my head!" It sounded like she was in danger, being tortured or in hysterics, certainly in some pain. Has someone gotten in to capture her? What now?

Hearing the noise, Eustis rushed out into the hall and saw the pretty, petite blonde at the top of the stairs, dressed in semi-sheer night clothes, with her hair in disarray, clutching her son.

"They are going to kill my baby! Neddy is in danger. God help us!"

Eustis turned to Arnold's other aide, Major Franks, who had come into the hall. Peggy's slave tried to restrain her, and Neddie's nursemaid attempted to secure the baby's safety. They were having no luck. She struck out at them. "No, no! Let me go! Go away! Where is the general? Don't come near me! No, God help me. God help me!"

Her robe hung open, revealing much more than any modest woman would allow. It was as if she was having some kind of hysterical fit, and she certainly did not seem to know where she was.

The woman continued screaming, and Colonel Varick, trying to rest in Arnold's office, staggered into the hall, joining Eustis and the aides who had been stunned into inactivity. Teetering at the top of the stairs, Mrs. Arnold pressed a squirming, kicking Neddy to her breast.

"Bloody bowels. What next?" Hamilton muttered and started up the stairs. Eustis and Franks ran to join him on the landing and carefully approached Mrs. Arnold. The three of them managed to secure the baby, hand him to the nurse, and half carry the distraught woman back to her chamber to put her on her bed. She was not calmed by finding herself in her bedroom and continued kicking and thrashing around on the bed. Because she had asked if Washington was in the house, and not sure what else to do, Eustis decided she might respond to the general or at least say something to him. Maybe she had heard what was going on and that was upsetting her.

Varick, who had followed the others into her room, went back downstairs and asked the general to come up to see Mrs. Arnold. Once

Washington arrived, she started to shake with another hysterical fit, shouting, "That man cannot be the general," then accusing him of wanting to kill her child. "No, no, no. That is not right! Don't come near me!" She pointed a shaking finger. "He's the one trying to kill Neddy!"

Taking one look, embarrassed, the general quickly turned to go back downstairs to what he knew – working with Knox on strategy, re-staffing, and defending the fort.

All the gullible young men, taken in by the young woman's beauty and distress, were desperate to figure out what to do about or for her as she melted into tears. Lafayette came upstairs and told Eustis about the messages just received about Arnold's defection. Peggy's husband had met with a spy and had deserted her, probably running away. That explained everything. Her distress now made perfect sense.

Eustis did his best to treat and soothe her. She gradually calmed down again and began breathing quietly, lying in her bed. Hamilton held her hand and stroked her hair while Eustis checked her pulse and eyes. Smitten with Peggy Arnold and wholly sympathetic, the young men quietly retreated to confer in the hallway. What should they do?

"I wish I knew what to do. Povre Madame Arnold," lamented Lafayette. His sympathy was totally with the beautiful young woman. "By virtue of her marriage to Mon General Arnold, her character and reputation will be completely ruined."

Hamilton agreed, shaking his head. "She has no hope of a social life and will be in total disgrace. What advice can you give, doctor? Any medicine to calm her? We need to do something for her."

"I now understand," sighed Eustis. "The hysterics make sense," he explained. "Women do get into that state when they're desperate. She'll not be able to make any kind of life for herself." There would be no escape from the scandal and condemnation awaiting the wife of a traitor. "But what if she is arrested?"

As the attending doctor, the others were looking to him. Eustis thought quickly of possible remedies. Bleeding was a common treatment for calming hysterical women, and he had faith in the treatment for nearly everything. It might work to get her back in balance and perhaps able to speak with them sensibly. He went back into her room to talk with her and found her lying on her bed, her slave, Alpha, pressing a cool cloth on her forehead. Mrs. Arnold was a formidable woman when she wanted to be, very clear about her likes and dislikes, and he was not sure he could obtain her permission for any procedure, much less bleeding. Eustis took her hand, smiled, and settled in to be as persuasive as possible.

Fortunately, she agreed to rest, and in time her condition seemed to improve. She could breathe with less distress and appeared to relax. Eustis hoped it was a sign she was regaining her senses.

He left Peggy resting in her chamber, reckoning she was hoping to hear news from her husband. Or she could be looking for a chance to leave. She must realize how much danger she was in. The young men did not realize that her husband had visited her in their bedroom before he left or that they had made plans together then.

The aides hovered, waiting for orders from Washington. He had been staggered, of course, and struggled to make sense of everything that had happened and what needed to be done. He had totally trusted Arnold, much more so than several of his other generals. Rivals Charles Lee and Horatio Gates came to mind. They had both tried to destroy public confidence in him, and Gates, looking for personal advancement, had even spoken to Congress against him.

Somewhat surprisingly, everyone was called to attend their early-afternoon dinner with the general as had been planned. Washington had decided to follow routine as a stabilizing factor for his men as well as himself, although he was clearly upset and ate very little. He said he could not give them any reassurances, nor would he discuss or go into detail about what had happened. He needed more information and was still thinking it through.

Eustis, Hamilton, and Lafayette wanted to plead Peggy Arnold's case with the general. He had regained his equilibrium by the end of their meal and told them other matters required his immediate attention. Mrs. Arnold would have to wait. He would get to her when he could.

Soon a hive of activity, Robinson House buzzed and swirled into the evening as Washington, with Hamilton, Lafayette, and Knox, worked quickly on plans to restore patriot defenses at West Point. They feared that British General Sir Henry Clinton, in New York, may have taken advantage of their vulnerability and confusion and ordered an attack. Clinton might be sending two or three companies up the river to seize West Point, and they could actually be approaching now.

There were possibly other conspirators around as well. Arnold's chief aides, Varick and Franks, were restrained briefly, suspected of being involved in the treasonous schemes; and Arnold's personal guard was confined at Fort Putnam. An alert went out ordering a Connecticut regiment to come as quickly as possible to bolster West Point's defense.

Reports trickled in that Arnold had escaped in the Vulture and had reached New York City. With time, the story gradually became clearer. It seemed that on Arnold's advice, on September twenty-third André, dressed in an old coat and breeches, rode overland to New York. Arnold had provided him with a passport that allowed him to travel under the name of John Anderson, seemingly on matters of business.

André never made it back to the safety of the British lines in New York. Colonel Smith, after pointing out the route, had left him nearly fifteen miles from the British lines. Three men from the Westchester militia, taking the day off for hunting, spotted a rider who appeared out of place, wearing fine boots with shabby clothes. When they stopped him, the man first seemed friendly and then, after realizing they were patriot militia rather than British, attempted to offer money as a bribe to let him go on to New York. Although tempted, they searched him and discovered the plans of West Point concealed in his boots. The three promptly hauled the man off to their militia captain, Colonel Jameson.

Had Major André been dressed in his uniform, he would have received courteous treatment. Disguised in civilian clothing, he was clearly a spy. Although immediately conducted by the militia to

Jameson, and apparently closely supervised, André managed to get word sent to General Arnold that "John Anderson" was captured. He hoped for some kind of rescue.

It appeared, however, that once on board the Vulture and safe himself, Arnold's thoughts turned not to André but to helping Peggy. He composed a letter to General Washington pleading his wife's blamelessness and sent it back to Robinson House under a white flag of truce. His plea worked. Wanting to believe in the hysterical woman's innocence and, even more, to be rid of her, Washington issued an order later that evening enabling Peggy Arnold to leave Robinson House immediately and travel to her family in Philadelphia. He put Dr. Eustis in charge of overseeing her departure.

By the next morning, Peggy, miraculously recovered, directed her slave in the process of packing all of her goods. Within two days, despite a steady rain, an elegantly dressed Mrs. Arnold descended the stairs and proceeded to the yard where the Arnolds' carriage waited, fully packed with everything she had brought not that long before. She graciously gave her hand to the officers lined up to see her off. Arnold's former aide, Major David Franks, released from arrest, would travel with her to make sure she arrived safely in Philadelphia. The nurse, already in the carriage, held Neddy, while Peggy's slave was seated outside with the driver. They rocked down the drive, leaving wheel ruts, puddles, and mixed emotions.

Hard-riding General Nathaniel Greene arrived to assume command of West Point. After lengthy discussions with Washington, he settled in to get the final construction and planned alterations back on track. Relieved, Washington could then leave, secure in the knowledge he had a good man in charge. He rode out with his escort, heading for Tappan where he would have to oversee arrangements for the trial of the disgraced and captured spy, John André.

After waving farewell to Mrs. Arnold, Eustis returned to caring for sick and injured soldiers quartered in the outbuildings and the wretched business of finding the one or two killers in his murder cases.

Chapter 14

Feeling somewhat out of step with what had been going on at the hospital, Eustis felt exhausted mentally and physically and realized he had not yet circulated the sketches of the young victim found by the river. He assisted Burnet throughout the morning with surgery on a young man's leg. Hopeful the man might walk again, Eustis left the barn feeling steadier but still in need of some quiet time to clear his mind.

He took a deep breath, considering. He did not want to proceed immediately into their usual pre-dinner routine of discussing medical matters or scandalous events of the past several days. Roaming down the driveway, he came to the path to the boat landing. The pier was bathed in clear afternoon light, and he sat at the end and swung his feet out over the river.

The water sparkled as if it actually knew something. Its life seemed centered and reliably regulated by the dependable tides and unconcerned with questions that bothered the doctor. But then, he reflected, the weather had something to say about that too; that nothing is guaranteed. I cannot count on anything except change each day, he thought.

Thoughts of the restless dead kept intruding into his mind. The unknown man found across the road near the tavern had been carefully prepared for burial after sketches and notes were taken. Wrapped in a shroud, he was interred in the hospital's cemetery. Although the man might be buried, the mystery of his identity did not go away. The other murdered man across the river had been buried in the cemetery there with the hope he too would be identified at some future point. And now it was left to Eustis.

Two men murdered. No apparent connection. But it seemed just as possible that there was. They had to be connected somehow. The odd conversations he had with various people had gotten him nowhere. He seemed to be going in circles.

He had to follow up on Mistress Tobey's suggestion to check in at the cooper's shop. And Jonathan Reed had not returned with answers as he had said he would. That man was a cypher in himself, not to mention his strange namesake. It had been nearly two weeks now since Reed left. And he'd said he would return within a day or so. Maybe he was a spy too. Could his identity be false?

Other thoughts intruded. Was there an unknown courier? Perhaps Reed could have been a contact? How had information been passed to the British by General Arnold if André was sixty miles south in New York all the time? And that brought to mind the fancy Frenchman.

By God, he needed information! There were at least three areas of questioning, probably more, that might or might not be related to the murders. He counted on his fingers.

First, it seemed odd there was so much mysterious and needless distraction about Norah Lindholm's pregnancy and this new rumor involving Elijah. Could anyone else in the Sixteenth Massachusetts Regiment be involved besides Norah's husband? Those men had been gone throughout the fighting season and would not return until it ended, probably not for another month or more anyway.

Second, did the counterfeiters and barrels have anything to do with Arnold? Has Mugford delivered his order?

Third, what about other spies working for Arnold? If these two dead men were spies, are all spies dead or are others still free? He could almost feel his head starting to spin.

Sitting at the end of the pier and gazing at the moving river was almost hypnotic. As his mind relaxed, there flashed several thoughts, and a possible idea. It might explain a lot, but it was easy to come up with ideas. He still needed to talk to several people and determine a killer's motive. He would talk to Burnet and figure out their schedule. With luck he could get across the river in the morning.

The day began with a dense, dreary covering of gray clouds. Coffee helped as did the friendly morning greetings and good news about their most recent surgical patient. Dr. Burnet had checked on the man before breakfast and seemed astoundingly cheerful. He agreed that Eustis should get back across the river to wrap up the murder inquiries. A little success goes a long way to lift the spirits, especially after the past difficult and confusing week with too many losses. The surgical success was just what the doctor ordered.

Elijah asked to go along, to check on his gran. He assured both doctors, in great detail, that his still room where his assorted herbs hung drying was well supplied and ready for their needs. Thanks to a successful expedition, he'd acquired new vigorous leeches, and an infusion of willow bark was ready. Noah would remain and could tend to medical tasks as well as the four-footed creatures.

So they set out, Eustis riding Hector and Elijah borrowing Noah's Sally. It took many assurances of supervised care to have Sally released for their travels. Hector approached the ferry with astounding calm this time and managed to get almost up the ramp before changing his mind and trying to turn back. But his escorts were forearmed and equally determined. Boarding was carried out almost efficiently.

The rain held off, and they rode to the fort along the familiar wagon road, acknowledging the path to the women's settlement as they passed and planning to return later. An increase in security at the gates to West Point and then Fort Putnam was evident. Entire companies crowded into the road, either arriving or leaving on assignments. There was more activity than they had ever seen during earlier visits. Once cleared for entrance and vouched for by several officers, Eustis and Elijah checked in at the commandant's office.

General Nathanael Greene had instituted these and other changes immediately after arriving. He could stay for only a few months because his next assignment was commanding the southern division of the Continental Army in the Carolinas. But he urgently needed to get West Point straightened out first.

Colonel Amos Kendall did not seem to be present, and Eustis wondered if he had been transferred in the aftermath of Arnold's disgraceful departure. When asked, the officer replacing Kendall vaguely explained that the colonel had been reassigned to other duties.

As they waited to meet with Greene, Eustis introduced himself and Elijah to the other two men who were waiting. A fair-haired young man, leather-dressed for hard riding, introduced himself as Consider Harris, a courier for the Sixteenth Massachusetts from Barnstable.

"Aha," said Eustis, "and what is the news? I know the good Dr. Thacher. I might even say that some persons of the female sex are eagerly awaiting the arrival of that regiment."

"If all goes as hoped, they should be here much earlier than expected for their winter encampment," the courier reported. "Should arrive in about two or three weeks, sir. Construction of a new encampment is planned about two miles west of the forts, and their manpower is needed."

"Good news, then. And you have had a successful campaign?"

"Not a particularly outstanding year, sir. I can say that we have been grateful for fewer deaths, but we're not happy with the continuing lack of food, money, and gunpowder. All the usual complaints." He smiled with the understanding that it was normal in their world.

The other waiting man interrupted to introduce himself. "You think you have complaints? That's nothin' new. Some years back, I remember at Cambridge up in Massachusetts when I was there with my

New Hampshire company, we went to complain to General Washington about the bread we was issued. It tasted like it had sawdust mixed in. There we was in line in his tent, waitin' to speak to him. We'd brung a sample of that bread, and we'd put it on the corner of his desk while he walked the other visitor toward the tent flap. When he came back, he reached out, picked it up, tore a piece off and started to eat it! Our whole protest died out. I'll tell you, either the general was the smartest or best-informed man in the entire camp, or he would eat anythin'!"

"And who do I have the pleasure of greeting?" asked Eustis, chuckling.

"Oh, sorry sir. I got into my story. Nehemiah Porter at your service. I am just passin' through, carryin' messages south, from Portsmouth, New Hampshire, down to Congress."

"Well," said Eustis, "I have friends living up there, so I know where you were. And as I said before, you will make your family as happy as I reckon the Sixteenth will, just by coming home."

Harris grinned and said, "We will be mighty joyful ourselves." At that point, he was called into the general's office.

Elijah had been particularly quiet. He'd been standing, arms crossed, staring at the floor. Eustis wondered what was keeping him silent; maybe news of the return of the regiment with Norah's husband. But they were friends, right?

When it came their turn, the doctor introduced himself and Eli to General Greene, a large, efficient and determined man, who had been born into a Rhode Island family of Quakers. Eustis explained his assignment from Arnold to solve the two murders of the past months despite being stationed at the hospital across the river. Greene asked if he had been assigned any support or assistance. He seemed concerned that Eustis had been trying to handle it alone. "Let me look into this. Come back tomorrow morning, doctor, and I may have some help for you. It would be good to at least get this resolved."

After obtaining approval to be at the fort for the next two nights,

Eustis and Elijah went to see the cooper. They could tell from a distance that the forge and shop were busy as the air rang with the clang of hammer on steel. Pausing in the doorway, Eustis looked around for Danny. He missed the usual shout of greeting. Mr. Mugford came over and, when asked for the boy, said Danny had not come to work that morning. Mugford was somewhat annoyed. "I've a backlog and several orders to get out today so I need his help. If you see 'im, tell 'im to get his butt movin'. He was just goin' to be away overnight, ye know, go see his mother.

"Doesn't sound like him," said Eustis. "We'll keep an eye open for him."

Stepping outside the shop, he looked at Elijah. "Seems we should have stopped at the settlement first. I'm worried. Let's head back there now." Eli hustled ahead, untied their horses and brought them over to Eustis. It appeared he was eager to see his grandmother too.

Riding briskly back down the wagon road, Eustis had time to think about their young friend, Danny. Someone, was it Sam? had said he should be watchful of him. Danny could so easily hear something and get into trouble. Elijah seemed to be concerned as well, judging by his silence and tight lips.

In fact, Eli was truly worried. He remembered too much about what had happened at the settlement that no one would talk about. Earlier in the spring, when four men had ridden in and tried to take control, his grandmother had tried to hide any worry from him, but he had snuck out the back door of their cabin into their garden. He had watched from behind the corner of the cabin as the men talked with several of the older women then grabbed Norah Lindholm and shoved her ahead of them to her little cabin. Maybe the other women thought she knew who they were. None had attempted to go along or visit her despite the sounds of a struggle. He tried to remember. Had there been other threats against the women? Since that wicked day, they had secured weapons and were now ready to defend themselves.

Eli was never to know details. About two hours after taking Norah into her cabin, the men had emerged and left, riding quickly out to the wagon road. He had seen only one of them come back, but that was last August. At that time, he'd hidden and watched as Norah crept behind that man at a distance out the path toward the road. She had her serious face on and appeared determined, and Eli did not dare to interfere. He guessed she wanted to make sure that the man did not return, and he had not. That was about when they first met Dr. Eustis, and the corpse was found on the wagon road. Although it had been taken away before anyone saw it, what he did see of it laid out at the fort had appeared somewhat familiar. But he did not want to go close to look. Perhaps he should have said something.

Elijah helped Norah whenever he could and kept her company through the long summer. He thought she was the most beautiful woman he had ever seen, and he yearned to comfort her. His gran kept telling him that he should not follow Norah around, and then she had the idea of him going to Robinson House to help. He had, and he really could make a difference there. He just missed and worried about Norah.

They turned onto the path to the settlement, as usual looking along its sides. Eli was not much interested. He knew the route well after all, but Dr. Eustis was always observant and studied the undergrowth as they went along.

Eustis halted as the path ended. Something was not right. He could tell that Eli felt the same way. There was no activity, no sound. No cheerful voices. Even the birds and squirrels were silent. The center of the settlement was unusually still. There was no laundry underway or any women out on their porches or in their gardens.

Then, over to the right in front of a cabin a little larger than the others, the one with faded lilacs by its front door, several women were huddled closely including Mrs. Grady and her two youngest children. She was carrying a musket. Elijah's grandmother, Mrs. Eldridge, was there as well, armed with her recently-acquired rifle. They were all staring toward Mrs. Grady's cabin in the distance.

Eustis and Elijah rode over, and Eli jumped from Sally's back to hug his gran. She thanked him for getting there so quickly and asked, "How did you know?"

"Know what?"

"Some men have got Danny in the Grady cabin," said one of the other women. "They came for Norah, but we've got her with us."

Several more women offered their opinions at once, including their plan of just waiting the men out. "But they might hurt the boy," said one, looking especially anxious.

Eustis realized he needed information right now. He went into what he thought of as his surgeon mode. "Can we go somewhere to quietly discuss this? I want to get it all clear in my head before I send Elijah to the fort for help," he said. "And we should get out of sight."

"But they said they would hurt Danny if we sent for help," said Mrs. Grady, wrapping her arms tighter in her shawl. She seemed near tears, on the edge of her sanity, her breathing ragged. "They want cooperation from Norah again, if you understand me," she added, looking intently at Eustis.

The doctor had dismounted and now led his horse around the side of the cabin to the back where there was a porch. Mrs. Eldridge, Elijah, and the other women followed, moccasins shuffling through the fluttering leaves.

"Now," continued Eustis, "can one of you become the spokesperson and tell me clearly what happened right from the beginning?"

Several started talking at once. Mrs. Eldridge's whistle startled them into silence.

"Alright," she said. "Let's start again."

Mrs. Grady's two youngest children clung to her skirts as she started talking, clearly and calmly with obvious effort. "I was stirring up my porridge and putting some dried beans on to soak when I noticed them going by and along to Norah's cabin. Three men it was, and they seemed very determined. I think Norah must have known somehow. Maybe she heard them. Her door was barred, and she had escaped into the woods in the back. They slammed around a bit then headed over to my place. I had sent the two little ones into the loft. Danny was with me because he was getting ready to return to the cooperage. They probably knew he was there. That's the problem, Dr. Eustis. They seemed to know too much about us."

"One of the men shouted from outside that there was something wrong with the cooper. They needed to talk with Danny, and was he in this cabin? Now, Danny's a brave young man, and he was concerned about Mr. Mugford. He wanted to go talk to them, and I, fool that I am, agreed."

She started to tear up and raised her apron to her face. Mrs. Eldridge moved closer to wrap an arm around her.

"As the men were coming in the front door, I took the children out the back to get them safely away. God help me, I should not have left him. But I thought I had time." She began to sob.

"I understand. You could not have known," said Eustis. "Now why or how did they come to decide to lock themselves in your house?"

"Oh, this is awful," she sobbed. "They found nothing in my cabin they wanted, certainly not the woman they sought, so they decided to keep Danny and ask to have a trade for Norah. Or if not that, then some money."

"No one dares to go speak to them, Dr. Eustis. But I know someone has to go and make an agreement, or something. Can you help us? We're used to making our own way, and we now have weapons. But this thing has us stuck. We're strong enough, but this is one of our children! We need a spokesperson, and many of us just want to accost them, no matter what happens. But Danny is there!"

Eustis glanced at Elijah, who nodded his agreement. "Let me handle a few things for you," he said. "Elijah, you go right now and get help from the fort. Tell them what you have heard, and that the men have a hostage."

Then to the women; "We need to find out as much as possible. Is Danny still inside the house? And where is he? What room?"

128

"I'll go look," offered Norah.

"Oh, no, Norah," said Eustis. "Not a good idea. I think they would just grab you and add you to the bad situation. If some of you other women can silently go around the cabin, hide in the woods, and report back as to what you see that could help. If anyone talks to those men, it will be me."

Then, to give them something to do: "If the mistress of this household will make tea, that would be wonderful."

Two of the women indicated they would sneak carefully through the woods in front of the cabin. Another woman, brown hair under her cap and wearing an apron over her striped, homespun skirt and knitted shawl, spoke up.

"I'm Katy Bates, and I'll take care of that tea. Would you care to come into my home?"

"I can bring cups," said another.

Eustis was relieved to see that this seemed to settle everyone down a little. They had something to do, and hopefully help would arrive. He understood their impatience, could not stand waiting himself, and intended to circle the cabin. If anything he observed aligned with what the women saw, with luck they would know exactly where Danny was being held. The men from the fort would have to know that before they could attempt anything.

Seeing they were momentarily settled, and promising he would be back soon, Eustis walked down the path until he could see the roof of the Grady cabin. The two women had headed to the right, more toward the front of the cabin. He decided to try to circle around behind, cutting into the woods on his left. There was no path that he could see, and he began to wish he had grown up in the country. He didn't want to trip in the snarls of undergrowth. Leaves covered the uneven ground. Branches of evergreen and scrubby laurel thickets blocked where he wanted to go. Glad he was wearing boots, he slowly worked his way around and through the undergrowth of pine and small oak trees.

Wait! Did something move? He could see the back of the cabin through the brush and watched its tiny attic window intently. Had he just seen movement there? He continued to circle toward the far side behind the cabin, noting that the immediate back area was clear of trees and had long weeds, grass, and, unhappily, poison ivy. There were several apple trees with ripening fruit. A ladder leaned against one of them, baskets below it, ready for use.

Now do we do anything? And, if so, what?

Chapter 15

He had seen what he could. Again cutting through the undergrowth, Eustis stumbled his way back to the Bates cabin. They were not his best moments. Clearly, he was better at making decisions than reconnoitering. He arrived to find that the two other women had returned before him. Evidently they knew real paths, certainly more than he did.

They reported they had seen no overt sign of the men or of Danny. Eustis asked them about the window at the front of the cabin. Were there any guards visible? They thought there might be one person peering out at the edge of the window, or at least they had seen a shadow.

An idea was formulating in his mind, but Eustis had to wait until help arrived from the fort.

It did not take long before a half-dozen, stern-looking men cantered into the settlement, stopping by the first cabins. A wagon driven by one man with Elijah and the mule tied behind followed. Eustis saw Elijah and went out to talk as they pulled up in a cloud of dust. Mrs. Grady and several other women followed on his heels. The leader dismounted and came over to Eustis. Fortunately, almost everyone was still hidden from view of the farther cabins.

"General Greene sent me to see what we can do here," said the man clearly in charge. "I'm Colonel Edward Aldrich. What can you tell me?"

"First, let's move you farther out of sight." Eustis led the soldiers around to the side of the Bates cabin. "Thank you for coming so rapidly, colonel." He introduced himself and beckoned Aldrich to the side where they could talk. When Mrs. Grady and some of the other women started to follow, he waved them off. He didn't want a multitude of suggestions, nor did he want them charging into danger.

"Colonel, I have done a little poking around behind the cabin. If you can engage the kidnappers out in front, and if I am right, I think there is a way for me to get Danny quietly out the back. I just need Elijah to help me."

Eustis explained his idea to the colonel. "Sounds good to me, doctor. If you're sure it's not too big a risk, I'll start negotiations. And you say no other men have been seen but for those three?"

"That is what I am told, and it matches what little we have seen," Eustis said. "I am trying to keep the women from becoming alarmed and grabbing their muskets. They want to storm the house because one of their children is captive there."

Once their plan was in place, and crouching as low as they could, Eustis with Elijah started to drift around to the back of the cabin again. Elijah knew of a slightly cleared way to avoid some of the undergrowth. Reaching the back of the cabin, Eustis again thought he saw a hand against the second-story window. He pointed out the apple-picking ladder to Elijah and mimed they could stand it beneath the window, climb up, and look inside. If they spotted Danny, they might see a way to get him out. The difficulty was to do it without noise.

Elijah comprehended immediately and signed that he would do the climbing and for Eustis to hold the ladder. He just hoped Danny would remain quiet. They would try it. The two men moved the ladder but had some difficulty leaning it quietly against the wall. To Eustis's relief, he suddenly heard the voice of the colonel in front calling for negotiations. That distraction was just what they needed.

Looking up at the tiny window, he could see the movement he had noticed before and realized with horror that it might be one of the men watching their rear and not Danny at all. He wished there was some way to check if the three were in front talking with the colonel. There was more commotion in front of the cabin and he decided to take the chance. Elijah signaled that he was ready, pointed up to the window, and gripped the ladder rung. Eustis moved into place. Eli silently began his climb.

This was not unlike performing very tricky surgery or when he had helped Dr. Warren climb into the back window of the Old South Church in Boston, thought Eustis. At some point, you just start and hope for the best. It was not long before Eli, perched near the top of the ladder, peeked into the window. Eustis watched expectantly.

The window seemed to bulge outward, opened, and Danny, his hands bound in front of him, tumbled out into Eli's grasp. He had been watching. They rapidly, almost falling, descended to the ground where Eustis caught Danny and untied his hands, again indicating he must be quiet. He was nervous that they had already made too much noise. Eli kept a grip on Danny and slung him across his shoulders, running to the woods.

Once hidden in the undergrowth, they fell to the ground to catch their breath, struggling to contain their excitement and to keep quiet. Danny started to shout before both men grabbed him and covered his mouth. Then getting up and moving as quickly as they could, they headed back to Mrs. Bates's cabin where the other women awaited news. Flinging the door open, the women rushed out. Mrs. Grady, suddenly in tears, hugged Danny to her chest. Norah flung her arms around Eli. Clearly, she was overjoyed at the results of his efforts, but Eustis could see that Mrs. Eldridge was not quite sure it was proper.

Eustis went out to the pathway and looked toward the Grady cabin where he waved to Colonel Aldrich indicating success. Aldrich immediately rushed toward the cabin, ordering his men to arrest the kidnappers. Their spokesman by the entrance ducked back inside in an attempt to bar the door. Aldrich's men forced the door open and slammed in with their muskets aimed. It took only moments before all was over – without any shots fired.

Elijah and Eustis watched as, their hands tied, two men were led from the cabin and loaded into the army's wagon. But where was the third? Hadn't Mrs. Grady said three? Eustis hurried to speak to Aldrich.

"Wait, wait!" Elijah was on his heels. After a quick consultation, Colonel Aldrich led three of his men inside to thoroughly search the cabin.

Elijah whispered into Eustis's ear. "I know where he is. I can feel it. They should check the cellar, but I bet they don't know it's there. I'm going to tell them." And he stepped forward onto the wide front step and into the door. The colonel's men were distracted, but then one turned and yelled, "Hey, you there. Stop!"

Elijah quickly stepped to the small door concealing the entrance to the cellar steps, calling out, "Down there! Here!" He opened the door, pointed urgently down the steep, ladder-like steps, then started down. Aldrich's man who had yelled at him followed, shouting "Hey! What right have you? Stop, you scoundrel! Wait!"

But Elijah had reached the bottom and paused with the colonel's man almost tumbling into him. He looked back over his shoulder and whispered, "Look there," pointing to a dark niche under the arched foundation of the chimney. Several large barrels nearly blocked the area, but it was a possibility. The exasperated man, determined to capture his elusive prey, shoved Eli aside and approached the area quietly, musket with bayonet raised, peering into the rear of the cave-like root cellar.

There he was! He could see the culprit, crouched, and wedged under the bottom shelf among the remains of last year's old potatoes and beginning stockpiles of new preserves and produce.

"Colonel Aldrich! He's here, sir," the man yelled. A worn man dressed in shabby, dirty clothes rushed from the niche and toward the steps. Eli stuck out his foot and tripped him as he went past. The man fell face first into the bottom of the steps. Colonel Aldrich at the top, pistol in hand, headed down, yelled "Stop!"

With the musket-toting soldier and Elijah behind, and the colonel in front, the man was hauled up the steps and handed over to have his hands tied and musket taken. He joined his two cohorts in the wagon, and the three were soon headed down the path to Fort Putnam under heavy escort. They would be interrogated at the fort.

Eustis still had concerns to attend to, including a quick inspection of the Gradys' cabin with Colonel Aldrich to ensure that it was safe for them to return. The residents crowded around outside, sharing everyone's joy and appreciation for their rescue and trading stories about Danny and Elijah. Before mounting his horse, Colonel Aldrich saluted the women and turned to shake hands with Eustis. "If it was not for you, Dr. Eustis, this may not have turned out so well. I appreciate all your help."

The doctor thanked Aldrich for his quick response and with appreciation offered to treat him to a mug or two of ale at the nearby public house. It was decided that the colonel would meet Eustis and Eli there later in the day.

More revelations would likely come out as the army probed around the edges of the three men's activities. Eustis believed they were the same suspected counterfeiters who had been in Mugford's cooperage and could well be the ones who had frightened the settlement earlier. Danny would be able to identify them. Right then, however, he was regaling his family and the others with stories of his adventure and how he had not been afraid one bit.

Surmising that the women needed some time to settle themselves, Eustis said farewell to Mrs. Grady, promising her that he would return the next morning. He knew there was more to clear up and questions to ask, and he rode back toward the fort intending to meet Colonel Aldrich at the pub later, thinking he might be an excellent person to get to know.

Elijah had asked to stay behind. He wanted to spend that night in the settlement with his grandmother and forgo the venture to the tavern.

Eustis agreed. The settlement would seem safer if he stayed there.

After a late midday dinner at the fort, Aldrich and Eustis rode toward Peter Brouwer's tavern.

"Have you visited this place before, colonel?" the doctor asked. "I found that sometimes it helped me as a source of information when I tried to find out what happened with that dead man found on the road."

"What was that again?" Aldrich pulled up his horse. It appeared that he knew nothing of any murder or that Eustis had been assigned to solve the mystery. He was amazed. "But, doctor, had you no help from the army?"

"No, sir. Seems I was given the assignment by General Arnold and that was all."

Eustis told his story from the beginning to the incident at the women's settlement that afternoon, not finishing until they had made their way into the tavern's main room. He saw a table, waved at the publican. They sat and waited for Bridey to bring cider. Eustis was impatient to see Aldrich's reaction to her and to find out what he knew about any resolution, if there had been one, on John André's trial. Had a decision come down, and would he go to prison?

As it happened, Aldrich was less interested in the events down the river at Tappan. Instead, once he heard about it, he had more questions about the murder. It was disappointing for Eustis in one regard not to hear news of recent developments but refreshing in another to have someone take an interest in his quandary.

Aldrich wanted specifics, and their time together turned out to be strictly business. Eustis went into as much detail as he could, including his difficulties with identification, and said he was not sure if the murders were connected to the counterfeiting going on in the area or if the second murder across the river was separate. Aldrich frowned, staring at Eustis in disbelief. "Wait. What? Two murders?" He was still absorbing the information about the first one. He had seen no records about any of these events.

After his detailed questioning, Aldrich said he planned to brief

General Greene early the next morning and would meet Eustis in the mess hall at eight. One mug of ale finished, Aldrich stood up, ready to return to the fort. It was not quite what Eustis was expecting. He had hoped to settle in and go over the entire situation then get around to Bridey and Aldrich's impressions of the area.

Aldrich was not interested in staying, saying that any news about André would have to wait until his trial was finished. General Greene would be presiding. Completing his briefing as they rode back, Eustis explained how he intended to spend more time talking with Mugford after he met with Aldrich the next day. Aldrich was not a social man, not a talker, and did not comment on the doctor's plan.

By the next morning, a sunny though brisk one, Eustis was eager to go back to the women's settlement and get details from Danny. There was a lot missing. He had not been able to speak with Norah either. Or any of them for that matter. And he needed to speak with Mrs. Eldridge about Elijah and what was going on there.

But first an early breakfast and then meet with Colonel Aldrich. He walked to the mess hall when, as he was appreciating his first cup of coffee, Aldrich arrived to tell him they were to go to General Greene's office. Aldrich had briefed the general earlier as planned, and now Greene wanted to go over it all with Eustis.

Chapter 16

"General Greene, sir." Aldrich stood at attention in front of the general's desk with Eustis by his side. Greene was sorting through various piles of papers. Some seemed relevant to what he wanted to talk to them about. Eustis sympathized with the man. The general had to get this fort functioning efficiently in an extremely short time before presiding over Andre's court-martial in Tappan. Once through with all that, he had to hurry to the Carolinas to take command of the southern army for General Washington. General Horatio Gates had made such a mess of things by running away during the Battle of Camden that it would take a real effort to recoup that army's losses, morale, and fighting spirit.

"Please sit, Colonel Aldrich, and you too, Doctor Eustis," said Greene. "I am astounded with what you have been trying to do while still maintaining your duties at Robinson House. I believe you were given an impossible task but are on the right track and may only need a few more days here. I will send a surgeon's mate over to Robinson's for the next three days to add to their limited staff and help Dr. Burnet, and I will assign you, Colonel Aldrich, as the doctor's contact for daily check-ins, help with any questions he may have, and general needs.

And you, doctor, will stay here for those days, and bring me a report on what you have discovered before you cross the river. Let us plan on September thirtieth at 9:00 a.m. Keep me informed. Good luck."

Clearly dismissed with their orders, Aldrich and Eustis turned and went out. Eustis would have liked to discuss some generalities, but he was finding out that was not done. He bade a temporary good-bye to Aldrich and, with the day warming nicely, said he was off to the women's settlement. Perhaps they could have supper together later.

Without Noah or Elijah, Eustis went to the stables and asked to have Hector saddled. The delayed start gave him time to organize his thoughts while riding down the road. He was surprised to enter a subdued settlement with no sign of the exuberance he was expecting. The women had come too close to a disaster. He rode to the Eldridge cabin and, greeted by Eli, was pleased to be invited in.

The cabin's main room served for working, eating, and sleeping. A ladder rose to a loft overhead; probably where Eli sleeps, Eustis thought. In the center of the back wall was a large hearth with a roasting spit and various cooking utensils and iron pots. A bed with quilts and pillows was against the left wall, and a large wheel for spinning yarn was on the right. Two baskets of "lambs' tails," the result of carding the fleece, were parked around it, and a pile of washed fleece was nearby on the floor. A sturdy, well-scrubbed work table was in the center of the room.

Mrs. Eldridge was spinning. Eustis walked over to watch the process more closely. The yarn twisted as it wrapped around the long steel, nail-like spike protruding from the end of the spindle. Once a ball of yarn got large enough, it could easily be slid off the pointed end. He could see Elijah's repair work, the new leather straps that held the spindle to the main post of the wheel. It all looked extremely efficient, no doubt the result of decades of development and practice.

"How was everyone here last night?" he asked.

As she talked, Mrs. Eldridge walked back and forth in front of her large wheel, twisting the wool into yarn as she went backwards and then winding it on the turning spindle as she came forward. She said she had owned the wheel all her adult life and that it had come from her mother, who had also put miles and miles on it.

Elijah joined him at his gran's table, and Eustis felt he could relax a bit in the warm friendly atmosphere and chat as he sipped his coffee. He realized it was made with chicory and managed to stifle his surprise. He thought he did so bravely, but he realized Elijah was looking at him in amusement.

"Oh, alright." he said, "I was expecting something else." Both Eldridges laughed with him.

"Pray, can we just get serious for a minute?" asked Eustis. "I want to know the whole story of what happened last night and how those men got here. Was there any communication with them? How did everyone here settle in when it was over? And were they anxious or worried or is there anything else notable you could tell me?"

"Well, as you will soon find, Norah is now staying with me," confided Mrs. Eldridge. "She is uncomfortable alone, and I can understand that. If it helps her, she can sleep in with me until her husband gets here. By the way, do you have any news on that?"

"Indeed. You will be happy to discover that I do. It seems that they should be arriving within the next two weeks – by the middle of October. They will be assigned to build another cantonment or large campground about two miles inland of West Point."

"Eli," said Mrs. Eldridge, turning to her grandson. "I just remembered. Would you go check on Norah to see if she will be coming in for dinner? Dr. Eustis should talk to her."

Elijah looked momentarily startled, apparently hoping to stay. But after glancing at his gran, he got up and left to look for Norah.

The doctor looked at Nan Eldridge. "Was it the same men as were here months ago? Were they back after Norah or something else?"

"I'll tell you what I can," she answered. "When those deplorable men arrived way back in the spring, there were four of them. They seemed to know exactly where to go, and headed to Norah's cabin. I thought yesterday that I recognized at least one of them. That first time, she came out and told them to leave. But one grabbed her wrists and started to force her back into the cabin. He kept saying that she should remember him. She started denying it, but with a struggle they pushed her inside. Two of them came toward us in a threatening way, and we backed up to our own cabins. Next thing I knew they were blockaded in Norah's place.

"When we saw that, we sent for help from the fort. Later when the men emerged, they kept a tight grip on Norah. She looked rough, bruised, really dreadful. They may have beaten her as well as raped her. We were lucky that they released her when they mounted their horses and hurried out of here. I think they gave her a warning not to reveal who they were and were gone quickly, well before any help arrived from the fort. I also suspect one of them returned after Norah again, not that long ago.

"This time, yesterday, when they rode in, it was their third visit," she continued. "Norah was out of sight, and they went over to bang on the door of the Grady cabin and pushed their way in the door. I saw Goodwife Grady flee out the back with her two youngest. She turned back, but I think they had grabbed Danny by then and mayhap thought he might be good leverage. And I am sure he knew who they were from the cooper's place. Once they lost control of Danny, thanks to you and Eli, they must have realized they had gotten themselves into a mess. Without any hostage, their next stop would have been to get ahold of Norah again."

"I reckon I know who they were, and I wish the fort had responded more quickly to your earlier call for help back in the spring," said Eustis. "They were most likely the same men who were not sure whether Danny recognized them at the cooperage. Do you think I should examine Norah to see how she is?"

"I don't think she will let you. She is frightened and a properly modest young woman. She will defend and protect her privacy as much as she can. She has gone back into the woods to the little river to bathe.

It was good that we were able to keep her with us this time and that she is staying with me. I'll tell you I did look her over recently, and I think her pregnancy is undisturbed. As in first pregnancies, sometimes they take longer to become evident."

"Have you checked her in the last two days?"

"No. I didn't think I needed to."

Eustis looked at her. "I have to ask you, and I mean no disrespect, but what is this suspicion of Elijah? You did seem eager to get him out of here."

"Yes," she said slowly. "I was worried for some time that Eli had fallen for her and had gotten involved enough that he might have caused her pregnancy."

"But why suspect Elijah?" asked Eustis. "Was the timing wrong? What set you off?"

"I am responsible for that boy, and I take that seriously. I told his mother when she was dying that I would look out for him. I was and am aware that this place, all female, offers nothing for a growing young man. He was bored and tempted to flirt with young women, which is only natural at that age, but it may not have been for the best.

"And," she added, "he was close to Norah although she is older than he is. The other women had begun to look strangely at them both and would whisper, and I thought it was time to straighten it out. I was worried it would affect his reputation, if not his life. Well, you know the harm gossip can do, doctor. But Norah's pregnancy does seem to be progressing. She looks to be about six months along. She started out undersize, but, as you see, it is fine now."

Just then Elijah slammed open the door and cheerfully reported that Norah would be coming to dinner, and that he hoped Dr. Eustis would be there too. Eustis agreed. There were a few more items he wanted to discuss.

"Will you talk to me about that murdered man who was found by the entrance to your path?"

Elijah looked a little puzzled, but his grandmother answered.

"Certainly, doctor, but that was back in the summer. Maybe August? Why now?"

"Because it is not solved, Mrs. Eldridge. I am still not sure how he was killed, who did it, or why."

"Oh," she said, and turned to pace back alongside the wheel. "They buried him, didn't they? I thought it was all put aside, tucked away because so much time had gone by, and I'd heard nothing. So you will not be leaving it alone?"

"No. I cannot. I have orders to deal with it. I must find out who he was and why he was killed." He looked carefully at her, and she put her hand on the wheel to slow it and looked down at the floor. "Have you any ideas?"

When she did not reply, but only shrugged her shoulders, he said, "Well, I will go talk with Mrs. Grady and happily return later for dinner. Thank you for your help, Mrs. Eldridge."

She looked at him, considering his question. "It was weeks ago. I will think on this some more, see if I can remember anything, Dr. Eustis, and you are welcome for dinner." As he left, she went back to her pacing and spinning.

Wearing her shawl, Mrs. Grady had brought a stool outside her cabin and sat with her feet up on a log. She was knitting when he walked over, almost as if waiting for him. "Come in, come in, doctor." She got up, gestured to her door, and preceded him into her main living area. "Please sit," she urged.

"Thank you, Mrs. Grady," said Eustis. "There are several things I hope we can talk about." He sat on the bench by her table. She took the other across from him. Her two younger children hovered by the hearth, Rebecca on a stool working on a slate, and the boy, Seth, building something with sticks.

"What has been going on here, in this settlement?"

"Goodness, you are right to the point, doctor."

"Well, I think it is about time. There is a great deal happening which no one will mention, and it has been going on for weeks. I now have

143

instructions from General Greene to get it all straightened out. I think you would not want him to come here with other soldiers to do it. So talk to me."

"But the women, the others, we agreed."

"That may be, Mrs. Grady, and as fond as I am of you all, you are better off talking with me than stalling any longer. Again, what has been going on?"

"I understand." She sighed. "I think Danny must have heard more than he should have at the cooper's shop. Yesterday's intruders seem to be the same ones that were there. But I am not sure how they knew Norah. I don't think she was doing their laundry especially, but she did go to the fort to pick up laundry nearly every day. We believe those men are counterfeiters and smugglers of some kind."

"Do you know what they were smuggling or who they worked with?"

"No. Danny said they were interested in the small barrels that Mr. Mugford would make for them. Must be they wanted to move something special in them."

"I think it is more than that, Mrs. Grady. For them to come here to find him, I think Danny came to know what it was that they were making or smuggling. Do you have any idea?"

"He will not speak to me. I was getting angry with him yesterday just as the men came to our door, probably why he was late in leaving. Perhaps he will talk to you."

"Good," said Eustis. "Where is he?"

As she hesitated, Seth spoke up. "I know. He's out looking for Norah in the woods. I can show you where he went."

His mother looked concerned and was about to tell him not to do that when she seemed to realize she had better let him get on with it. The little boy led the doctor out the back door of the cabin and toward a narrow path. "This leads to the pond where we swim," he said proudly.

Along the way they came across Danny crouching behind some

shrubbery, and Eustis realized he was waiting for Norah. He also realized he would have to have a talk with the boy. Spying had gotten him into trouble in the first place, and it looked as if there would be more problems if he continued with it. At that moment Norah walked toward them along the path from the pond, wearing moccasins, her shift and skirt, with a shawl covering her head and wrapped around her shoulders. She had another piece of fabric, perhaps linen toweling, folded across her arm. It was evident she had been bathing. She looked up, startled to see them as she approached. The doctor saw that she had indeed progressed with her pregnancy and now had a substantial belly. Her breasts were considerably larger and fuller. She looked astoundingly attractive, even with her wet hair, and still had that demure appearance that had so intrigued him earlier.

"I beg your pardon, Mistress Lindholm," said Eustis. "I didn't mean to startle you. The boys said you were here, and I wanted to talk with you about yesterday. What can you tell me about those men?"

Norah did not seem eager to talk to him. "Can it not wait, sir? I need to get warm at home."

"Certainly," said Eustis. "Perhaps I can speak with you after dinner?" He knew she would rather avoid any questions, but persisted. "I understand you will be joining us all at Mrs. Eldridge's cabin."

"Oh, hmmm, yes, doctor," she said slowly. "I suppose we can work that out. I have no more information for you about that murdered man, nothing that you do not already know."

Eustis wondered how she had come to assume he wanted to talk about the murder. She had to have it on her mind. Interesting. Why? Could she know who the man was?

"Thank you. I understand." he said. "We don't need to go into that right now. I just wanted to pass on recent news that your husband should be here within two weeks. His regiment will be assigned to construct cabins and a new camp behind West Point. But you go get warm. I'll look forward to talking with you more later."

Delighted, Norah smiled at the news. Perhaps it alleviated some of her anxiety and let her know her long wait would soon be over.

"Oh, I'm sorry that I was rude before. Thank you, Dr. Eustis. I'm forgetting my manners, and I do look forward to chatting with you later."

She hurried along the path back toward the settlement, and Eustis, with the two brothers, went to look at their pond.

A wide curve in a small river made a fine pond that sparkled in the early afternoon light. It was surrounded by trees and various shrubbery. Birches and maples were beginning to drop their leaves to the surface, the current carrying a swirl of red, yellow, and orange down the stream. It seemed an industrious beaver had been at work and probably created a cozy dam home and an appealing swimming spot. It was turning into a spectacular clear and warm afternoon, boding well for a sunset of many colors. God's paintbrush at work, thought Eustis.

He was sorely tempted to swim himself but felt he could not give up his dignity entirely by stripping off his clothes and jumping in. The boys, Danny and Seth, felt no such concerns and, after assuring Eustis that they swam there all the time, did just that. Eustis called to them that they could not stay long because their mother expected them for midday dinner. He began to realize he might be facing a challenge getting them out, rubbed dry, and back to Mrs. Grady in time to eat.

Dinner at the Grady home was reminiscent of Eustis's days around his own parents' table, with adults and children all enjoying Mrs. Grady's squirrel stew and fresh bread, talking and laughing. A special treat, honey for their bread, had been recently collected from the wild hive the boys had found. The room was filled with the scent of their meal as well as the harvested onions and herbs recently hung from overhead beams to dry.

Eustis thought it was as warm and congenial as any meal he had enjoyed in the years since he last was in Boston. He rather hated ending the fun by asking Norah to take a short walk with him. He would have to get back to the fort that evening as he had other things to do, and he thought he might check in at the tavern as well.

146

Reluctant and shy, Norah could not relax with him enough to be of any help or to reveal any information besides what he already knew. Elijah had been a good friend for the entire time she was living here. Yes, her husband liked and appreciated him. She did not know the attacking men, she said, and was still not sure why they wanted to lock themselves in the Grady cabin with Danny. And why was everyone asking about barrels? She could not or would not say anything further about her experience with her attackers.

Clouds had moved in, and a breeze began moving the leaves. Eustis decided he had better head back to the fort before anything untoward developed. Riding in the rain was not his favorite activity. After cheerful salutes and thanks to Mrs. Grady, he headed off. He could try again tomorrow.

Back at the fort, after leaving Hector at the stables, he went to see if Aldrich was around. The colonel told him that a message had arrived from Jonathan Reed informing Eustis that he was finally headed back.

"Was Reed an acquaintance?" asked Aldrich.

Eustis, mentally questioning which Reed he meant – the tall dark man or the blond courier – answered, "Yes, sir. I met him when he was a patient at Robinson House. Is he expected today?"

All the while he knew he had to be careful with his answers as he was not sure which Reed had sent the message to him. He would have to wait and see.

"I thought he was already here. Interesting," said Aldrich. "I had not realized he was across the river as well. Was he hurt?"

"An accident with his leg. He's fine now," said Eustis. "Should not be a problem to him anymore." He could not tell what Aldrich knew about Reed and if there were two of them, but he did not want to go into any detail until it was clear who they were talking about, and if one of the Reeds was a spy. Instead, he mentioned his intentions to go to the tavern to ask some follow-up questions. "I'll return within a few hours."

Why was neither Elijah nor Noah around when he wanted them?

And Aldrich had not wanted to come along. Muttering, he set out for the stables to retrieve his horse and ride to Brouwer's. It turned out to be a less than productive evening. No one who he wished to see was there. Discouraged, he wondered if people were watching and avoiding him.

To his surprise the next morning, Eustis saw Jonathan Reed at breakfast, the tall, dark, bearded fellow who had been their patient at Robinson House – and he was right there in the Fort Putnam mess hall. Eustis asked if he could join him, and set his plate of bread, cheese, and coffee on the table. Cheese that morning. Perhaps an indication of a lucky day to come.

"Good morning, Mr. Reed. I am pleased to catch you here this morning and hope you have information for me."

"Yes, indeed, Dr. Eustis, it is a pleasure to greet you as well." Lowering his voice, Reed explained, "I was called away on a secret mission for General Washington, and I am concerned that I left you with no help and no answers."

"You are correct. It has been an adventure. Do you have another way I should address you in this space? Is mister appropriate or shall I call you colonel? You must realize that I have many questions."

"Mister is fine," said Reed.

"What can you now tell me about the dead man I had in my surgery several weeks ago? And have you any knowledge of the other Jonathan Reed who was supposed to be lingering here?"

"Yes, doctor. I understand you have many questions. But we may have to wait for a more private spot."

Eustis, sipping his coffee, wondered how much longer this man would stall. "I could tell you what I found out from my examinations of that second dead man found by the river."

"That would be interesting, doctor, but know that I am on limited time because I have an appointment shortly."

"Briefly, the man along the river bank was strangled before going into the water. There was no water in his lungs. He could have been

148

killed anywhere and then put into the river near there or elsewhere. I don't know yet if he was connected to the other man whose body was found near here."

"That opens up possibilities," said Reed. "I will tell you that the second dead man was likely watching for the transfer of smuggled goods. I am not sure yet why he was in the area or there on that road. Let us plan to confer this afternoon. I will be here for dinner at about two and will look forward to our meeting then." He arose and headed for the door, like a man on a mission.

Eustis called after him. "But I need his name, sir!" Reed did not turn or respond. Infuriated, Eustis closed his mouth, averted his eyes, and kept his oath inside. How much longer would this evasion go on?

Chapter 17

Retrieving Hector, Eustis left the fort and again rode toward the path to the settlement. The day was overcast but it was not likely to rain and, as always, he sought information. While watching bees and monarch butterflies floating through the milkweed and tall grasses by the side of the wagon track, he thought of the details he wanted to clarify with Norah Lindholm and Danny Grady. Later, he'd visit the cooper and try to get names from Mugford, although he probably would not succeed. Eustis would need to find some kind of leverage to use with him.

Arriving at the settlement's central clearing, Eustis was pleased to see more activity. They were getting back to business. He saw a wagon by the Bates cabin as he passed down the path on the way to Mrs. Grady's. She must have been watching and stepped out onto her front step.

"Good day, Dr. Eustis. I see you still have questions."

"Yes, I surely do, Mistress Grady. I hate to be such a nuisance, but once I get my puzzles resolved I can leave you good wives alone. Elijah will be working with me over at Robinson House, so I expect I will hear news of your activities, and the Massachusetts Sixteenth will be returning shortly. I'm sure you all will be very busy. I have just a few questions left for Norah. Also, has Danny left for the fort?"

"Not yet, doctor. I wonder if he could ride back with you. I do not feel confident in his being safe on the road. But do come in first."

Eustis tied Hector to the post by the door and went into the cabin to accept a mug of Mrs. Grady's creative coffee. Norah was helping with the Grady housework, washing dishes in a basin at the end of the table. There was a pail of water beside her on the floor. Another Grady child was drying the dishes with a piece of linen toweling and placing them back in the cupboard.

He wished Norah good morning and asked if she could come on a short walk with him. Overhearing, Mrs. Grady announced she intended to send the children out to look for fall berries along the path to the swimming pond, so Norah and the doctor could stay there and talk privately. She, of course, would remain just in case they needed anything. That said, she hustled the three young people out the door and closed it. Then she turned expectantly.

Eustis was concerned that Norah would reveal nothing under such close scrutiny. He was not sure how to put her at ease which was why he had asked her to walk with him. He decided to start with Mrs. Grady. He would insist on private time with Norah later.

"Tell me about those muskets, Mrs. Grady. I didn't see them when I was here earlier. Where did they come from?

"I generally keep mine under my mattress or behind the door. It seems best to have it out and close to hand now."

"Did your husband teach you to shoot?"

She looked at him in amazement. "Hardly, doctor. My honored father did. All the women in this settlement know how to handle guns. Ever since we were little. You've heard of the mama bear and her cubs? We'll protect our lives and our children any way we can."

"And I saw Mrs. Eldridge also has a rifle?"

"Yes, doctor. I don't understand your lack of understanding. As I just said, we all know how to defend ourselves and our families. We're alone here. You should realize that us women have no legal rights. The law expects us to have a male protector, either a father, husband, brother, or uncle. You must know that! We cannot even testify in court without a man, a family member with us.

"When we live here alone, it makes sense that we protect ourselves while our men are gone, and many of us have lived on the frontier west of here. Remember Elijah came to his grandmother because his family was killed. Many women now hide knives in their clothes for protection when they are out of their homes. It is as though we're fair game for any indecent male who is single or bored." She sighed in exasperation.

Eustis held up his hands. "I'm sorry, Mrs. Grady. I realize I can be difficult and a nuisance. In the home where I grew up in Boston, my mother did not carry any kind of weapon. Forgive me. The only other questions on my list are for Norah. I want to know if any of the men who were here yesterday were among those who came before, last spring or summer."

Mrs. Grady nodded. Being generous, she looked at Norah who was examining her fingers. Eustis realized this whole interview was not going well. He had to get the young woman away to a more private place.

The two women looked at him apprehensively. He realized it was useless to insist further. It just wasn't going to work. He rose and moved toward the door. "Well, indeed, yes. Ummm, I believe we should take a little break. Thank you, Norah. We can talk later whenever it is convenient for you. And Mrs. Grady, it is always a pleasure to enjoy your coffee and our conversations. Being this far from my own family makes it even more pleasant. I'll be moving on now with the hope I may see you and your family before I go back across the river."

Mrs. Grady looked baffled. She had hoped for more.

As Eustis opened the door, he remembered and asked, "Would Danny like to accompany me back to the fort?"

Danny, directly on the other side of the door, eagerly agreed so quickly that Eustis knew he had been listening. Indeed, it seemed

152

practical for Danny to go with the doctor. He could ride behind the saddle and get there safely, quickly.

"I'll come back for him as soon as I speak to Mistress Eldridge," Eustis said.

He walked the short distance to that cabin. Eli came out to greet him and assured him that Noah's Sally was fine and well cared for. They both had concerns about bringing an unhappy mule back to Noah.

As the men chatted, Mrs. Eldridge, ever watchful, came out onto the front stoop. "Greetings of the day, Mistress Eldridge" said Eustis, sweeping off his hat. He knew it pleased her. Her usually stern face broke into a smile, and her fluffy white hair peeked out from under her cap. She looked happier than he had seen her in several days.

He asked if she could spare Elijah for a few more of his nuisance questions, and she agreed, liking it that Eustis called them a "nuisance." Giving a pleasant nod, she went back into the cabin and to her spinning.

"Eli," said Eustis, "I am most impressed with the way your gran cares for this settlement and its people. She and Mrs. Grady were ready to defend everyone against those men the other day. She even had her rifle ready. I noticed that Mrs. Grady had a musket and wondered who else had arms."

"I do," said Eli. "Gran passed her old musket on to me. Mrs. Bates has one. Gran has made us practice too. She really is a fierce old woman. You don't want to cross her," he added with pride. "We realized we had to be ready if anything started to go amiss."

"I can certainly see that," said Eustis, thinking of the rifle missing from the dead man found at the end of their path. "Where and when did your gran get this addition to your arsenal?"

"I'm not sure," said Eli. "She came home with it. She probably traded for it. That's how she gets most things. Those items that she doesn't want, she sells or trades to someone else. You know she goes out on her trading journeys with her wagon packed with garden greens, linens, anything else she can sell."

"Yes, I do know she's a trader," said Eustis. "And I see she has been building up your capability for defense here. Now, are you going to come to the fort with me or stay here tonight? In which case, I'll stop by tomorrow."

Elijah wanted to remain and walked with him to the central area. Eustis wondered if it had a name. Most towns called them greens or parks or commons or something like that. But then, most towns that he knew in New England also had a sheriff or a constable and deputies to take care of just the kind of thing he was now trying to resolve. This business of being between countries, or not yet a separate country and in a war was frustrating to say the least. It will be so much better once it is all done and we have our own laws, our own commonwealth, our own country. Evicting the British was just the first step.

They parted, and Eustis, holding Hector, stopped for Danny, intending to drop him at the cooperage and go on to meet with Colonel Aldrich. He wanted to know if Aldrich knew anything helpful about the other Jonathan Reed or the Frenchman in Arnold's office. Elijah boosted Danny up behind Eustis. Reaching the main wagon road, with Danny holding on behind, Eustis turned left toward the West Point complex.

The doctor was growing impatient with his inability to get complete answers at the women's settlement. He had to overcome his mother's training and an innate urge to be polite, and just insist on answers. Interrupting Danny's eager chatter about his visit, Eustis half turned in his saddle and said, "That's fine, Danny. But I want you to tell me all that you know. I want to hear about everything that you have been told not to tell me. I will not reveal my source of information. Now talk to me."

Danny rode silently for several minutes. Then, as if the proverbial dam burst, he told Eustis all about the six months of anxiety in the settlement since April.

"It was them, doctor. I seen 'em every time. The same men that were at Norah's were at Mr. Mugford's. And they knew I saw 'em. They said they was watching me too. But I think they was not sure until this last time they came there. Then they questioned me a lot. I think they were wantin' Norah to help 'em, or they would take her away."

"Whoa, Danny. Let me just get this straight. Those men threatened you and Norah? And they were the ones who came here last spring and through the summer?"

"Surely so, doctor. I was scared of 'em too. But they liked Norah the best."

"Did they all return? Everyone? And how many was that?"

"Yes, sir. They was mostly all here. All three. Jus' not one of 'em who came this last time."

"You mean four all together last spring? And three this time? So one was missing. Now, names. What do you recall of their names?"

As they rode on toward the fort, Danny expanded on his information, relieved to finally talk about it. He knew the names of two of the men, but he could not remember the others. And, as Eustis realized, these might well not be accurate names anyway.

By the time they arrived at Fort Putnam, Eustis knew that the group that had been at the cooperage was the same that over the past months had harassed the settlement and focused their desires on Norah. It seemed that they were originally looking for a place to hide their supplies and in trailing Norah had found the settlement. It was ideal for their purposes. They would have space, could set up their counterfeiting, do their deliveries, and live like King George. And the women would accommodate them – or so they had planned.

Stopping to deliver Danny, Eustis asked to talk with the cooper. He could see that Mugford was worried. His apprentice was getting into trouble and he, Mugford, might be held accountable for bringing outsiders into the fort. He had realized those men were up to no good but thought that once they left with their barrels, he would be rid of them. He suspected they were using his barrels for illegal activities but was anxious to not be involved, asserting over and over that he knew nothing. And now it might involve a dead man.

"Hmm," said Eustis, his head as usual filled with ideas, but none that seemed absolutely right. "I may need to talk to you more. Don't go off anywhere."

He tied Hector to a ring near the main office and then went in to seek Aldrich, finding him hard at work. After being invited in, he sat down and waited for the colonel to finish his paper shuffling and sorting. Aldrich gathered some into a pile and asked, "Have you had any luck? I have been too distracted to get away to do any poking around myself. One bit of news. I have learned the name of the man killed out along the road by the women's settlement. Wee Gordie Wallace, he was called. One of that lot we caught in the settlement identified him. Seems he was part of that group."

"Wallace, eh? Very good news, sir," Eustis replied. "I have had some luck too, but now I want to know who that odd man in General Arnold's office was. Probably not French. But in disguise? Also, is there any listing of missing persons – or of men not being accounted for in a company? More information is needed to wrap this up. And then there is the identification of the murdered man across the river. I hope you can help me with a few more answers."

Aldrich took notes of Eustis's requests. "I have not been very good as a backup for you. I do apologize. As you can appreciate, with General Greene rushing to get everything done and heading off to run that court-martial, we are in a constant state of activity here. I have not had a minute."

"I understand, sir, but you realize that we also are trying to get our answers for General Greene before he leaves. I hope to get my thoughts clear soon. If you could just get me some answers, it would be a help.

"Also as their surgeon, I am needed back at Robinson House. Unfortunately, I can't linger for days here. Yesterday was wasted at that tavern. No information came from it at all. I'll try again later today to see if I can learn anything."

Eustis said he was off to the mess hall and his midday dinner. Then, as he was leaving, he turned to ask if Aldrich knew the whereabouts of Jonathan Reed. He wanted to talk to Reed.

156

"Ah, there I can help you, doctor. He is here, and I can get a message to him to meet you at Brouwer's. And check to see if those drawings got circulated. I do understand that we need to find that other identification for you."

"Thank you, colonel. That would be very helpful. I'll come by tomorrow morning to see if we can put it all together before I leave, or at least establish where we are."

The colonel did not seem excited at the prospect, nodded distractedly, and resumed his paperwork.

Chapter 18

Brouwer's public house was alive with patrons when Eustis arrived later that afternoon. He stood by the door and looked around the room; spotted Reed, tricorn placed aside, very smartly groomed with a recent haircut, beard trimmed, sitting at a table with several other men. Barely concealing his irritation, Eustis maneuvered toward him, dodging happy guests and Bridey loaded down with a tray full of mugs. She smiled, raised her eyebrows, and rolled her eyes. "I'll be findin' you later, sor."

As he approached, all but Reed rose and started toward the door. Eustis grabbed a vacated spot on the bench, and waited for Reed to speak. Reed turned, and perhaps realizing he had been deficient in his attention to Eustis's problems, smiled sheepishly and apologized. "Good day, doctor. I do have some news for you, and I hope I can regain your good graces."

Eustis just looked at him. "How long have you been back, Reed? I heard that you arrived a while ago, so when were you going to contact me?"

The tavern was crowded, and the noise of various conversations threatened to block comprehension. Then Bridey hurried to their table asking, "Ale for the both of you?" Eustis requested cider, and Reed opted for ale. There was a slight pause as the men admired the buxom Bridey before she hustled away.

Then Reed continued. "Back just a few days, I assure you, doctor. But I do have news." It appeared that Reed had been busy with a new group of rebel spies who would be going into New York, gathering information to bring back to General Washington.

"Tell me what you can," said Eustis.

Reed leaned forward. "That man you saw in Arnold's office, pretending to be a French officer, was an agent for the British. It seems he used various disguises to gather information when Arnold needed to get updates from Major André and General Clinton. By the way, there was indeed a plan to kidnap General Washington during his journey to Hartford, but the British canceled the attempt because it had leaked somehow. Do you know anything about that? Appreciation goes to whoever passed the warning. You perhaps?" He raised his mug of ale in salute.

Eustis declined to acknowledge his part, but was pleased to know that their efforts may have prevented a possible disaster, although he had no idea from whom the coded letter had come. He resisted Reed's attempt to mollify him and continued as a straight-faced interrogator. He was not going to give in yet.

"Back to that Frenchman," he reminded Reed and took a sip of his cider. "Have you a name?"

"Peter de Vos was one of the names I was given. Did I mention him? He seems to have disappeared, possibly in another disguise. But I don't believe he is either of your dead men. He may have run messages from here down into New York as a courier and then tried to gain information on the French as well. He certainly made too exaggerated an appearance here to go unnoticed, but he may have meant to be a distraction. There were at least two, maybe more, undercover agents working in the area who passed information to André in New York. You do know he was the head of General Clinton's spy ring, right?"

Eustis nodded.

"And," Reed went on, "you also asked about the identity of the dead man found on your side of the river, along the road to the Queen's Head. I did receive permission to reveal his connection to the counterfeiting and smuggling rings. There are several smuggling groups around us here, as you probably know. Many folks are trying to get what money they can with the Continental dollar now almost worthless, but it was the counterfeiters, not the smugglers, I had been asked to investigate. That counterfeiting has done huge damage to the patriot and Continental Army finances."

"Go on," said Eustis.

"As you surmised," Reed continued, "that man found along the road was known to me. Although he did not know all our plans or who was working with us, within his space he was often helpful. He sometimes used the name of Ephraim Bowen. If he was trying to reach you, I suspect he may have been a double agent, bringing that cane as evidence. He might also have been trying to reach General Arnold."

As he said that, Eustis suddenly remembered where he'd seen a fancy cane. Yes! It was with the fake Frenchman in Arnold's office.

Reed went on, "Perhaps he had particular information for General Arnold. We think he was killed to prevent him from reaching one of you. Arnold may even have heard he was on the way and sent one of his men out to intercept him. But I don't understand why Arnold would not want to retrieve that cane, unless he thought it could not be connected to him, or did not know Bowen had it. We may never find that out."

Reed paused and looked intently at Eustis. He seemed to be wondering if he had said enough? Eustis for his part needed a minute to think. He thought he remembered that Reed had earlier given another name, that of de Vos, not Bowen, to that other victim across the river. This multitude of identities just confused the issue. And who did he mean by "we." He thought it likely that the one called Bowen or de Vos wore various disguises and beards as had that Frenchman. He waved

160

toward Bridey who hovered nearby. She seemed to be waiting for the signal to approach.

"And how has your day been, sors? Can I make you any happier with another tankard of ale or cider? Or I believe they have some delicious stew available. And by the way, is that nice Mr. Adams comin' by anytime again?"

With some surprise and amusement, Eustis understood why she seemed so eager to come see them. It was Adams! A note about it would delight Sam. He would have to write to him. Bridey waited, and he asked for cider, looking expectantly at Reed. "You as well?"

"I am sorry to have to decline, doctor. I need to be on my way and catch up to one of the men who left as you arrived. Perhaps we can meet here again and go over other questions you may have."

"I will be back at Robinson House within two days or so I expect," said Eustis. "And I am eager to go over this and other questions with you, as soon as possible. Just send me a note or take the ferry as soon as you can. And one more thing. I want to find out more about this false Frenchman, this Peter de Vos, or was it Bowen?"

Waving off the question, Reed drained his mug, rose, and headed for the door, acknowledging several men coming in, and stopping for a few words with one of them. To Eustis's surprise, it was Colonel Amos Kendall. Now here was an interesting opportunity. Wondering what had happened with him after Arnold left, Eustis rose, waved in his direction.

"Colonel Kendall, sir. Good evening to you. I have a table just here. Please join me." Kendall looked startled, and expressions of wariness, reluctance, then submission crossed his face.

"This is an unexpected meeting, doctor," he said. "Thank you. My time is limited, but I will join you briefly." He sat, looking for Bridey, then turned back to Eustis. "To what do I owe this pleasure, running into you here?"

Bridey came to take his order. Eustis, hoping to find out about Kendall's situation, said, "Just wondering if all's well. I have not seen you for several weeks and wondered if you were still here or on reassignment."

"And I am surprised to see you here," replied Kendall. "Have you been re-assigned to the medical staff at West Point?"

Eustis, amused, responded, "Alas, sorry to say, no. I am still across the river. Indeed, I am enjoying my time on this side more and more. Mayhap I will be transferred sometime. What are you up to?"

"Hmmm. I have been reassigned, as you expected. Seems I was too close to that traitorous disaster to keep me around, so I have been sent to one of the outer redoubts. Purgatory, really. I liked just keeping things organized, quiet you know, running smoothly for the general. Bloody British! With luck, I can work my way back here soon. Meanwhile, I like to come in here to get a whiff of the good life."

Eustis took a sip of his cider, watching Kendall. "Who was that absurd French officer I saw with General Arnold? He had to be false. His whole act was so obvious and hardly effective."

"Yes. I know what you mean, but I understand it worked out well in some places. He was considered a successful courier and carried messages for General Arnold. He and that other courier named Reed seemed pretty thick."

"Hmmm," said Eustis. This was new to him. Yet another description of Reed – as a courier for Arnold and friend of the Frenchman. Just to clarify, he said, "I thought I saw Reed across the river when he was a patient. Who did you mean?"

"Could be, I guess," said Kendall. "I did not pay too much attention."

"But just now at the door you seemed to know him," said Eustis. Before Kendall could fumble for an answer another voice interrupted.

"Hey, doc!" It was Sandy MacDougal striding toward them with another man, a shorter, redheaded Scot, trailing behind. He turned to his friend and said, "'Tis the sawbones who I was tellin' you 'bout, the doc who was workin' on that corpse out in the icehouse."

Men at nearby tables turned to look, interested in this new bit of tantalizing gossip. MacDougal pulled over a stool and sat. His friend did likewise. Not waiting for Eustis to comment, he went on. "You find out anythin' inside that body?"

Kendall seemed relieved by the distraction. Tossing off his ale, he rose and said, "I do have to check in with some other fellows here, and I thank you for your company, doctor. Perhaps we'll meet again."

Bridey McGuinness came to the table, MacDougal swung her onto his lap, and seemingly settled in for a good talk.

"Me darlin' boyo," purred Bridey. "I do have to keep me job, so if you'll be lettin' me go, I can fetch you boys a glass."

She gracefully untangled herself and went off toward the corner bar, stopping at tables along the way to chat. The neighboring men hitched their stools slightly or leaned closer hoping to hear something.

"It's always interesting to talk with you, MacDougal," said Eustis. "But to answer your question. Could be Gordie Wallace. I know how he died and have been told he was decently buried, but I was not in attendance."

"Yeah, may the divil take 'em, it could be Wee Gordie," said MacDougal. "Ah heard he was stuck with a fancy saber. Did ye ever find it?"

"I have not found one that could do that job yet. Do you have any suggestions?"

"Again, what ah heard was that 'twas that snail-eatin' frog, ye know, the Frenchie, who did it."

"Well, your guess is as good as mine at this point," said Eustis. "You hear anything about the smugglers who kidnapped that boy Danny?"

"Ah doubt they're connected, but ah'll listen around. Ye know ah got a slew of relatives who might have heard somethin'."

"You could check one thing for me. I am still wondering what happened to Wee Gordie's horse."

"Aye. Well, ye see, that one I can tell ye, doc. One of my friends found 'im wanderin' alone down the road, and bein' a fine fellow of

163

sympathetic sentiment, an' feelin' sorry for tha' poor 'orse with the great weight of 'is saddle, relieved 'im of it. Then, he realized that 'orse looked starvin', so he took 'im along to a new pasture. An' ye know? 'E was verra happy there."

"Thank you, Sandy," smiled Eustis. "You cleared up a large question for me. It sounds like a good solution for a lost horse. Now all I have to do is find out what else is going on."

Two men at two other tables offered their suggestions. "Take a look at those men goin' in and out at the cooperage up at the fort," said one, which brought another opinion from the opposite table. "Ah, yer arse and parsley. Those bombats are worthless. They know nothin'."

"Ye shut yer gob, Barney. Wha' do ye know."

It went on this way for a bit until Eustis rose and thanked them for their company, moving as best he could among the tables toward the door. Behind him, he heard the talk continue cheerfully, the men happy to have a new argument. With several ideas swirling in his head, he decided he'd look over the cane as soon as he got back across the river to Robinson House. For the moment, he would go to the cooperage and see Mugford before heading to the ferry.

Chapter 19

Just before leaving the tavern, Eustis glanced back over the room and was surprised to spot the man himself, James Mugford. He sat at a back corner table with two other men, his hand wrapped around a tankard. Probably ale, Eustis thought as, holding his own mug, he walked over, turning sideways to fit between two laughing groups. As he approached, he thought for a moment that Mugford seemed alarmed, almost as if he would flee. Why he seemed to create this feeling in those he greeted was a mystery. Sam would laugh.

"Greetings of a splendid evening, Mr. Mugford."

Mugford focused on him, "Aye. 'Tis. Good, that is. What're you doin' here?"

Eustis looked for a place to sit, pulling over a free stool. "Just having a break in my investigation. May I join you?"

The two other men rose to go. Bridey approached for an order, nodded at him, and paused, interested to see what would happen next. Eustis thought Mugford looked discouraged. Had he hoped for more time with those men, or time alone with Bridey? Most likely it was Eustis's presence as a killjoy.

"I wonder if you heard the latest news about the counterfeiters?"

asked Eustis as he sat down. He went on to relate, with a little dramatization, how the men who had been holding Danny had been caught in the women's settlement. They were now in jail.

"Yeah, I heard all that from Danny. I'm real glad you found the boy, doctor. I just don't want 'em to think it was me that ratted 'em out," said Mugford.

"I rather doubt that," said Eustis. "I wonder how they found the place to begin with."

"What place?" asked Mugford, looking puzzled and annoyed.

"You know. The women's settlement."

"Oh, yeah. Mayhap I gave them directions, long time ago, spring mebbe."

"Do you remember what they wanted?"

"Just talkin' about the area around here. Where things was."

Bridey interrupted the less than stimulating conversation, asking, "Is Danny really well? Not scared and upset or anything?"

Eustis reassured her and remembered to ask if she had seen the Frenchman around.

"The fancy gen'lman? Can't say as I 'ave. 'E's off into thin air," she said, gesturing an explosion with her hands.

Eustis could not help but notice how cheerful Mugford became as soon as he said he had to return to the fort.

"I am sure you can keep Miss Bridey amused," Eustis said as he rose, leaving his tankard behind. Then, taking Bridey's hand, he bowed over it with a flourish and wished her a good evening. He had learned that by watching Sam, and it seemed effective.

Waving to Mugford, he moved toward the door again. It had been amusing getting Mugford irritated, but he had learned that the counterfeiters had used Mugford as a source of information far longer than he thought, and it confirmed his suspicion that they were the same bunch who began terrorizing the area last spring.

He untied Hector, mounted, and ambled back to the fort where he left the horse in the care of the stableman. One stop at the necessary out back and he retired to his bed without further distraction, hoping to get some rest despite all of the theories and stories dancing a reel in his head. It would be better when he could return to Robinson House.

A final check with Aldrich would wrap up this visit, and it should not take long. Eustis wanted to ascertain how long he had before General Greene departed. But as before, it was not clear and could be any day, just as soon as Greene received the schedule for the court-martial. The best Eustis could do was promise he would be back with the answers Greene sought as soon as he could. That might take a couple of days depending on the situation at Robinson's.

***

He woke to the sound of rain on the roof and stormy skies, but the rain began to let up by the time he finished his coffee and corn cakes. After firmly pulling down his hat, and despite the wind, he set off, saddle bags packed, and stopped briefly to see Colonel Aldrich who he found in his office, distracted, trying to give orders and make plans to travel down river to Tappan. The colonel took a minute to make sure Eustis knew they had the firm identification of the dead man found on this side of the river.

Known as "Wee Gordie" for his size and demeanor, obviously an inside joke among the men, he was likely the fourth member of the now imprisoned counterfeiting group. Eustis said he remembered what Aldrich had said before. Apologizing, Aldrich made it clear he could not give Eustis any further time.

***

One more visit to Mrs. Grady and Mrs. Eldridge on the way to the ferry. With the help of the wind, leaves were deserting the trees, and as he turned into the path to the settlement, he could see farther into the brush on either side. He rode slowly, examining the sides of the path as was his habit. He still felt he should be able to find something, but the leaves were now thick on the ground.

There was a stone wall he had not noticed before, parallel to the path and about ten feet away in the woods. The wall and the path had

167

probably been created at the same time many years before, possibly by early Dutch settlers. It seemed far north of their hub in Manhattan, but perhaps an ambitious farmer had settled here.

As Hector ambled along and Eustis mused, a lighter colored spot caught his eye, a light tan patch against the gray wall. It took a few seconds for it to register. Eustis pulled up Hector, dismounted, and poked through the underbrush and branches. The object lay against two large stones at the base of the wall. It was a bag of sorts, a haversack, and soaking wet. He picked it up, undid the buckle, and peered in, realizing he needed a better place to examine the contents. Taking it back to Hector, he tied it to his saddle, proceeded briskly into the settlement, and pulled up at the Eldridge cabin.

Several women were already at work, building their fires in the center area. Perhaps a sign of normalcy returning. Two were looking at the sky obviously hoping to see more signs of clearing weather. It would affect drying the laundry.

Mrs. Eldredge heard him, stepped out, and invited him in for coffee. He was not sure where she got it, but he was happier to drink whatever her coffee was than her tea.

"Thank you, mistress. And a good morning to you. I had hoped to catch you for a few moments before I headed for the ferry. I have something to show you."

"Dr. Eustis, you are not leavin' us? I am sorry," she said and led the way into her cabin. "I must have had a premonition as I just knew it would be good to have some coffee on hand. And 'tis hot too." She smiled, then made him comfortable at her table and turned to get her pot from beside the fire.

"You will be havin' a few more questions I suspect," she surmised.

He had placed the bag on the table and waited for her to turn around to see it. When she did, she stopped moving and stared. Putting the pot down, moving to the table, she sat and stared for another minute. He nearly got up to go to her aid.

Finally, she said, "'Tis a shock, you know. If it is what I think it is,

I never thought I'd see that again." Another pause.

"Do you want to tell me about it?"

She gave a big sigh and stared at the table top.

"Have you looked inside?" she asked. "There should be some things I would guess. Maybe identification."

Eustis asked for a rag or some other piece of cloth to put on the table for any wet contents he took out. After Mrs. Eldredge brought it and sat watching again, he opened the bag and removed its contents. First a soiled homespun shirt, then woolen stockings, then some sort of ledger, so wet that Eustis doubted they would be able to read anything in it. He opened the ledger and separated some of the leaves with his penknife to determine if it was possible to dry them. At the bottom was a knitted scarf and a small bag with a surprising number of Spanish coins.

It appeared the owner or someone else using the bag was able to write. Inside the flap at the top was the word, written in faded ink: JReed.

Surprised at seeing the name, Mrs. Eldridge said, "Oh, I don't understand! There has to be some mistake, unless it was stolen."

"Mrs. Grady said that Jonathan Reed came here to bring your mail, Mrs. Eldredge," said Eustis. "Could he have been using a false name and he was someone else? Perhaps it's some name he had heard? Or someone else was using his name. Have you seen him recently?"

"I'm sure I do not know! When I followed . . ."

"Who did you follow?" Eustis interrupted. "What did you say? You understand I am worried that Jonathan Reed may not even be alive."

"Oh my! Well, there was nothing else I could do back then. I didn't know anything about Mr. Reed. I was worried about the women and children right here. That horrid, wicked man was here, threatening the women. God rot him. And Norah was watching him. I wanted to know where he was going, and she must have followed too."

"I know you meant well, but perhaps you had better tell me about it," Eustis urged.

In bits and pieces, starts and stops, Mrs. Eldredge told her woeful tale. She had watched the man start to leave after he had threatened the women and spent hours with Norah in her cabin.

She related how, after the man had become sick and fallen from his nervous horse onto the path, the horse had bolted away. He'd continued on, walking down the path, and she'd followed him. Norah disappeared earlier. Maybe she'd stayed in the woods or had run back. Mrs. Eldridge accosted him along the path to tell him not to return. But he told her to stop bothering him and that he would do whatever he wanted. Soon the settlement would be his to control anyway. "Stupid cow! You've got no rights. I own you, granny. You think you can protect those people. Well, soon you'll do whatever I say, or regret it."

Then the man turned his back to her, stumbled, recovered his balance, and went toward the road. At one point, he dropped his rifle and flung the bag aside but kept walking on. He staggered in an oddly dizzy fashion, perhaps drunk, or about to lose consciousness. Seeing the rifle left on the path, she said she picked it up and ran as fast as she could back to the settlement. She did not see anyone, but she felt that someone was watching.

She never told anyone about thinking someone else might have been there and believed no one had connected the man with their settlement until Eustis came along. The rifle could easily be explained as one she acquired on her trading and swap expeditions. They needed it for defense, she said, and it was a good one. Rifles shoot so much straighter than muskets.

"I'm glad you have told me about this, and I may need to go over it again with you," Eustis said. Hoping to confirm the name, he asked her, "Do you know what that man's name was?"

"I'm sorry. I don't. But maybe Norah heard it. She was held by those despicable monsters for hours on several occasions. Short of killing them, I did not know what to do."

"I'll be back to talk with you in a few days. Meanwhile, I do have to return to Robinson House. I'm going to check with Mrs. Grady before I leave. We need to find out about Jonathan Reed. You should stay right here and, if you can, find out what Norah knows."

"Doctor, please, please do not hold anything against Elijah!"

"Not at all. But I emphasize, you should stay right here until I return," he cautioned. "No wandering off on a trading expedition."

Mrs. Eldredge was bent over the table, her face in her hands, as he rose to go, picking up the damp ledger and other items.

Leaving the horse tied but with the ledger and haversack in a saddlebag, Eustis walked farther along to the Grady cabin. He knocked at the door and was pleased that Mrs. Grady opened it.

"Good day to you," said Eustis. "I'm off to Robinson House. I'm not comfortable leaving Dr. Burnet with that large patient load for so long."

"A good day to you as well," said Mrs. Grady. "Have you any other news?'

"I plan to be back as soon as I can, but if you could, check with Norah whenever you get the chance. Send a message for me if you or she require further help. I need her assistance with solving this murder, especially whatever she may have heard from those men. I must have their names. She avoids talking to me, but she may share her experiences with you."

"Rest assured. I'll see what I can find out for you, and we will miss your presence until you return."

"My appreciation, Mrs. Grady," said Eustis. Then turning to leave, he tipped his tricorn and bowed.

Standing, holding Hector's reins and gripping the railing on the barge, he stared ahead at the shore, his thoughts wandering over all possibilities. There was something about crossing this river – this must be the fifth time – that helped him think. He had a lot to ponder. JReed on the bag. Which Reed? How many could there be? Had the blond courier owned it and someone mayhap stolen it? He could try drying the ledger and possibly make out some information there.

171

But could he believe everything that people told him as being accurate? Mrs. Eldridge probably knew more but did not want to talk about it. He had learned that people would usually not tell all the truth when asked. Even when backed into a corner, they would lie. Which one could be protecting someone? By God, he needed Sam to go over it with him. Perhaps once he got any problems straightened out at Robinson's, he could have time to think and then write to Sam. And he had to report on Bridey's interest, too.

Hector alerted him by snorting and tossing his head. Their impending arrival distracted him as the barge neared the shore, and Hector began to dance. Other passengers moved out of his way and they disembarked in a homeward rush.

Clinging to his saddle until Hector quieted, he hoped that Elijah and Noah had done well while he was away. At least he was confident of their abilities, but he owed them something for leaving them. Then there was Burnet, and his own promise to stand in for his colleague so he could get away. And Mrs. Nardy.

And Jonathan Reed! An odd thought intervened. If this man was a British spy, could that name be an alias and an inside joke, perhaps a jab at the "real" Reed? Maybe he'd stolen Reed's accounts and bag to pass on. He knew the British sometimes referred to the rebels as "jonathans," meaning some local dullard or peasant. Really? Could that be possible?

There was an aura of peacefulness as he arrived at Robinson House and rode into the barnyard. Several sutlers' wagons were lined up as usual in the side field. They had small cooking fires and their laundry spread out to dry. The sound of some repairs indicated other work or preparatory activity. It reminded him he'd better get his shirt over there. It needed to be washed, and he was already wearing his spare one. He needed more stockings for winter too. Drat! That was what he was going to talk to Mrs. Eldredge about. Luckily his boots would hold out.

The weather had cleared, and patients wrapped in blankets were sitting on the benches in the brightening sun. It almost made him nervous to approach the barn. Could it be working this well without him?

Elijah and Noah greeted them; Noah hugging Sally and Hector's necks, Eli saying, "Welcome back, doctor!" Dismounting, Eustis patted him on the shoulder and reported his grandmother was doing well, as was the entire settlement. They would talk more later since he had much to share about his days away.

Burnet, hearing of his arrival, came from the barn followed by Mrs. Nardy. Both seemed calm. Perhaps all was functioning well.

"Greetings, foreigner," said Burnet. "Let me give you an account of our few days. You probably know all the news from across the river and can tell us plenty. Are we moving to Morristown?"

Then Eustis realized why Mrs. Nardy looked worried. Was the hospital in danger?

"Bloody hell! What has happened, Burnet? Oops, sorry." He looked in apology at Mrs. Nardy, realizing he'd spent too much time in taverns and at Fort Putnam. He'd better get himself in line.

"Rumors have been circulating ever since the army's most recent winter in Morristown, and I wondered if you knew whether His Excellency will be returning there or coming here for the winter?" Burnet queried. "They seem to have plans to build a new campground, calling it a cantonment, so it does sound official. We need to know in regards to provisioning."

And suddenly Eustis was launched back into the management of the hospital.

"Let's set aside some time later today to go over all this," Eustis suggested. "Agreed? Perhaps after dinner?"

With all in accord, Eli left to take the doctor's pack up to his quarters, Noah would make Hector happy in the pasture, and he could make rounds in the barns with Dr. Burnet. He took a deep breath and sighed. He was back.

Burnet had several cases to discuss and a difficult surgery for Eustis to consider. A man in agony had come in with bladder stones. He could not seem to pass them and was in exceeding pain. Burnet did not do that kind of surgery. As a physician, although he was certainly capable with wound care and basic stitching, his training was not the same as a surgeon's. Eustis immediately asked about laudanum and rum, any kind of mind-numbing possibility for the patient, and was determined to tackle it early the next morning. He needed to go over his supplies and talk to Elijah about herbal possibilities to get the man through the night.

Another patient had dropped a boulder on his foot while trying to repair his stone wall. The toes were purplish black and looked unlikely to recover. He would handle that one as soon as they could prepare the patient. Removing his jacket, he called for his apron while walking to his surgical shed. He was pleased that someone – probably Elijah – had swept it recently and had clean rags available.

The young man, a captain of a nearby militia company, was brought in and propped up on the surgical table, his legs extended and feet bare. Elijah and one of the stronger women positioned themselves. Eustis smiled at her in greeting and gratitude. He remembered her as an excellent nurse and a very practical mother of six who worked at the hospital. Another of the surgical mates joined them to observe.

There was no question about three of the smaller toes. They had been crushed and already looked gangrenous. The other two might be saved and would help with the patient's balance. Eustis decided to take it in steps and see if he could salvage the two. Checking that his patient had had plenty of rum, signaling his two helpers who leaned in and gripped the man, he quickly took his sharpest pincers and cut deftly through the toes in question. He followed with a sizzling cauterizing iron, then pressing a poultice in place, he wrapped the foot tightly, and looked up. The young man had been caught so unawares he'd not managed much of a scream, and he now moaned, looking at his edited foot.

"You will do well," said Eustis, wiping his hands before leaving to get his dinner, while Elijah with the nurse prepared to move the patient to a bed in the barn. The surgeon's mate admired the quick work. Eustis smiled to himself. Once the plan was made, doing it rapidly always seemed to work best.

As arranged the spring before, the women serving in the kitchen had traded a large amount of garden produce for half a pig. Slaughtered at a farm next to them, the pig provided pork for dinner and ham to come. It was so much better, more delicious, than he remembered. Why would he even consider going back to Fort Putnam and West Point?

Before going to the barn to check on his patient and make preparations for the next morning's intricate surgery, the doctor dashed upstairs to look at the cane he had kept, the one found on the road to the tavern. Holding it carefully, he looked it over, recognized its decorative head as similar to the one he saw on Arnold's desk when the Frenchman was visiting. Carefully drawing the sword out, however, he could see that it would be hard for it to be the weapon he sought. It was thin and indeed dangerous but certainly longer than necessary. Awkward to use in a raised manner. Very close though.

Why was Bowen carrying the Frenchman's cane? It did seem that they could be one and the same. Oh well, more to consider.

Before returning downstairs to go to the barn, he removed the still damp ledger from the bag and laid it out in hopes of recovering something once it dried, if it did. What he needed next was time to think.

Checking in his surgical shed, he saw that Eli had laid out the supplies, the scalpels, the curved needles, and thread that he likely would need the next morning. That young man was becoming invaluable. This meant that he could steal away to do some thinking at the dock beside the river where he had found a peaceful respite a week or so earlier.

In his head, he could hear Sam saying, "What if?" The pondering and musings. And some things began to make bizarre sense. But the picture was not yet clear.

Tomorrow, he would perform the surgery on his patient with kidney stones, and when everything seemed stable here, later that day or the next, cross the river once again to report to General Greene. Perhaps he should send a message about when he would be there. Meanwhile, he had some peace and a place in which to think.

***

Drawn downstairs by the smell of baking bread the next morning, Eustis sat in the dining room slowly waking up, yawning, clearing his head and mentally preparing for the tricky procedure he anticipated. Cutting for stone meant he had to make a cut in the man's bladder to excise the stone or stones.

When he went out, Elijah was preparing the shed, laying out the herbs that would be needed for pain, and heating cauterizing irons in the small fire just outside the door for use if necessary. They had already plied their patient with rum and laudanum, and Eli had one of his pain preparations ready and gave him the potion to drink.

It had taken both of the surgeon's mates to get the patient into the shed because he could barely walk. They had him lean over the table with his legs spread, strapped them to the table legs, and gave him a strap to hold, with more ties to keep his arms in place. He could bite on a particular piece of thick leather saved for the purpose and positioned in his mouth.

Behind him, sitting on a low stool, Eustis examined the area around the man's testicles and determined where to cut to access the bladder. It was necessary that the man not move. Mentally thanking Dr. Warren for his lessons in anatomy, Eustis picked up his sharpest small scalpel and carefully made his first cut. Within five minutes his patient had passed out. They hoped he would not awaken from the pain.

Chapter 20

Walking to the river and the pier, his thinking spot, was a renewed pleasure. The end-of-afternoon light slanted toward him from the west across the river, highlighting its ripples and eddies. He sat on the end and looked down. The river was transparent and shallower than the last time he had been there; different tide of course, he thought. Outgoing or incoming? Either way it would bring ideas. The morning had been tense and busy, and he felt tired but good, the surgery having gone well.

Then he heard Eli and Noah running down the pier toward him. "Doctor!"

Now what? Eustis wondered.

"A man came over! They are sending a barge for you," said Eli, out of breath. "My gran has called for you to return as soon as possible. Norah is in a bad way, and the baby is stuck."

That said, Eli pointed into the sunset. There it was, small in the distance, the barge oared by six men and headed for him. They must have sent for him at the fort and found he had returned here. The message was confusing. He had been here barely two days. He sighed. He had better prepare to go along.

Beginning to run, Eli turned back toward him. "I'll get your pack!"

He returned with Noah carrying Eustis's gear, his surgical kit, and a bundle of cloth-wrapped herbs. "For pain," he explained. "The women can make tea. And I'll come across and bring Hector tomorrow. Help Gran, please. I know she was worried that the men's threats to Norah might start somethin'." Thrusting the pack toward Eustis, he said again, "Please!"

The barge looked like a whaleboat, a rather large launch. "Good day, doctor. Come on aboard," called the lead oarsman as they pulled up to the pier. "No one knows more about birthing babies than Nan Eldridge and she needs you. Must be having some kind of big problem."

"Do you know when labor started?" asked Eustis.

"Probably last night. I hear it has been going on a long time," he replied grimly and applied himself to his oars. Eustis felt the best he could do was to get mentally prepared. In the army, he had not dealt with many women's issues; but back in Boston, he had worked with Dr. Warren who knew almost as much as the midwives and more about the surgical end of giving birth.

Approaching the western shore, they were greeted by an anxious young woman riding one horse and leading another that Eustis recognized as Mrs. Eldridge's Belle. Mrs. Eldridge was organized and in charge over here, he reminded himself. The woman hailed him as soon as Eustis stepped from the barge. "Here, doctor! I've got a horse for you. Come quickly. We must save Norah!"

Tying his pack behind the saddle, Eustis mounted Belle, and they set off at a fast pace for the settlement. His escort did not talk but just kicked her mount to go faster. Everything was bathed in a sense of urgency. The entire settlement seemed worried; a dozen or so residents were huddled outside the Eldridge cabin. After leaving the horses in someone's care, Eustis hurried into the cabin.

He was stunned at the scene before him. Norah was propped up in Katy Bates's lap, on Nan Eldridge's bed, and looked close to death, sweaty hair plastered to her head, her color absolutely gone to gray, her lips almost blue. The bed had been pulled away from the wall. Anna Grady was to one side, sponging Norah's forehead, while Katy stroked her hand, whispering encouraging words.

A distraught-looking Mrs. Eldridge in a bloody apron took Eustis aside. "Her labor started early yesterday mornin', and she came over to me. I think it was the most recent attack by those men and her anxiety that got it started. I should 'ave shot him!

"I've done everythin' I can think of, and I cannot shift it. The babe is lying across the womb opening blocking it, or something is – and nothing can get through. I'm thinking it might be the placenta. Please, do you have ideas?"

Needing a moment to think, Eustis called for a basin of water and soap so he could wash. Then tying on his apron and assuming his medical mode, he soaped his hands while he considered. Placenta previa? Detached and launching itself first? Good possibility. Mrs. Eldridge said she was bleeding with bright red blood. But it meant the babe had little chance to survive and might already be dead, although Norah might pull through. To save her, he would have to get the womb cleared, and he looked at his sharp scalpels and the ugly iron hooks to dismember the infant – if he had to.

"Let me see what I can find," he said. Then asking Mrs. Eldridge, "Will she mind? I know she was averse to me examining her before."

"She is barely in this world. Go ahead and I'll explain to her." Mrs. Eldridge moved to the head of the bed and bent down to whisper to Norah, who barely stirred.

Eustis lifted the covering sheet and was surprised by the amount of blood seeping onto the bed. It seemed too much. Perhaps the placenta really had begun to separate. Then gently, cautiously, inserting two soapy fingers, he checked Norah's cervix. It was barely dilated and clearly blocked. It could be the baby lying sideways or it could be the placenta. Hmmm. Try shifting the babe first.

To Mrs. Eldridge he said softly, "Let's see if I can turn it. Anything else in your collection of herbs that can numb her further? Any laudanum? Or opium? And, you know, if I cannot turn it, then I will have to operate to save her life."

"I understand. But oh, it is so sad, so awful." she whispered.

Then, more loudly: "Can someone get some more water? More rags and cloths?" Pulling herself together, Nan Eldridge directed another woman who moved quickly to get the water.

"We have no opium, doctor, and we have run out of laudanum," she continued. "All I have is whiskey. But can I also be of some help to you? Earlier, I could feel where the head was."

Eustis agreed, and standing on both sides of the bed, they positioned themselves, with hands on Norah's bulging stomach. Together, they began to exert pressure to turn the infant. If this rotation did not work, at least one life would be lost, maybe two. Her friends tried to sooth the mother, keeping her calm until she moaned, then screamed. Eustis and Eldridge continued to press in.

***

In her barely conscious state, Norah could see it all. It was like a dream. She looked down upon the struggling people. It was so interesting. There was Dr. Eustis. And there, dear Nan Eldridge, all trying to help her. And Katy Bates. And Anna Grady. But there was no need. She did not feel worried. In fact, it was quite pleasant, floating here with nothing left to worry about. After a while she watched as they spoke urgently, moved around, and acted excited. Then, suddenly, they had a tiny, blueish creature laid out on the bed as well. Dr. Eustis was working on it, pressing its chest with his fingertips, and leaning over it. But soon the little blue creature just floated up and came to her breast and she could hold it. How lovely and warm. She looked at them all fondly. She wanted to say how much she loved them and not to worry. She was fine.

***

The dream ended. Pain shot through her body. She screamed again, coming abruptly down onto the cold, wet, bloody bed. They were still there around her, looking at her, those caring friends. And she could

180

tell, looking in their eyes, that it was not good. Why could she not go back? But this was reality. It was not lovely and not nice.

Nan Eldridge, with tears in her eyes, softly told Norah she had lost her baby but might survive to see her husband when he came home. Dr. Eustis looked just as sad. He, too, patted her hand, and said she might well recover, but it would be difficult. She would have to do exactly as told and stay in bed. Her feet and hands did not seem to work. She could not feel them. Only the longing, the ache of loneliness.

As the other women surrounded her and changed her clothing and the bedding, she could hear Dr. Eustis and Nan talking by the table. She still felt barely part of this world. One of the women, Anna Grady, lifted her head and helped her sip a hot herbal fluid. Perhaps willow bark tea.

Eustis and Nan looked at the little wrapped bundle that lay between them. "I can take it back with me for burial," he whispered..

"Oh no, doctor. We'll tend to this small soul and give her body a nice spot here. We have other graves back near Mrs. Grady's still. Flowers and all," Mrs. Eldridge whispered back.

The comment about the Grady whiskey still nearly stopped Eustis's thought process; he had been so focused on what he had to do. He had not heard they made whiskey, and he instantly realized that was how and where Mrs. Grady was making extra money. Of course, selling or trading for whiskey! Clever woman, he thought.

"You know I can never thank you enough, dear Dr. Eustis. You have saved our Norah. Will you stay the night?"

"I believe I prefer to go back across the river for the rest of the night, if you can get the boatmen. I have a few things to prepare and then can explain all to General Greene in another day."

Eustis felt the need for the security offered at Robinson's but began to realize he was being foolish.

Nan Eldridge looked at him warily. "I'm not sure the boatmen will be able to take you this late. And I have not heard General Greene has left, but I expect he will leave very soon. It might even be tomorrow. Have you any answers for him?"

"I do but there are, as expected, some bits that I hope will become clear as I talk it out with him," Eustis replied. "If I cannot get to Robinson House now, I will go to the fort for the night and then see where we are tomorrow."

"You know we are very fond of you, doctor, and appreciate everything you have done for us. Norah is tough, and I think we can get her through this. There is always the promise of her husband coming, and he better be up to it, or he will have a bevy of women to answer to!"

Eustis smiled and looked around, suddenly realizing, coming out of his medical or what Sam called his business fog, that he was exhausted, and that Mrs. Eldridge was right. The sun had long gone and it was later at night than he realized. He had barely time to get to the fort before they barred the gates.

"May I borrow Belle for one more day? Elijah is bringing my horse across to me tomorrow. And I will, of course, check Norah again."

"Very well, doctor. You do need some rest." She smiled. "I'll call for Belle and then see you off."

"And," he looked at her, "you'll send for me at any time during the night if you need me. Right? Norah needs liquids. I have always believed milk is best, and sleep."

Chapter 21

Riding through the gates of Fort Putnam, Eustis felt wrung out, with no ability left to think or focus. He'd borrowed a lantern to get there. Visibility was low though it was a clear night. He checked in with the main office, got permission to sleep in the officers' barracks, visited the stables to leave Belle, went back to the now familiar place, and collapsed onto his cot.

He woke about two hours later, realizing he needed the necessary, and then made his way to the mess hall. Much too late for any proper meal, there were platters of leftovers and essential supper utensils laid out, plenty for a worn-out, starving man. A deep sleep restored him. By breakfast, although still concerned about Norah, he remained confident in the women's abilities and was eager to finish up his own mission. Perhaps General Greene had time today.

Eustis went to the main office and asked for the general. The response was hugely disappointing. He was gone. As it happened, Greene had just left for Tappan and his role of presiding over the John André court-martial. The new aide in his office said he would not be back for at least three to four days. Eustis could wait or spend his time however he wished. It was a huge letdown just when he figured he had completed his mission with most of the answers. He asked for Colonel Aldrich and was told he'd gone to Tappan as well.

As he was leaving, feeling dejected about his inability to wrap everything up, Elijah burst in, asking for the doctor. He had made his way across the Hudson River to bring Hector. Indeed, thought Eustis, they might as well go to the settlement, return Belle, and follow their usual routine of hoping the right question would elicit some sterling bit of information that would enable them to further unravel the mystery.

A stop at the stables, a saddle on Belle and both men mounted to head out from the fort. Just then, "Wait! Dr. Eustis. Dr. Eustis!" and Danny was running toward them. It was as if he had the eyesight of eagles or some other perceptive power, thought Eustis. How does he know when I am here?

They waited for the boy to approach. "Who're you lookin' for?" he asked. "Mebbe I can help. I know most ever'thin' around here."

"I am sure you do," said Eustis. "We are headed to the women's settlement to see your mother and the other women there. We'll perhaps see you later. Watch out and take care of yourself here, Danny."

"But, doctor," interrupted Eli, "maybe we should hear what he has to say now."

"Well, you're right, Eli. I'm actually in no rush. We can do that, but where is a good place to sit? Can we tie the horses?"

"Just follow me," said the boy. And they did, finding a shaded alcove with convenient rings in the wall. Sitting down, Eustis looked at the boy. He seemed in good health, cheerful, and, as usual, eager to tell them something.

"And what is your report, sergeant?" asked Eustis. Danny grinned, amused by his new title.

"I think there's a spy left around here. One with a diff'rent name and a disguise. Maybe a wig. And he changes it all the time. He could be three or five different people, or more!"

"Where did you hear this, Danny?"

"I am the sergeant, 'member? But really, I heard some men talkin'.

They didn't like General Arnold's old helper, that Corporal Kendall. He got sent away. But they say he's still comin' 'round. Lurkin' and spyin'.''

A thought flashed into Eustis' mind of running into Kendall at Brouwer's public house. He had seemed uneasy to see Eustis at the time, and it was odd. He should not have been. Hmmm. They would have to go look for Bridey, see what she knows about Kendall.

"Thank you so much, sergeant. This report of yours is actually very interesting to me. I want to think about it some more. But now Eli and I are going to see your mother, and we'll find you again later."

The boy seemed satisfied to have delivered his report and cheerfully ran beside them as they made their way to the gate, waving them off.

Eli had not been that interested in the "sergeant's" report, but seemed to have other problems on his mind.

"Can," Elijah hesitated, "can I talk to you, doctor?"

"Certainly, Elijah. Don't be concerned or uneasy. I hear many things and deal with lots of people's problems. You will not shock or surprise me. Anything you say is fine with me, and we can keep it between us."

"I've been talkin' to Noah. He is anxious about the end to the war, and we talked about goin' west together. Mayhap Ohio. We thought we could try our hands at adventurin' and could offer some herb doctorin' too. We got those skills now. And Noah's real good with animals, even doctorin' 'em. But I don't know about how to tell Gran."

Eustis saw the problem, and he was not sure Nan Eldridge would go for the idea, especially given the history of the death of Eli's family in western Massachusetts. She'd want him to stay here safely in the East. He searched for a reasonable response.

"I see the problem, Eli. But I do think you have to tell her at some time. You cannot just leave. You have valuable skills that the homesteaders in the wilderness will appreciate. Can I suggest you stay another six months or so and learn as much as you can about what is out there and what you can get here? Stay through the winter here then plan to leave next spring. Noah too. And we can tackle your gran together. It may be that the war will end by then for all we know."

Eli was silent as they turned onto the path to the settlement.

"Think about it, and talk some more with Noah," urged Eustis. "He will be better off staying with you. It is just the way things are now, and you know that. It's up to us to help him, sort of protect him, until our new country gets safer."

Thinking about the boys. No, he had to adjust his thoughts. They were young men. But they would be well suited to go exploring with Noah's gift for caution and reticence and Elijah's eager sense for adventure. Each could help the other, and they would be safer that way. He, on the other hand, would be in a state of anxiety all the time they were away. This must be what parents feel, and probably the closest he would come to it.

Riding into the center clearing, Eustis was relieved to see several women at work. The ones he wanted to talk to were not there, and he surmised they would be in the Eldridge cabin. They tied their horses in front and walked to the door, hearing sobs as they approached. Alarmed, Eustis hurried in. He was immediately relieved to see that it was the youngest Grady child, Seth, who was weeping against his mother's skirt.

He exhaled, turning to Mrs. Eldridge. "News?"

She shook her head. "We had a good night. Norah slept through most of it, and between us women, Anna and Katy and me, we kept watch. She does not seem much stronger or in pain, and she is still sipping her water and milk."

"Is she conscious?"

"Yes, most of the time, but not talking."

"Hmmm. Let me take a look." He approached the bed, looked at Norah lying quietly, carefully tucked under several quilts. Taking her hand, he checked her pulse and then felt her forehead for fever. The silence disturbed him and, despite understanding how close she had come to death, the doctor had hoped for a quicker response. But the human body needs time to recover no matter how impatient we are, he reminded himself.

Leaning over Norah, he asked how she felt. She stirred herself, looked at him, and then averted her eyes, mumbling something. He leaned in closer and asked what she had said.

"Did it," she muttered.

"You sure did," Eustis exclaimed. "You survived a horrendous time, and you will continue to get better."

"No, "she whispered. "Did it." And she closed her eyes.

Eustis decided not to question her further because she seemed so exhausted. He lifted the quilts to see if there was blood. The amount he saw, although less than yesterday's, confirmed his suspicions. And he was not sure what else he could do beyond packing the area with lint and clean rags, adding more fluids to her diet to offset the loss, and hoping for the best.

Norah must know she is not recovering as quickly as she might, and that is why she rallied to speak to him, he thought. Perhaps he could talk with her again a little later. He exchanged a glance with Mrs. Eldridge, and she turned to get more bandaging, returning with two other women to help change the bedding.

Eustis stepped outside the cabin. There was not much else he could do here. It was all about waiting. The women were good at what they were doing, and he had no more suggestions. He told Elijah he was going to go see Mrs. Grady and then return to the fort. He planned to check on everyone later in the day on the way back to the ferry.

Elijah could stay or come with him. Eli had been stunned by Norah's appearance and opted to stay in case he could do anything. He knew of some herbs that might help stop the bleeding.

Leading Hector, Eustis walked on to the Grady cabin. A subdued Mrs. Grady waited for him at the door. Her look told him how disturbed they all were.

"I am so sorry, Mrs. Grady," he said. "I have no magic cure. I wish I did and that I knew more. We'll have to wait for nature to do its work, one way or the other.

"Come in," she said, "and I'll give you something stronger than tea.

You look like you need it." And he remembered she made whiskey. She could give some to Norah too. Might help.

"Has there been a prayer group formed, Mrs. Grady? That is sometimes soothing to its participants. And try a little whiskey too."

As the day moved on toward noon, Eustis went back to Mrs. Eldridge's to get Elijah and go back to the fort. He would check Norah once more.

She was conscious and lying slightly propped up on several pillows with Elijah sitting on the bed. The doctor went over to her as the other women hovered.

"I'll stay here awhile so you all can take an hour or so to tend to your own families," he told them. "You've been a tremendous help all around, and I thank you. Please, go see your families."

Several slipped out the door to dash to their own cabins.

Norah looked at Eustis. "I told you," she whispered. "I killed that man . . . in the end . . . our road."

Elijah interrupted. "No, Norah. Don't say that!" He looked desperately at Eustis. "She's just dreamin' this up."

"No," she said. "Want my conscience clear when I leave you all."

"But you are not leaving!" insisted Eli.

Eustis drew closer and leaned down. "Just tell me what you think you did."

"That slimy, disgustin' man. Made me do it. Tol' me I had to do wha' he said. Later I gave him that stew. He said to get him somethin' to eat. Put leaves in it . . . make him sick. Eli's poison leaves." She sighed and closed her eyes.

"But that could have killed him," gasped Elijah. "No, you couldn't have. I think you've been havin' a bad dream."

"I was goin' to stab him. With the spindle from the wheel."

Eustis broke in. "How could you do that with a piece off the wheel? I examined his body. There was only a very small hole in his ear."

"I jus' undid the leather fastenin', bu' then I dropped it, on the trail," she paused. "When I ran," she added. "'Twas back, the ol' leather cracked, an' Eli repaired it with new leather. Had to protect myself, and he would not stop." Her words slurred. "Ye un'erstan'?"

Unfortunately, he did. And shockingly, it seemed justifiable to him after she had been so attacked. Just because her husband or the other men were not around, these men thought they could do whatever they wanted. But what to do?

"Never thought it'd kill him! Jus' a little skinny thing. I thought t'would hurt and make him un'erstan' we did na' want him here. Wha' can any woman do?"

Eustis needed to recover his thoughts. "I do believe it may have been the thing that killed him, Norah. That and the poison. I'll have to think it over more. Now you need to sleep."

She slipped down under the covers like an obedient child and closed her eyes. Elijah looked utterly devastated. Tears ran down his cheeks.

"Come with me, Eli," Eustis ordered. "We'll go back to the fort, and we will not speak of this with anyone until we have thought it through and are sure of our facts. Come now, say good-bye to your gran outside."

Mrs. Eldridge was out by the horses, waiting. She looked devastated. She could see Norah was not recovering as quickly as she had hoped. It would take some miracle, Eustis thought, and she might not want Eli to leave. He shook his head and shrugged slightly as he looked at her. There was nothing more he could do. She nodded, moved to Eli, hugged him, and urged him to be on his way with the doctor.

They rode back to the fort in silence. Eustis wanted to get his midday dinner and hoped Eli could eat something too. Then they would go see the cooper. Eustis wanted a few more words with James Mugford.

Not much later, passing large barrels stacked and ready for delivery, they entered the shop and walked over to where Mugford was hammering away on his anvil on a piece of red-hot iron recently removed from his furnace. Turning as they approached, he nodded in greeting, holding the glowing iron rod. There was something oddly menacing about it.

"Stopping by to say farewell to Danny, Mr. Mugford," said Eustis. "Our investigation is near complete, and we are headed to Robinson House. We'll only return when we can report to General Greene."

"So, ye got ever'one ye wanted? Thought 'twas a few left."

"Maybe so, but I am satisfied with what I know," said Eustis.

"Yeah? So wha' can ye tell me? Ye got the one who is tellin' secrets?"

"Which one do you mean?" asked Eustis.

"If ye know, ye tell me. I'm talkin' about the new big cheese, not that traitorous bugger who skipped out."

"Yes," agreed Eustis. "I've got him on my list too. Just wanted to say thanks for your help." And he turned to go, knowing it would irritate Mugford, and he might learn something more.

"Wait!" Mugford said. Eustis stopped and turned. "He's still around. I saw 'im earlier."

"Does that bother you?" asked Eustis. "Is he holding something over you?"

"Well, if he is the fellow I am hearing stories about, he'll go after Danny, then me, and more after that. He's a killer. So, yeah, I'm worried."

"But you don't dare say his name?"

"Course I do. It's prob'ly that Kendall. He's prob'ly been running that spyin' crowd from across the river all along. There're others in it too. I hope you can catch 'im."

"Thanks, Mugford. I do too. But General Greene and Colonel Aldrich are away, so it may take a few days. Meanwhile, keep a close watch. And keep quiet. Whoever this strong man is, he may have the British Army behind him."

"Yeah, I understand, doctor. I'll keep watch on Danny too."

"And I am going back to Robinson House to clear up a few things on that side of the river. But first I'll check in at Brouwer's." He tipped his hat and strode out of the cooperage.

Mounting, he said to Elijah, "Let's look to see if we have mail then head to the tavern, see if anything is new there. I have one more thing to discuss with Bridey McGuinness." Elijah was still silent, appearing to follow with no purpose, absorbed in his thoughts.

Eustis stepped into the main office to pick up the packet of mail for Robinson House, and they set off, soon arriving at the tavern. Ducking through the door, Eustis looked around. It was early yet, and many tables were empty. He chose one and indicated Elijah should sit while he went over to the publican at the corner bar. Bridey was there chatting.

As he arrived, she delivered her happiest smile and asked what she could do for him. He had several immediate thoughts but limited his response and smiled. "I have just one question for you. Have you seen that man called Colonel Kendall in here often lately? And what about that Frenchman?"

"That is two questions, sor," she grinned. "And if ye go sit, I'll bring two mugs of our cider. I think that is what ye preferred. And we can talk."

Pleased to be so warmly welcomed, he replied, "Thank you, I'll be waiting."

Within minutes, she arrived with two foaming tankards, placed them on the table, and sat on the bench beside Elijah. She twinkled at them both. "What can I explain for ye?"

"I dunno," sighed Elijah, and before she got too distracted, Eustis intervened with his question.

"What can you tell me about the Frenchman? And have you seen Colonel Kendall?"

He imagined a sassy response, then she seemed to realize it was not the time, and reformed her answer. "That colonel, 'e's in most nights now. He watches ever'body. 'E's not very friendly, or at least 'e doesn't seem to have friends. And the Frenchman? No, haven't seen 'im. Prob'ly the last time was mebbe two weeks or more ago."

Eustis thought he was likely in the West Point cemetery and said, "We'll let him go for now. Back to Kendall. Does he meet with people? Or is he just watching others?"

"The ones 'e does talk to, 'e tries to convince them of somethin', but I'm not sure they believe 'im. They do a lot of serious talkin' about some other new man in charge. Not jokin', ya know? Strange. They seem nervous and stop any talkin' if I am around. I thought it'd get better onct that traitor left, but somethin' or someone new seems to have made them anxious."

"I know what you mean, Bridey."

"An' what's this I hear about Robinson's bein' closed and you movin' to the new campground they're buildin'?"

"We're at Robinson House for now as far as I know, Bridey."

Just then, a man at the neighboring table rapped with his knuckles, and she got up, waggled her fingers at him, and went over to take their orders.

"That's it, Eli," said Eustis, putting down his mug. "All I need. Are you ready to go back to Robinson's?"

"I don't care, doctor. I suppose it might be better, but I really want to be with Norah."

"Hmmm," he considered. "You might be a comfort to them there. If you want, as we ride to the ferry, you can take the path to the settlement. I do want to get the last ferry back. I have my obligations to the hospital."

Eli readily agreed, and they set off, Eli for the women's settlement, and Eustis for the ferry.

Chapter 22

Riding into the barnyard at Robinson's, Eustis felt a wave of relief about coming home. But he couldn't shake his puzzling question about how Kendall could somehow manage to form a rogue group. He did not seem like a strong leader, and Eustis felt there had to be a British spy or two somewhere in the mix for guidance. He'd have to cogitate some more, and fortunately he was back at Robinson's, his best thinking spot. And he owed Mistress Annabelle Tobey a visit. And her coffee! But first to open his mail, talk to Dr. Burnet, and find out what was on his list of tasks here.

September 30, 1780
Dr. W. Eustis
Robinson House

My Dear Eustis,
Just wanted you to know we are plenty busy here holding off and mending those involved with defending the northern line. I did hear some gossip I wanted to pass on. One of the wounded men who was brought in was raving about a new leader who was particularly vicious

– called the Cobbler. He seems to have been operating for several months in Manhattan near you and has gathered a bunch of disgruntled Loyalists to do some spying and maybe counterfeiting. This man, not the redcoats, slammed one of my patient's fingers, then sewed them together so they would never be able to hold a musket again. Ugly! He may be the person controlling all the nastiness happening, perhaps trying to get someone positioned inside West Point. I have repaired what I could of the man's hands but we surely could use your skills here. Have you heard anything? Be careful, my friend.

> *Yr ob't serv't,*
> *S. Adams*

After his hospital rounds with Dr. Burnet, Eustis escaped to sit at the end of the old pier, staring down into the shimmering, sky-reflecting water, Sam's letter in hand. Sam was on the job! His message did seem to clarify a great deal, filling some gaps in his information and revealing an identity for this recently-discovered predator.

Eustis had heard earlier indications of a band of counterfeiters operating in Manhattan and thought they were scattered, operating independently. Now it seems someone may have seized this opportunity to organize these outlaws and take control. It could explain several things. That lot terrifying the women's settlement might have been a part of an expanding operation. It could be a huge effort to regroup after Arnold's failed efforts to sabotage the American cause.

But was Reed involved? Hadn't he said himself that he was working as an agent or spy? But for which side? What if the spy ring was led by this crazy cobbler person? Images of a shoemaker flashed through his mind. They work in leather, cutting and sewing shoes. Make belts and saddlery too. All kinds of knives, needles, hole punches for tools. But sewing a person? It was hard to believe.

One sympathetic friend he still wanted to talk to was Annabelle Tobey. It was getting toward dusk when he left the pier, headed to the house and barnyard, looking for the sutlers' wagons.

"Good evening, Mrs. Tobey."

"Out for an evenin' stroll are you, doctor?" She was sitting on her log near the fire and seemed to have just finished eating oatmeal or something in a bowl with a small wooden spoon. "I hear you been investigatin' t'other side of the river." She picked up her coffee pot and a mug for him and indicated the other log for his seat. "I'm curious if you found out what you were lookin' for."

"I have to say, mistress, that I was eager to get back to your coffee," he said, sitting and raising his mug in salute. "It is the best on both sides of the river, but I do have a question."

"And why does that not surprise me," she said, smiling at him. "What do you want to know? Maybe I can help you."

"I am wondering what you can tell me about Amos Kendall. Who has he been talking to, and what is he doing?"

"Interestin' fellow, Colonel Kendall. I suspect he holds a grudge against Arnold and his superiors from way back for not awarding him the post of commander at West Point. He's been passed over, time and time again. Now, being from Virginia, he could become dangerous and harbor thoughts of lost honor. Those sort are very concerned about it. And they may join others."

"Not just Virginians, Mrs. Tobey." Eustis smiled. "Many in the army, my brother Benjamin included, are all concerned with personal perceptions of honor. One said to me, my name and my honor are all that I truly have in this world."

"Hmmm. I understand, but I do not agree," said Mrs. Tobey. "I have heard that Kendall said to someone, who passed it on to me, that the odd Frenchman in General Arnold's office, the one you saw, was a British spy in disguise. That one seems to have gone back south into New York for the moment or at least disappeared."

Eustis wondered how Mrs. Tobey found all this out. People must talk in front of traders like they do around servants, as if they had no ears.

She continued. "And Mr. Reed said that Frenchman was also the

195

one who was murdered by the side of the road here."

Eustis frowned, wondering which Reed she meant. "Did you know there were two men posing as Jonathan Reed?"

"Aha. Interesting idea," said Mrs. Tobey. "That may explain some of the confusion."

But, thought Eustis, was this Reed bearded and dark or fair without a beard? "Who have you talked to, mistress? Was it the Reed that was blond, served as a courier and traveled north and south, carrying notes and news for the Americans? That Jonathan Reed stayed mostly on the other side of the river. I think he served as a legitimate courier. I am not sure about the dark-haired one."

"I have only spoken to the blond man," said Mrs. Tobey. "He seemed perfectly fine and loyal to the cause. There is another?"

Eustis grimaced. "And I have talked to him too. He was here briefly as a patient. Leg injury. I'll have a great deal to ponder as I try to sleep tonight. Some people seem to keep moving around. I have no idea where or if they are located on any semi-permanent basis. Any local families around here who might offer shelter to questionable folk? Like some of these transient types?"

"I think there might be," said Mrs. Tobey. "But you need your supper and a good night's sleep. Then perhaps it will all become clear in the morning."

Eustis bid her goodnight and walked back to the house for his own supper of bread and cheese.

The talk at the table that evening was the sobering news that André had been hanged at Tappan two days earlier, on October second, and that General Greene was on his way back, expected within another day or two. They had heard about the negotiations by General Washington with British General Clinton to trade André for Arnold. Washington really wanted Arnold. But Clinton had refused. He just would not or could not make any arrangement that recognized the Americans as the legitimate opposition, even for his best officer.

Once he knew his fate, André had requested to die as a gentleman by firing squad. But as a spy, he would hang. Many of the officers were sympathetic to his plight but could offer no arguments on his behalf. After this conversation, the Robinson House residents retired quietly to their rooms without the usual cheerful wishes.

***

Come morning, the grim mood was somewhat elevated by a crisp, sunny day. Eustis decided to send a message across to the fort asking for an appointment in two days to brief General Greene. Meanwhile, he would give his attention to the hospital. Noah hovered, and Eustis realized he had been neglecting him too. And Mrs. Nardy. And Dr. Burnet. Actually, the entire operation required his undivided attention for a change. And there was no news from Elijah.

That evening the sun was starting to illuminate the sky in farewell colors as it retired for the night. Eustis, exhausted from a day filled with business, despite the cool evening, sat on the side porch. He invited Noah to join him. After a few minutes of companionable silence looking at the stars and the fireflies, he asked, "Are you worried about Elijah?"

Noah certainly looked as worried as he had been for days now. "No, doctor. Eli knows the situation. He'll work it out. He's been through hard times afore. An' he's got us."

"But you, Noah, you're still not happy. Am I right?"

Noah seemed to be deliberating whether to speak or not. Then he observed, "I wish I knew how this would turn out. You know, this war an' all."

"I sure do know. You hope for the comfort of having a plan. I think we all do. But you have to understand that none of us know how this will turn out. I can tell you that in the end we Americans will win merely by surviving. We have the advantage of our home ground, and we're able to retreat farther toward the west for as long as it takes. The British cannot afford to continue to wage a war this far from their supplies. And I hear that Parliament is beginning to get tired of the huge expense."

"I," Noah hesitated, ". . . but what about me?"

"You remember what Sam said?"

"I do but I'm not like you. I was owned by someone! An' I got no real education."

"I understand. And it is very hard to trust us after the life you've had. I wouldn't be ready either. Here is a suggestion." He paused, "You stay here until spring, and Sam and I will make sure you have all you need to move west. I truly hope Elijah will be ready to go on the road with you. He wants to. I have talked to him about this. Can you do this, trust us that long?"

"But I still go over it an' over it in my mind," Noah countered. "I get to thinkin' too much about what can go wrong. I can be caught an' sold again!"

"Well, for the moment, it is not very likely if you are with me. And right now, I can at least offer a distraction. Come with me when I head back to West Point. I need to report to the general soon, and we must see how Mrs. Lindholm is doing. Elijah has not sent any news, so it would be good to check on him, talk it over too."

Noah still looked wary but nodded and agreed. Eustis did not think he was completely reassured or relieved. Maybe talking to Elijah could help. It came down to trust, and he could see why Noah could not trust them yet. Then he had an idea. He would write a letter to Sam tonight. Perhaps they could create a document of manumission for Noah, certifying he was a free man instead of hoping the country would do it. The paper could say that they, as his owners, had given him his freedom. Sam's father might help.

***

When a courier arrived with news that General Greene was back at the Point only a day later than expected, Eustis arranged to go there immediately, taking Noah with him.

The river crossed, the men rode to the women's settlement, intending to pay a short visit on their way to the fort. Eustis was apprehensive about what he might find after their days away. As they approached, his fears were somewhat allayed. They did not see a cluster of worried women outside the Eldridge cabin. Instead, the usual laundry business simmered and dripped.

Eustis called out to Mrs. Eldridge as they secured the horses.

"Dr. Eustis! How nice to see you! We've unexpectedly good news for you."

"Good day, Mrs. Eldridge. Pray tell. What news?"

"Come inside and see." She smiled broadly. "And perhaps Noah can go get Elijah. He is out back of the cabin working on preparing my garden for winter. And I'll make some tea."

Eustis was surprised by the change in atmosphere and entered the cabin to be amazed by the sight of Norah propped up in Mrs. Eldridge's bed, still obviously weak but clearly improving, certainly better than the last time he had seen her. He was relieved that his worst expectations had been wrong.

"Good news, indeed," he said, approaching her bedside.

"Not only that," added Mrs. Eldridge from where she had begun setting her table for tea, "but we have had news that the Massachusetts Sixteenth will be arriving within four or five days. Good news always brings its cures."

Eustis felt as pleased as the women. He noted that they had wrapped Norah's breasts tightly to discourage milk formation. The women knew what they were doing.

"You do look so much improved, Mistress Lindholm. I am delighted. Can I help you with anything?"

Norah smiled.

"You have done everything we could wish for, doctor," interrupted Mrs. Eldridge. "Saved our Norah for another day and another year. We will not be able to thank you enough."

"Hmmm," Eustis hesitated. "Could you answer a few questions?"

Mrs. Eldridge and Norah both laughed. "It would not be you without questions, doctor. Make yourself comfortable." She dragged one of the stools from the table to the bedside. "Here, sit."

199

Eustis sat and sipped. Could he call it tea? A rather different warm beverage, he thought. "Thank you, Norah. I realize this has been an ordeal, but you appear to be well through the worst parts, and I do just want to clarify a few points if I may."

She smiled over at him expectantly. "I'll do what I can, doctor."

"Please tell me again about what happened after that scoundrel left you. Did he say where he was going, or why?"

She frowned, looking down at her hands clasped on her lap. "Before he left, he threatened me that if I talked to anyone, he would kill me. He said he would soon be in control of the whole area. I could not quite understand what he meant. Maybe it was about the British and that he was working for them."

"Then what happened?"

She visibly steeled herself to talk, taking a deep breath, exhaled. "As I said, after he forced me to do what he wanted, he then demanded food. He said he was my master and I should get him something to eat. I offered him some stew that I had over the fire. But I chopped some of the leaves and berries that Elijah had brought for Mrs. Eldridge to dry and stirred them in. I thought they might make him sick, and it would serve him right for being so evil and disgusting. I threw the rest of that stew away."

She looked down at her hands, clenched her lips, took another breath, and went on.

"When he finally left, I felt so hurt, so worn down, so tired, doctor." She glanced quickly at him. "But I wanted to make sure he left so I followed. I had the spindle in my pocket. I had taken it off the wheel just before I left the cabin. I was afraid if he saw me, he would attack again. He seemed to get dizzy and fell from his horse on our main path out to the road. Then he began to mutter to himself and stumbled and wobbled along.

"I could hear him wretch and saw him fall down almost at the end of the path. But he crawled up to his feet. That is when I turned to run back. But the strange thing is I don't think I was alone in following

200

him. I could not see anything or anyone, but I could feel it. Do you know what I mean? I don't know if 'twas because I was asleep or unconscious or just feelin' exhausted, but I did feel someone was out there. I think I dropped the spindle then, when I started to run back."

"Yes, I do know what you mean. And you are certain you dropped the spindle? How did it get back here?"

Mrs. Eldridge had been hovering, this time watching Norah intently. "That was me. I found it later. I thought I recognized it and brought it."

"Indeed. Thanks to you, mistress. And you have been a great help to me too, with caring so well for Norah. You both relax now. I will finish this, uh, tea, find Noah, and get on back to the fort."

As it was, Elijah and Noah wanted to stay together longer. Mrs. Eldridge said she would give them supper, and Noah could stay there for the night. Going out the door, Eustis looked hard at Mrs. Eldridge and said softly, "Are you sure you have nothing else to tell me?"

"Outside," she said, narrowing her eyes and following him out. "I don't want Norah punished. 'Twas I followed her."

"I thought that was possible," said Eustis.

"I did accost that wicked man again. I caught up to him as I said and from behind I grabbed at his shoulder. He was so angry. When he rounded around to hit out at me, I stabbed with the spindle. I thought to get him in the eye and ended up hitting him in the ear as he turned. Then I turned, grabbed that rifle and ran away. I think that was when he fell down."

"I'm glad you've finally told me. I know it was difficult, but so was the situation you were in. My remaining worry is how Norah will adjust and if her husband will accept her after what has happened. I don't know if he has a forgiving nature. Perhaps the rest of you can help with that."

She nodded. "We'll do our best."

"I am not sure what is next at the fort," he said, "but I'll tell you if any decisions have been made when General Greene is settled. And I will be back by tomorrow for the young men." Arrangements completed, Eustis left to ride to the fort alone.

The day remained a perfect example of what is enjoyed most in the fall – crisp air, changing leaves, and bright sun. Eustis could almost feel Sam riding along, this time saying, "What now instead of what if?" He continued his pondering until the fort and its sentries loomed before him. Information checked, he was allowed through the open gates, visited the stables, left Hector, and walked back to meet with General Greene. He did not have to wait long.

The general rose behind his desk to greet him. "Good morning, doctor. I hope you can alleviate one of my problems or at least shine a light on it. Here, please, sit." He indicated a chair. Greene, although not young at thirty-eight, looked much older, swamped with worries and tired to the point of exhaustion because of his travels and the disagreeable task of presiding at André's trial and his execution in Tappan.

Eustis removed his tricorn and placed it on his lap as he sat. "I have been trying to think of how to begin, general. There are several parts to this story. And you missed out on the entire beginning."

"Yes?" Greene indicated he should go on.

"I first thought that these two murders were unrelated. I now realize that they come under the control of a single person whose name I am not positive about but I hope it becomes clear before I leave here."

"And who do you think it is? This murderer?"

"Let me start at the beginning, sir." He stood up, placed his hat on the chair, and began to pace. "First, a man's body was found lying at the side of the road near to the entrance path to the woman's settlement back in August. General Arnold assigned me the task of identification and answering the question of how he was killed. I performed an autopsy on this body and was puzzled by the manner of death.

"We could get no identification from anyone in the area although he looked to be dressed as a rifleman. There was the remainder of vomited residue in his throat and a small puncture in his ear. After the autopsy, he was buried at the fort, and I began talking to people, hoping to get some useful information to lead me to understand what had happened. Now thanks to you, we have his identity as Wee Gordie Wallace."

He looked at Greene to see if he was being clear enough. When Greene impatiently nodded, he then went on.

"The second dead man was found about a month ago, September eighth, on the other side of the river near the Queen's Head public house. His body lay at the edge of the clearing across from the tavern down near the river. I thought at first that he had drowned because his clothes were wet and he was found so close to the water. We then carted the body to Robinson House where I could examine it more thoroughly. I discovered that he had been strangled, and although in wet clothes he had not drowned but died before he went into the river. He is presently buried in the hospital's graveyard as an unknown.

"I hope you understand, I am new at this kind of assignment. The closest I can come to identification in an autopsy is when we look for clues in the body for cause of death. But that did not answer the questions we had as to personal identity. Drawings of the man were circulated, and I wandered around here and the other side of the river whenever I could, taking time from my real medical obligations, and talking to anyone who might have information. I tried to understand what happened and who these men were. The man by the river has been variously identified as de Vos or Bowen, but I am not confident of either.

"Several weeks ago, my friend, Sam Adams came for a visit of a little over a week and was helpful as someone with whom I could go over what I had for facts and develop a plan to find answers to questions about what we did not know. Sam asked important questions. It freed our minds to wonder beyond the obvious and look for other motives."

"Please continue, doctor. Let's get on with this. What have you concluded?"

"Hard to call them conclusions, sir, but in the overall picture, this area has been out of balance – almost in dis-ease – since midsummer. Rampant suspicion undermined everything. There has been no organization providing stability. It's as though the brain became idle, perhaps through exhaustion, and it lost control. General Arnold did not offer this essential direction or stability. Instead, he seemed to do the opposite. He also had people secretly working for him as couriers and spies, reporting on what was happening in New York as well as in the villages and countryside around here.

"One of those random groups developed their proficiency in counterfeiting which, as you know, has been very problematic for our patriot effort. These men moved about in upper Manhattan Island, not far from Robinson House. That group recently grew to have a strong leader who I have heard is sometimes called the Cobbler. He is amazingly devious and effective as a spy too, seeming to move around freely by adopting many different occupations and appearances.

"What he could not do was keep track of or manage all those who worked with him. Some groups that were originally working together began to have ideas of their own, and they developed their own small fiefdoms. It was all about the money. Because, of course, no one has any. Without the immediate control and backing of the British Army, this group dispersed into small bands of roaming, overconfident cutthroats, pirates if you will, profiting through counterfeit dollars.

"And when Arnold left, his contact inside the fort . . ."

"What?" interrupted Greene, leaning forward. "Good God! Have you any idea of who this kingpin is? And who this other inside man was? Do you know where they are?"

"Yes, sir, I do, and I can explain most of it."

"May the devil take them! Let me call Aldrich in. He'll have to act on this immediately."

"I hope so, sir. And I think there will be other deaths unless you act soon. I believe there may be a developing rivalry."

Just then there was a knock on the door, and an aide offered the information that the lead scouts from the Sixteenth Massachusetts had arrived and that the regiment was only a few days behind.

"Very well," said the general. "I'll want to welcome them and direct them to the site that they'll develop into a new campground for the winter." He rose saying, "I'll get back to you, doctor. Please be sure to let one of my men know where you'll be."

The general left the room with his aide, and Eustis was left staring at empty space.

"But I know the answers," he said aloud, thinking they could not or would not take the time to listen. And he was just supposed to wait?

Chapter 23

He stared glumly into his cider, having walked to Brouwer's tavern to while away a few hours. Might as well have something to eat as his breakfast was many hours ago. He felt the urge to punch something as well as the desire to just leave for Robinson's. There seemed to be no understanding about the life and commitment of a medical man. Huh! I suppose all I am is just a hack, a sawbones to them. No other value.

Bridey came by and patted his shoulder. She seemed to know he was in a bleak mood. "I smoked it, Bridey. I figured out the answer! I have the solution to the murders, and they've gone off without hearing me out!"

"Don't ye worry, sor. It'll all work out." She sat quietly with him for several minutes before leaving to attend another table.

There was no one of interest in the tavern, that is until Colonel Kendall came in. He looked around and may not have seen Eustis, or did not care, as he settled at a table and welcomed several men to join him. He acted as leader of the small contingent as they huddled over the table. Planning something?

There was a sudden lull in the usual tavern noise as two women entered and went over to the publican seemingly to ask a question. In the sudden quiet, Eustis heard, ". . . need you back inside, sir." One man glanced over his shoulder and leaned in closer so that Eustis did not hear more until Kendall, clearly irritated, stood up, smacking the table. "I'm workin' on it, ya eejits!" At that, the man who had looked over at Eustis signaled for quiet, then stood up and left.

It seemed to Eustis that everyone was angry, annoyed, or discouraged lately, including himself. He put down a coin for Bridey and left to walk back to the fort and, with luck, get more time with General Greene.

It was another hour before he stood before the general. Greene briskly urged him to explain further from where they had left off, asking about the first murder and for more details about Gordie Wallace.

"Yes, sir," said Eustis, taking a seat and beginning again.

"I believe he was a deserter, originally from New Hampshire, and in and out of the army, ours and the British, several times. He got in with a small group of counterfeiters that had picked out the woman's settlement as a perfect base of operations. Unfortunately for them, the women did not agree and resisted at every chance. He repeatedly raped an attractive young woman over a period of months. Without other recourse, she gave poison to him in some stew just before he left, and although he would have died, he was also later stabbed on the road.

"I found a haversack Wallace dropped when leaving the settlement that last time. I was unable to recover any information from it, other than the name JReed. It was just too long out in the weather and soaking wet, having lain outside for several months on the forest floor. I believe it had been stolen from Jonathan Reed to enable use of his name. A useful prop."

He paused looking at Greene to see if he was following his explanation. Greene nodded and waved his hand, indicating he should continue. Eustis stood and paced while he extended his story.

"The other dead man, possibly Ephraim Bowen, was found across the river, attempting to defect from an organized small group and bring me the cane that the false Frenchman had used as a prop. Jonathan Reed identified him with different names. The one of Bowen seems to fit best.

"It was Bowen who likely played the role of the Frenchman I saw in General Arnold's office. He was attacked near the Queen's Head, his body rolled down toward the river. The murderer then just went on into the tavern. I am not positive of Bowen's motive in coming there. He must have thought I might use the cane for identification, or it could have been part of the admission that he played the Frenchman himself. Or wanting to sell information about his contacts with Arnold. Arnold would certainly have wanted to stop him. He was murdered before he could reach Robinson House, attacked, as I said, near the Queen's Head. And he had a contact here in the fort."

Greene stiffened. "Yes. . .?"

"I believe that Colonel Kendall served as a go-between for Arnold and these outsiders and is now unwisely trying to assemble his own group. The main leader, however, and the most dangerous is the one called the Cobbler. We've got to find him."

Eustis hurried to present all of his information before he got cut off again.

"This Cobbler is clever and very adept at manipulating people. He knew just how to talk to these disenfranchised people, how to play on their fears by promising a new order under his own leadership. And they supported him because they believed their lives would somehow be improved. He required extreme loyalty, and those not loyal suffered miserably. All his men had to do was believe in him. Their grievances would all be addressed. And he benefited from, really reveled in the sense of power he had."

"Thank you, doctor," Greene said. "This is an amazing revelation. Do I understand that Bowen is buried in the Robinson House cemetery?

"Yes, sir. Likely killed by the Cobbler who later went into the public house there."

"I will follow up from here to find this Cobbler. I am completely indebted to you. We'll get out a notice immediately. You have a name?"

"I suspect he is still using the alias of Jonathan Reed. Although that may be far from his real name."

"But you have a description? I thought Reed had been a courier through here and was blond. But you say this one is tall, bearded, dark, and another person altogether. Are you sure, doctor?"

"Yes, sir. There were two fellows who claimed the name Reed. Or more correctly, one who was indeed truly the courier Jonathan Reed and another who took the same name as a confusing coverup and a tease to the patriots. Do you know if the true courier is still alright? I am worried he might have been targeted."

"I have not heard otherwise," Greene said. "I certainly appreciate all your work and thank you for straightening out what may well have slipped through the cracks while we were focused on other aspects of this war. As I said before, I am astounded. Rogue traitors operating independently in small groups!"

"You should put Colonel Kendall on your list, sir. You'll need to lock him up before the Cobbler or Reed, whoever he is, kills him. I understand that he is ruthless when crossed."

"Thank you, doctor. I will get these orders out immediately. Oh, and the Cobbler killed Ephraim Bowen?"

"As I mentioned, I suspect it was the Cobbler, and he was able to just blend in with those in the public house. Funny thing, general. This rogue group operating with small groups reminds me of what we did ourselves, back in the old days protesting the British in Boston. Except our cause was not personal gain." Eustis smiled. "You know where I am, and I'll be off now and leave it in your hands."

Arriving at the women's settlement in the afternoon, Eustis approached happily, ready to pick up Elijah and Noah and head across the river yet one more time, the last he hoped for a while. He was surprised to see them both sitting on Mrs. Eldridge's door step.

Elijah called out. "We're ready to go, doctor! Don't need to stay here anymore, and now I can get back to buildin' my life with the army. I've explained to my gran about our plans for after the war, and she understands my need to go adventuring.'"

Hmmm, thought Eustis. Not completely likely, but Mrs. Eldridge was no fool and she would not stand in his way, at least not yet. "Well, come along both of you then. Let's catch the next ferry. I am sure they need your services in the apothecary shed at Robinson's."

Mrs. Eldridge came to wave them off as did Mrs. Grady who stuck her head out of her door and called her farewells and thanks.

Suddenly there was shouting and cheers of "Huzzah! Huzzah!" coming from the path as two men strode in, dressed in makeshift dirty uniforms and loaded down with muskets, powder horns, canteens, and haversacks. Women squealed and ran out to greet them. It would seem the lead scouts of the Sixteenth Massachusetts were beginning to arrive. And more of those men would soon follow.

***

A few days after celebrations and catching up at Robinson House, Eustis called his two assistants, Noah and Elijah, to join him down at the old dock before they went in for their supper. He wanted to make sure they understood how much he appreciated their devoted help during the past two months of near insanity when too many things called for his attention. Now they could go forward with a nearly normal life at the hospital, prepare for winter, and look forward to spring. The three of them sat together at the end of the pier and watched the sun begin to set over the river.

"Don't you all make the prettiest picture!" Hearing the voice, Eustis rose and turned, dreading to see who he knew was there. The two young men turned to look at the tall, dark-haired man as well.

Eustis cleared his throat and said, "Greetings of this beautiful evening, Mr. Reed. Please join us."

"I rather think I will," said Reed, smartly dressed in black and drawing a large pistol from his belt, exuding arrogance as he sauntered closer.

210

"I appreciate your hospitality, but I do want to clear up a few things." He stopped, feet slightly apart, holding his pistol in both hands. "You have made some problems for me, Dr. Eustis. Got my men taken by the army. You should know that no one crosses me and lives."

Eustis could see that he was allowing his rage to build, to take over his being. His squinting eyes became almost black under heavy brows. He was enjoying it.

The doctor's mind was feverishly working as he knew both Elijah's and Noah's were. What to do? By God, he could not let the young men get hurt! He moved a step closer to Reed, and keeping up the facade of being friends, held his hands out, said, "You don't need a pistol, Mr. Reed. Please. Come sit down. We're hardly a danger to you. You can tell us about your earlier life in New York. Didn't you say you worked with the British officers?"

"Indeed. That was my old life. I want to know who has been ratting me to the Continentals? And why should I do anything you suggest? Seems to me that you are the difficulty here, doctor. That lily-livered, lobster-lovin' traitor thought you would not be any trouble. Wouldn't be able to figure it out. That's why he asked you to take it on. But you're still getting in the way! A nuisance that I intend to remove right now."

Reed smiled. The malice in his smile did not ease anything.

"And is that your solution to anyone who is in the way?" Eustis asked.

"Sure does take care of it, and you're one of 'em. Many others have found they should never have questioned my orders."

"Ephraim Bowen, for instance? What did he do? Disagree with you?"

Elijah and Noah had slowly inched apart from where they sat, moving slightly toward the edges of the pier on either side. Reed's focus was on Eustis in the middle as he raised his pistol to aim. A living menace in black.

Then, a blur as Noah dove to his left, pushed Eustis off the end of the pier, and followed him into the water. At the same moment, Elijah,

211

who had one foot up on the dock, partially rose stooping low and charged to tackle Reed. The gun went off. Eustis, in mid-fall, knew only that he did not know anything. He hit the water and surfaced sputtering. Noah's head rose nearby, and Eustis looked to see if he was swimming, decided he needed help, grabbed his shirt collar and, pulling him along, swam toward the small landing.

But what had happened? There were some scuffling noises and then total silence up on the pier. Eustis could see nothing overhead as they struggled toward shore. Eli?

Standing, sloshing ashore in the grass, Eustis looked for Elijah, saw him grinning, sitting astride Reed who was snarled in rope from a nearby rowboat used for fishing. Dripping, Eustis and Noah hooted and laughed relieved from their distress.

Eli was holding his own arm where blood seeped through his sleeve. He had managed to wrap enough rope around the momentarily stunned Reed after knocking him down to immobilize him. Noah rushed to add his sodden weight on Reed's legs.

"How did you plan that?" wheezed Eustis, still laughing. Relief led to joking. He said to Eli, "Your gran is not going to believe this! You, Noah! How did you think of doing that?"

Both young men laughed delightedly back at him, thrilled with their success.

"Let's look at your arm, Eli," and with that, reality intervened. People were running toward them from the house. Someone had heard the shot.

"We jest getting' ready for the wild west," joked Elijah. Noah, eyes sparkling, grinned.

The arriving hospital staff took over, efficiently secured Reed, and Noah helped Elijah walk back to the surgical shed where Dr. Eustis could dress his wounded arm.

"Best send a message to General Greene that we are still doing his job," said Eustis. "And ask him to come get the Cobbler."

Epilogue

Barely a week later, while on his way south to New Jersey, Dr. David Townsend rode into the barnyard to join his old friend, Dr. William Eustis, for midday dinner at Robinson House. They had known each other for years. The men as well as Sam Adams had been fellow students at Harvard College and they had been apprentices together with Dr. Joseph Warren.

Although from Barnstable, not Boston, Dr. James Thacher, another longtime friend, joined them as well, crossing the river from West Point. He had finally gotten a day's leave from the Massachusetts Sixteenth to join his friends for dinner. They reminisced about their time as new doctors during those early days in Cambridge.

Having attended the hanging of John André, Thacher could provide all the details that the doctors craved. Commenting on how André had befriended most of his captors, he told about the sympathy felt by many of the watchers for the elegant young officer. They admired his composure when he realized his request to die like an officer rather than a spy had been denied, and he had climbed upon the cart and put on his own blindfold. Maintaining his dignity, he had died as a gentleman.

The men in Thacher's regiment were assigned to build another series of log cabins for the new cantonment to be called New Windsor on acreage behind West Point. They were happy to build their own encampment, leave the fighting until the next spring, and see their families. In the end, they would also build a new hospital. The Robinson House doctors would learn that Robinson House would be closed within a year and operations moved to New Windsor.

William Eustis looked around the table at his friends and reflected on how much he valued them all, how much he enjoyed working with them. Then Thacher asked about how his campaign season had gone, and Dr. Eustis began his saga . . . of lust and murder.

And in this case, what some might call murder, others might call justice.

Author's Note

I have based the characters in this story on my research about real persons who lived and served in the Continental Army in the Hudson Highlands in 1780. Dr. William Eustis was a surgeon from Boston and served at the Robinson House hospital, working there for about three years.

Dr. William Burnet was also assigned to Robinson House. Mrs. Nardy was their matron in charge of nursing. When those medical facilities were moved to the new cantonment at New Windsor, Eustis became the lead medical officer and remained at West Point through the end of the war – another three years – when he was the last to leave, locking the door behind him.

The story of Benedict Arnold's residence at Robinson House and defection to the British is accurate, as is the death of John André. General Nathanael Greene was indeed called in to straighten out the mess left by Arnold at West Point. After our story ended, Eustis's friend Aaron Burr married his lady love, the recently-widowed Theodosia, within a year. They had a daughter together also named Theodosia.

Close Eustis friends, Sam Adams Jr. and James Thacher, were doctors practicing in the West Point area, although Thacher, as a regimental surgeon, traveled with his regiment during its campaigns. The other young men – Alexander Hamilton, Henry Knox, and the Marquis de Lafayette – were at Robinson House as described, as was General Washington. An attempt to kill Washington was planned in conjunction with his trip to Hartford. It was canceled or dissolved, but information today is scarce as to exactly how it was stopped.

The women's settlement and all the women are fictional as are the counterfeiters, the murdered, the murderers, and Norah's husband. Claudius Smith, however, really existed. He was arrested for counterfeiting in upper Manhattan. Almost everything else happened in that exact time and in the Hudson Highlands.

Some years later, William Eustis gave up medicine to pursue a political career with adventures of its own. He was elected to Congress when Thomas Jefferson became our third president. He later became an ambassador and then governor of Massachusetts.

www.ingramcontent.com/pod-product-compliance
Lightning Source LLC
Chambersburg PA
CBHW031958240626
47153CB00003B/1023